inarticulate

EDEN SUMMERS

To

friendship and love.

Without both in my life this book wouldn't exist.

One

"**My sweet Ms. Hamilton, we've got a problem.**" The deeply growled tone came from the office across the hall.

Savannah slumped over, resting her head on the elegantly polished wood of her desk and fought the need to bang her forehead. "What is it, Spencer? I'm kinda busy."

As far as understatements went, hers was gargantuan. The To-Do List currently stapled to the back of her mind was growing with every disgruntled staff email that slid gracefully into her mailbox. She had property managers to call, PR issues to resolve, and profit reports to analyze that, at first glimpse, showed a lot of red, instead of soothing black.

"It's important. Get your butt in here. *Now.*"

A hissed chastisement came from Spencer's office and she cringed, knowing his father was also in there. Mr. Rydel, *the* Mr. Mathew Rydel from the Rydel hotel empire, was her boss. So was his charming son, Spencer. The former was a demanding man. He cracked the whip like an ancient Roman on a power trip, without apology or remorse. It was a challenge to work under his leadership, and she thrived in the role.

Spencer, however, had a different work ethic, one that revolved around flirtation and perfectly worded compliments. He'd seduced her into an eight-month relationship that ended six weeks ago, when he forgot to remain monogamous.

But she hadn't been hurt. Crazy, huh? Eight months of companionship had come to an end and all she could think about was stocking up on AA batteries. Because that's all their time together had been. One scripted sex scene after another. It was merely colleagues with benefits.

Convenient copulation.

Only Spencer disagreed. Apparently, their future held the un-mistakable sound of wedding bells and a honeymoon somewhere warm and exotic. Her reluctance to agree was merely stubborn pride because he'd slummed it with the manager of the Rydel Chicago property in a moment of weakness.

She actually felt sorry for his unrealistic perception. She could never love a man like Spencer. He was too pretty. Too perfect. He'd never worked a day in his life, he merely skated along the pristine path his father laid for him. He had no drive, no commitment.

In the last six weeks, his self-righteous attitude and love for himself had scrubbed away any aesthetic appeal, leaving her to see the egotistical man he hid beneath.

He was, however, a perfect asset in the bedroom. A woman couldn't live on the company of battery operated products alone, and for a brief eight months he'd given her the opportunity to unsubscribe to her favorite sex toy website.

"My life is but to serve," she muttered and pushed to her feet, shimmying her ass to lower the thigh-high skirt now hiked up her stocking-covered legs. As she shuffled around her desk, she swiped at her mug and stole the last dregs of coffee, placing it back down with a relieved gasp that spoke too much of her reliance on the heavenly liquid.

With a pasted on smile, she held her head high and strode across the hall. When she entered Spencer's office, her footsteps faltered at the matching scowls etched across the faces of the father and son duo. "What's wrong?"

"There's problems in Seattle." Mr. Rydel's hazel eyes were a darkened shade of we're-in-huge-fucking-trouble.

"Problems?" She frowned. "The paperwork for the sale has already been finalized. There's less than three months until settlement. There shouldn't be any problems." Well, nothing worthy of the high level of concern focused her way.

Over time, the Seattle property had slowly become their profit decimator. The cause of their sinking bottom line. This year the decision had been made to cut and run, sacrificing their worst performer to benefit the rest of the portfolio. It was an emotional and stressful conclusion none of them liked to acknowledge. And as soon as the sale was complete and staff began working for their new employer, Savannah planned on kicking off her heels and dancing around her living room while simultaneously guzzling a bottle of merlot.

"Less than three months that will bring us to our knees if our employees continue to quit," Spencer muttered. "They're leaving in droves."

"Why?" It didn't make sense. "Our terms with Grandiosity were specific. They promised to take on incumbent staff. You told me that was non-negotiable."

Spencer leaned back in his chair and crossed his arms over his immaculately tailored suit. "That's what we agreed on with Patrick, but it looks like his team is playing dirty to get a better deal. If any more staff leave, we won't be able to reach the minimum hotel occupancy we committed to in negotiations. Which means the fucking settlement figure will fall."

"*Son,*" Mr. Rydel grated.

"What? You know it's true. They also made it clear our staff are sub-par. Getting them out of the way means they can slide their own into place instead of wading through three-month probation periods and possible payouts for those who need to be fired."

"Just show her the email."

Spencer's lips pressed tight as he slid a sheet of paper toward her. "We've been receiving information of unrest since we announced the upcoming sale, but this came from the shift manager this morning."

Savannah picked up the email and skimmed over the text.

Dear Mr. Rydel. Yadda yadda yadda. *Staff are seeking alternate employment in fear of the inevitable loss of work in the future.* Yadda yadda yadda. *They're intimidated by the presence of future manage-*

3

ment. Yadda yadda yadda. *Please advise how you would like me to proceed.*

She slammed the paper back down on the desk. "This is a breach of contract. Their management can't terrorize staff. They shouldn't even be in the building."

"No, they shouldn't," Mr. Rydel agreed. "But from the amount of concerned phone calls we're receiving, someone certainly is."

"Who?" She slid into one of Spencer's hard leather seats beside his father. "Do we have a name?"

Spencer squinted at his computer screen. "It's the assistant to the CEO. A Miss Penelope Augustine."

Savannah's stomach dropped. What was the chance of two women with the same extravagant name living in Seattle, Washington? *"Fuck."*

Mr. Rydel stiffened, his gaze narrowing on her in concern. "Savannah…"

"Sorry." Her composure was usually solid in the office, her profanity contained to the inner spheres of her mind. But this… This wasn't good.

"Are you familiar with her?" Spencer's expression was more impressed than distraught.

"You could say that." They'd grown up sharing summers together. And a thinly veiled annoyance for one another.

Hope twinkled in Mr. Rydel's eyes. A misplaced hope. One she wished he would wipe off his face, so she didn't have to do it herself. "That's perfect."

No. No, it wasn't. "We're not close. We haven't spoken since I was seventeen." The same year Savannah kissed the guy Penny had been crushing on, sending her younger cousin into a rage that probably should've been calmed with pharmaceutical intervention.

"But familiarity will work in our favor." He pushed from his chair, as if a conclusion to the problem had already been found.

She tracked his movements to the door and refused to bite her lip. "So you want me to place a call and gently ask her to back off?" Awkward wouldn't come close to the way the conversation would pan out.

4

"No. I want you to go to Seattle and talk to her." Mr. Rydel peered down at her, the faith in his expression weighing heavy on her shoulders. "I also want you to track down the staff who have resigned and convince them to return. And make sure all current employees are comfortable and familiar with how the changeover will occur. There's a lot of miscommunication over there, and you're the perfect person to clear it up."

"Perfect person?"

"Yes. You're bubbly and approachable."

She raised a disbelieving brow and stared at Spencer, hoping he was noticing his father's rapid descent into psychosis. "I'm none of those things. The sarcastic wit and humorous charm is a front. I honestly despise people. I like to consider myself as more of a dictator that staff are confident in but scared to approach."

Mr. Rydel laughed.

Laughed.

She wasn't joking, goddamn it.

"Mr. Rydel—"

"You'll get the job done, Savannah. I have faith in you."

She blinked once, twice. "But..." What? What possible excuse could she use to get out of saving the company a large chunk of settlement money? "I'm entirely smothered with work. I can't drop everything and leave for a few days."

"We'll figure something out." He stood in the doorframe, an undeniable force. "And it won't be for a few days. I want you to remain in Seattle until this is over."

Eleven weeks. "But, sir—"

"It's a big ask, I know."

She sank into her chair and met Spencer's focus, wordlessly pleading for him to say something to his father. Anything.

He shrugged. "We'll give you a week to pack your things."

"That's much better." She rolled her eyes. One less week wouldn't make much difference. "What about the backlog of work I currently have? I'll never catch up."

"The staff here are capable of taking some of your duties for the duration. The rest you can do while you're there," Mr. Rydel's voice was filled with confidence. Annoying, authoritative confidence. "I'm relying on you to fix this, Savannah."

She turned to him, hoping her puppy dog eyes would work better on the aging Rydel man, but he was already gone. Deal done. No begging or pleading possible. She slumped into the chair and tried to ignore the growing list of tasks that made her brain throb.

"I'll handle reporting while you're gone," Spencer offered.

She scoffed. He'd completely mess them up. The benefit of being the boss's son was that you could fuck up absolutely anything and get someone else to deal with the fallout. "Thanks."

"Think of it as an opportunity." He eyed her, his lips twitching. "You can let your uptight hair down and start dating new people without me hovering over your shoulder. That's what you claim to want, right?"

"It's not a claim, Spencer." She shoved to her feet, glaring. And she wasn't uptight. She was a hard worker. The most efficient and forward thinker they'd ever had. Being with him had tainted the facts. New employees considered her merely a skirt that clung to Spencer's coattails. They didn't realize it was the other way around. "And I could start dating right here, right now, I just don't have time."

"It's not time that you lack, sweetheart. It's enthusiasm." He grinned at her. "You know we're meant for each other. You'll quit being stubborn and forgive me soon enough, and when you do, I'll be here waiting."

"Spencer..." She sighed.

He needed to understand they would never ever get back together. Unless the powers of vodka and wine teamed up to create an un-defeatable army against her resolve, she would forever be committed to keeping her thighs closed in his presence. The only problem was that she didn't know how he would react when the information finally sank past his impenetrable ego.

"You need to move on."

He inclined his head. "But that's impossible when I see you all day, every day."

Was that the first hint that her job was in jeopardy?

"You say you can live without me, so prove it. Go to Seattle," he continued. "I promise you'll be missing me within days."

She held back the cloying need to roll her eyes into the back of her head and let them hibernate there until summer. "Fine." It was a small price to pay. "I'll take care of the settlement." She didn't have a choice anyway. "And when I return, everything between us will be laid to rest."

"Okay." He leaned back in his chair, the sparkle in his eyes gleaming at her. "If you last until settlement without needing me, I'll pretend like we never happened."

Her chest loosened with unmistakable relief. "Great."

"Perfect," he purred.

Christ. So much for the reprieve. He was far too confident of her failure. He practically stripped her and took inventory with his eyes. "While I'm gone, why don't you take Rebecca out on a date?"

She was going to hell for throwing her assistant under the bus, but tough times and all that... "She thinks you're gorgeous." It wasn't a lie. Rebecca remarked on his physical appeal all the time, she just always backed up the compliment with a comment on how much of an ass he was.

"Been there, done that."

Her mouth gaped. "Are you kidding?"

"That's why I know the two of us are perfect together. I've played the entire field. From the single mom in accounting, to your assistant, and any welcoming bed I've come across when I do the yearly reviews on each of our hotels. No one compares to you, babe."

"You're disgusting."

He chuckled. "You didn't have a problem with me for all the months we were together."

She whimpered. She didn't have the patience to reiterate her perspective. They'd been over it more than once. He thought they were a match made in heaven because she didn't hound him. She hadn't questioned his fidelity. There were no conversations about the future, or whispers of love and commitment. They shared meals and sex and spoke about business tactics whenever words were necessary.

That was it.

He considered it a perfect relationship. A ball and chain, without the ball and chain.

She considered it enjoyable sex without emotional connection.

End of story.

"This has to stop," she muttered and turned for the door. "I'm not going to put up with the bullshit once I return."

"You know where the door is, Savannah. I'm pretty sure you know where the unemployment line is, too."

And there it was, the unmistakable threat. *Asshole.*

"Oh, and one last thing," he called.

She stopped in the hall, refusing to face him.

"I should thank you for mentioning your connection with Penelope Augustine. My father was determined to send me to Seattle until you enlightened us. God knows I don't want to spend Thanksgiving or Christmas in that hell hole. I appreciate you taking one for the team."

She ground her teeth and trudged into her office. Seattle wasn't a place she dreamed to be during the holidays either, but the more she thought about it, the more she knew it would be the perfect opportunity to regroup and reassess.

Spencer's unenthusiastic work ethic had rubbed off on her. She'd become complacent and distracted. It was time to remind the father and son duo that she was an invaluable part of the team.

The best way to do that was to prove she wasn't here to kiss ass, she was here to kick it.

Two

ONE WEEK LATER

Savannah tugged her suitcase into the hotel suite and was thankful for the loud click of the door as it closed. Peace. Quiet. She wanted both, and lots of it. After enduring a three-hour delay at the airport, then sitting next to a mother with a newborn baby on the plane, her nerves were frazzled. And today hadn't come close to the stressful week spent training her assistant, Rebecca, to take on new tasks, or the hours spent arguing with Spencer over how to run the profit reports, or the unending phone calls from the Seattle hotel in preparation of her arrival.

She needed a bath, or a glass of wine. Both would be best. Obviously, at the same time.

Staff had whispered nervously as she checked in. Their hope-filled eyes tracked her movements. They expected her to fix all their problems. And she would. She just needed a chance to catch her breath and start fresh tomorrow.

She dropped her handbag and the suitcase handle at the end of the short hall, and shuffled the five steps to plant face-first on the bed. Movement wasn't necessary for the next twelve hours. She'd eaten an airport sandwich on the cab ride to the hotel, and staff didn't expect to see her until morning. From now until then, she would rest in a coma-like state.

Within two minutes her mind was fading to black, sweet dreams hovering on the edge of her consciousness, then the loud trill of the suite phone tore a groan from her throat.

"Go away," she mumbled into the comforter.

The phone continued to wail its siren call, disrespecting her plea. She gave a soft whimper and clawed her way to the other side of the mattress, picking up the receiver from the bedside table.

"Yes?"

"Ms. Hamilton, it's Kelly from reception. I'm sorry to disturb you, but there's a man here asking to see you."

She pressed her forehead against the pillow and closed her eyes. "Are you sure he's here for me?" Nobody knew she was here. Nobody except hotel staff and her colleagues back in San Francisco.

"Um..." The receptionist's nervous hesitation was clear. "He said he's your cousin."

Savannah pushed to a seated position and kicked off her heels. "Are you sure he asked for me?"

"Yes, ma'am. He asked for you specifically."

"Come on, Savvy, let me know your room number."

Savannah grinned at the masculine voice calling in the background. The tone was unfamiliar, far too deep for the teenager she knew from her childhood. But the long-forgotten nickname wasn't. Dominic was the only person who called her Savvy.

"It's okay," she told the receptionist. "Send him up."

"Will do."

Savannah couldn't wipe away the grin as she hung up the phone and padded to the bathroom. The unfavorable reflection in the mirror slaughtered her happiness. She looked like a drug addict. Her blouse was crushed, her light-brown hair a tattered mess. The bags under her bloodshot hazel eyes were something she couldn't ignore, the dark smudges announcing her exhaustion, while her pale complexion told of an unfavorable amount of hours spent in a high-rise office without a glimpse of sun.

She rushed back into the main room of her suite and yanked her handbag off the floor. She scrounged for her compact concealer and dabbed it under her eyes with less than artistic flare. A quick slide of lipstick later and she was ready for the loud knock that echoed through the room.

Anticipation bubbled in her belly as she padded to the door and pulled the heavy wood open.

"Whoa." She needed to raise her chin to meet Dominic's eyes. "How long have you been on steroids?"

Dominic chuckled, his brilliant smile whacking her with a heavy dose of déjà vu. "Is that any way to greet your favorite cousin?"

He stepped forward and pulled her in for a hug. The scent of his aftershave was all wrong. The feel of his hard muscles, too. Her short and skinny cousin was nowhere to be seen. He was no longer the kid she remembered dragging her under the water on summer vacation. He was a man. Tall, broad, and professional.

"You got big." She pushed back from his chest and scrutinized him from head to toe. His blond hair and blue eyes hadn't changed, but everything else had, including the bump in his once perfect nose. "And you learned how to dress yourself." His white collared shirt was in better shape than her blouse, not a crease in sight. His charcoal slacks and matching tie were in perfect order, too.

"And you became completely stunning." He eyed her with appreciation. "If we weren't cousins, I'd totally hit that."

"*Oh, Jesus.*" She slapped a hand over her mouth to stop an encouraging laugh. "You're still as inappropriate as ever."

He held up his hands in surrender. "Just paying you a compliment, Sav."

"Let's not make this awkward." She shook her head and indicated for him to come inside. "I don't want to regress to the time where I had to punch you in the face to stop you from trying to kiss me."

"I was eight." He walked past her. "It was dark out, and I thought you were someone else."

"We were ten, and it was in the pool before lunch."

He snickered. "You have a good memory."

"It's not easy to forget the first time your cousin tries to lay one on you."

"First and last. I learn from my mistakes." He slumped onto the corner of her Queen-sized mattress, dwarfing the bed with his large frame. "So how have you been?"

"I'm good." She settled against the tiny desk opposite him, unable to stop mentally noting all the ways he'd changed. His feet were so big. His hands, too. "But I'd love to know how you found out I was here. And why you turned up on my doorstep."

He pulled a face, a cross between a wince and a smirk.

"Don't tell me." She put up a hand to stop his explanation. "My lovely Aunt Michelle."

He winked at her. "Guessed it in one."

Christ. Savannah's mother couldn't keep a secret to save her life, especially when it came to her sister. For as long as she could remember, her mother and aunt had been inseparable. They endeavored to lessen the miles between them, from San Francisco to Seattle, by daily phone calls and weeks on end in a family cabin during summer.

"I gather you didn't want us finding out," he drawled.

"It's not that." It was a tricky situation. She hadn't kept tabs on her cousins' lives. If she had, maybe she could've foreseen the current drama. Years separated the last time they spoke, and she wasn't confident in assuming they wanted to see her again. Especially when Penny's involvement in the sale of the Seattle property seemed like a personal vendetta. "I didn't know your sister was working with Grandiosity. I'm actually here because..."

How should she put it? Her relationship with Dominic had always been solid. They were born within months of each other. They reached the same milestones together and became long distance best friends.

Her communication with Penny was in vast contrast. She was the younger relative neither herself nor Dominic wanted to play with. She threw tantrums and demanded attention. She was immature, annoying, and daddy's little girl even at the age of fifteen when they'd last spoken.

However, the past didn't dictate her favorite cousin's current bond with his sister. He could've outgrown the annoyance toward his sibling.

"She's stirring up trouble again?" Dominic straightened.

"Kind of." Merely scaring grown men and women from their long-term employment. "Is she still a—"

"Bitch?" he interrupted. "No. I think she's evolved from that. Being a bitch was mere child's play."

"Perfect." Savannah chuckled, ignoring the flush of annoyance heating her cheeks. "You still haven't told me why you're here."

"Yeah...about that." He flashed a smile at her. "I was supposed to call and make sure you came to a family dinner tonight. I was actually going to do it days ago, but it completely slipped my mind. So instead of calling now and getting an inevitable last-minute rejection, I thought I'd show up and drag you along kicking and screaming."

"Kicking and screaming?" It was a possibility. She wasn't in the mood for a family reunion. Dominic was enough for now.

"I'd prefer your ire to my mother's. That woman can hold a grudge."

So could his sister. "I'm exhausted, Nic." She slumped her shoulders for effect. "I don't want to leave a bad impression after all this time apart."

"You'll be fine."

"I've been in my suite less than half an hour. I haven't even opened my suitcase." The opportunity to catch Penny in a friendly, family situation was favorable, but Savannah needed a certain mindset to approach danger. A mindset she didn't think she had the determination to muster.

"Don't waste your time with excuses. You know what my mother is like." He stood, hovering over her. "If I show up without you, I won't hear the end of it."

A smirk pulled at her lips. "That's a risk I'm willing to take."

"So you've decided on the kicking and screaming option?" There was no inflection in his tone. No humor. Only a formidable determination in his features. He was going to make good on his promise; she could see it in his eyes.

"Damn you." She pushed to her feet and glared at him. He hadn't changed. Not one little bit. And apparently, neither had she, because she was still succumbing to his stubbornness. "I'll get my coat."

Three

"Family dinner?" She shot Dominic a scathing glance as they approached a familiar house. The curb on either side of the street was banked with cars. The driveway, too.

"I think she may be a little over excited." He parked in the drive behind a shiny silver sports car and cut the ignition. "But it's free food, right?"

There were no words. All she could do was glare.

"Okay, okay, I'm sorry." The laughter in his tone said otherwise. "I may have known there were a few additional people invited."

"A few?" Savannah released her seatbelt and shoved open her car door. "The least you could've done was tell me to get changed." She was still wearing her travel clothes—old comfortable jeans, her crushed blouse that was now hidden under a black suede coat, and a shimmery pink scarf she'd hoped would detract from her laziness.

It detracted nothing.

"I'm going to look like the homeless cousin stumbling to the doorstep for a free hand-out."

"Don't exaggerate." He slammed his car door and rounded the hood. "You look fine. And besides, I wasn't going to wait for an hour while you tried on a million outfits and plastered your face with make-up."

"Now who's exaggerating?" She walked backward, shooting daggers at him as she approached the single-story brick building. "Just remember payback's a bitch."

"And so are you, my sweet cousin."

He was a jerk, but gosh, she'd missed him. The banter and the fun. The laughter and the snarcasm.

She swung around to the house to hide her smile and bounced up the three stairs toward the front door. Movement nudged her periphery and she slowed, taking in the sight of a man standing in the shadows at the far end of the porch. His hip was cocked against the bannister, his eyes hooded.

Her concentration latched on to him, unmoving as the world around her dulled to a faint hum in her mind. She wasn't sure what intrigued her. It could be his narrowed stare, the way he didn't greet her with warmth or kindness. Only sterile appraisal. Or maybe it was the package his arrogance came in—the tense expression, stubbled jaw, and lush lips pressed in a tight line.

Her tongue tingled. Mouth salivated. She would've liked to think it was due to the heavenly aroma of her aunt's cooking drifting in the air. Would've liked to...but that was a load of bull.

"Hi." She gave him a friendly finger wave as Dominic came up behind her.

The man continued to stare, his face still unwelcoming in the shadows.

"Keenan, don't be a prick." Dominic tugged on her arm, stealing her attention. "Come on. I'll introduce you later."

She kept her focus on the stranger, their gazes entwined, hers soft and inquisitive, his harsh and fierce, as her cousin dragged her inside, the door slamming shut behind them. "Who was—"

"Oh, my sweet Savannah!" Aunt Michelle hustled up the hall, wiping her hands on an old apron tied around her waist. "It's so good to see you."

The familiar face held more wrinkles than Savannah remembered, her aunt's long blonde hair now gray and thinning. But the beautiful blue eyes were still the same—loving and gentle.

"It's good to see you, too." She ignored the strangers poking their heads into the hall from different doorways and fell into a comforting embrace. "Thank you for the dinner invitation."

"Oh, please," her aunt chastised. "You don't need an invitation. Come around any time."

There was a whirlwind of introductions. Her aunt took position on her right, gushing with affection and compliments, while Dominic remained on her left, muttering snide comments that threatened to make her laugh.

A timer dinged from the kitchen, a welcome reprieve as her aunt excused herself and left Savannah to take a breath. There had to be twenty people crammed into the small house. All of them smiling and friendly, unlike the man outside who still lingered in her thoughts.

"You want a drink?" Dominic nudged her elbow.

Hell yes. "Please." She followed him to the back of the house, into the laundry, and toward a fridge stocked full of beer, wine, and pre-mixed drinks.

"Help yourself."

He held the door open while she grabbed a small bottle of something red and no doubt comatosingly sweet. "Thanks."

"I'm gonna hit the bathroom." He closed the fridge door and looked at her in concern. "Can you survive for a few minutes without me?"

"I guess I'll have to. I'm not going to follow you to the toilet."

"*Obviously,*" he drawled. "You gave up that opportunity when we were eight."

"Twelve."

"Ten." He chuckled and walked from the room, leaving her alone with the hovering threat of chatter from the other end of the house.

It was time to go incognito. She didn't have the energy to smile at strangers. Alcohol would help, but for now, she needed cool fresh air...and maybe another glimpse at the menacing eyes of the man she'd met on the porch.

She shoved the bottle into her coat pocket and sauntered down the hall, measuring her steps to lessen the clap of her heels. She reached the front door without notice and pulled it open, slipping into the darkness of twilight without a word.

The man was still at the end of the porch, a beer bottle now visible in his hand as he leaned over, resting his elbows on the bannister. He didn't acknowledge her presence. She supposed a man with arrogance ebbing off him in waves didn't have to. His dismissal gave her the opportunity to appreciate his ass stretched in well-worn jeans and the perfection of how his black jacket rested at his hips to give her an unhindered view.

"Hi," she offered for a second time.

He didn't move, didn't even spare her a glance as she approached the bannister. He continued staring straight ahead as he lifted the beer bottle to his lips and took a long pull.

"It's a lovely night for a family dinner." Was he a distant relative? God, she hoped not, otherwise Dominic's inbred tendencies were rubbing off on her.

He replied with a jut of his chin. *A jut of his God. Damn. Chin.*

What an asshole. And wasn't she just the stupidest set of ovaries to walk the earth, because it only made her itch to push his blatant need for solitude, to poke at him with questions until he acknowledged her with the respect she deserved. The respect *any* human deserved.

"So... you like beer..." she drawled, glib as hell.

The corner of his mouth twitched as he continued to focus on the street. But still, no answer.

She could smell him, could practically taste his delicious aftershave on her tongue with each inhalation. He was a taunt to all her senses...well, except her ears because the pretentious ass wouldn't say a word.

He took another swig from his bottle and straightened to face her. She could see his eyes now, the steely silver, almost blue, that made her shiver with their ferocity. He was tall, too. At least an inch above her even with her heels.

She pulled the pre-mix bottle from her jacket pocket and twisted the lid to keep her hands busy. She could see two outcomes eventuating. Either he would smile, knocking her off her feet with the brilliance of his appeal. Or he was going to pull a gun from the inside of his jacket and blow her brains out.

Player or gangster. He could totally pull off both.

"I'm usually a wine drinker myself." She raised the bottle of bubbly red liquid in her hand, slowly tilting it to her mouth. She took a sip, licked the alcohol from her lips in a deliberately seductive provocation, then lowered the bottle again.

Still, he gave her nothing. Noth-ing. He was the most accomplished jerk she'd ever come across, and yet she still couldn't ditch the intrigue and walk away. Without a word, he had her tied around his little finger, begging for attention.

"I like your jeans." She ogled his crotch, wanting to return the discomfort of how humiliating this one-sided conversation was becoming. "They're snug."

His lips quirked, giving her a glimpse of straight white teeth. Asshole. *Asshole. Ass-hole!* He was gorgeous, the faintest hint of humor turning his dangerous eyes playful. She lifted the bottle to her mouth again, this time ignoring any pretense of seduction as she gulped at the liquid.

"Are you always this charm—"

The front door creaked open and she turned to find Dominic eying them both skeptically. "What's going on?"

She smiled, the biggest, fakest smile she had in her arsenal. "I'm having an in-depth conversation with this lovely gentleman."

"Really?" Dominic frowned, his brows pulling deeper with every passing second.

"Yep." There was gushing amounts of sarcasm in her tone. "First we conversed about our drinking habits, then fashion. I was about to bring up the topic of politics and world peace when you rudely interrupted."

She glanced at the man in the corner, an arrogant smirk now curving those sensuous lips. He wasn't the only one capable of being a jerk.

"Well, that's strange..." Dominic came closer. "Because Keenan doesn't talk."

It was her turn to frown. "What do you mean?" Her skin prickled with goosebumps as the weight of both their attention focused on her.

"I mean, Keenan doesn't talk." Dominic shot his friend a questioning look, but she was too focused on her cousin and shocked from his words to bother with the silent stranger's response. "At all."

Keenan cleared his throat. It was deep and gravel-rich, demanding her attention. When she turned to him, he raised a brow, throwing the rudeness she'd been wordlessly accusing him of right back in her face.

The muted accusation sent a shiver of unwelcome stupidity down her spine. She became uncomfortable in her own skin. Ashamed. But who the hell did he think he was? Just because he couldn't, or didn't want to, speak didn't mean he lacked the skills to communicate his inability.

"Oh." She smiled sweetly. "That clears things up." She turned her attention to Dominic. "I thought he was just an asshole."

Her cousin snorted. "Don't worry, he is." He bridged the distance between them and flung an arm around her shoulders, pulling her into his side. "Savvy, this is Keenan. He's practically family. And Kee, this is Savvy, she actually *is* family, so stop being a prick and treat her nice."

Her throat tightened and the moisture coating her mouth evaporated. Keenan stood there, taking another long pull of his beer, suave as hell, before placing it down on the bannister and holding out a hand.

She could already sense the exhilaration his touch would ignite. Her arm was tingling, all the way down to her palm and through her fingers. She stepped forward, sliding her hand into his, and tried to appear unfazed by the jolt that followed the brush of their skin. His mouth was mesmerizing. Both lips equally lush and soft. She wondered what he would look like when he smiled. A full, beaming smile. Would his eyes light up? Would the dark mysteriousness wash away?

"So you don't talk?" She pulled her hand back even though a little part of her wanted to keep the connection.

He shook his head. Once. Stilted.

He definitely didn't overcompensate for his lack of speech. Everything he did was calm and controlled—a jerk of his chin, a curve of his lips, a tilt of his head. The asshole knew he was intriguing. It was probably his calling card.

"Then how did the two of you become close?"

19

"Why don't we talk about this later?" Dominic pulled on the crook of her arm. "It's time for dinner."

"What about Penny?"

Dominic winced. "Now, don't get mad…"

Too late. "She isn't coming, is she?"

He shook his head. "She won't finish work for hours."

Savannah slid her tongue along the edge of her teeth, feigning annoyance even though she was relieved at not having to deal with the wicked bitch of the north. "You realize you owe me, right?"

He inclined his head and made for the front door. "I'll make it up to you next weekend."

"Next weekend?" She sauntered after him, sensing the silent stranger a few paces behind her, his presence making the hair on the back of her neck stand on end.

"We'll discuss it later." He held open the door, allowing the rush of chatter and laughter from inside to echo into the front yard. "Let's get through dinner first."

Four

Numerous serving plates were spread over a long trestle table. Eighteen people in total, all of them smiling from the effect of delicious food and friendly conversation. Savannah sat next to Dominic, across from Keenan, with her aunt graciously seated at the head of the table.

"So, he never talks?" she murmured under the hum of chatter.

Dominic cut her a glance as he chewed the food in his mouth. "He has his own way of communicating."

"I bet he does." With his hands, and his lips, and his tongue. The evil death stare said a lot, too. "He's attractive, has perfect dress sense, and doesn't talk. I think I want him to father my babies."

She'd caught Keenan eyeballing her over dinner. More than once. It was a look with narrowed eyes. Not quite a glare, but close enough to show his annoyance. She wasn't sure what she'd done to piss him off, but she'd give him a gold star for animosity.

"You and every other woman he's met since I've known him."

"Is that jealousy I hear in your voice?" She nudged his shoulder and winced when his knife clattered against his plate. "Sorry."

"No jealousy here." Dominic jerked his chin in Keenan's direction. "He's good people. It just takes a while for him to warm up to strangers."

Warm up? She merely wanted to get past the stage where she thought he wanted to stab his dinner knife through her chest.

He still intrigued her, though, and it wasn't all due to her fluttering ovaries. Everyone spoke to him during the meal. There was no discomfort or lull in the conversations he was involved in. Yet she noticed nobody asked him questions that required more than a yes or no answer. Nothing that needed more than a subtle jerk of his head.

"Who wants seconds?" Her aunt stood and held up a dish of potato bake.

There was a mass of groans. Guests leaned back in their chairs, rubbing overextended tummies while others shook their head, or waved away the possibility of more food.

Savannah chuckled to herself at the dramatics, skimming her attention over everyone until she reached Keenan. Their gazes collided and her breath caught. A rush of adrenaline slid through her veins as she waited for another one of his glares.

The nasty look didn't materialize. This time his focus was blank. No emotion. No expression. She broke eye contact, unable to match his unblinking stare without the threat of doing something silly like snorting, giggling, or blushing.

The man was a damn robot.

"The meal was lovely. Thank you." She pushed from her seat, placed her dirty cutlery onto her plate, and then poked Dominic in the shoulder. "I'll wash if you want to dry."

He peered up at her with incredulity. "What century are you living in? We have a dishwasher. You rinse, I'll stack."

"Deal." She beamed at him, her full smile holding until she turned back to the table, and her traitorous eyes focused back on Keenan. *Damn it.* She needed to stop seeking him out. She was too young to be shot. Or stabbed. Or kidnapped.

She was tempted to poke out her tongue, flip him the bird, even flash her bra covered tits to see if he was capable of more than an impassive stare. *Whatever.* She would ignore him from now on. He didn't deserve her attention. No matter how attractive his brooding was.

"I'll meet you in the kitchen," she muttered to Dominic.

She ignored Keenan, who pushed to his feet to stack empty plates, and strode from the room. As soon as the dishes were done, she was out of here. Her mood had deteriorated, and she didn't want to risk seeing Penny when holding a professional façade would be near impossible.

"About next weekend—" Dominic came up behind her and clattered a stack of plates into the sink, "—there's a bonfire on the outskirts of the city on Saturday night. You should come."

She sidestepped, moved out of his way, and bristled at the sight of Keenan in the doorway. "I'll keep it in mind. I'm not sure what my schedule will be like by then."

Dominic grinned and addressed Keenan. "Does that sound like a brushoff to you?"

The other man rested his shoulder against the frame and inclined his head. *Gah.* What she wouldn't give for him to show some enthusiasm. A smile. A thumbs up. Even shooting her the bird would be a relief from all the thinly veiled disdain.

"A bonfire in the middle of nowhere isn't my idea of fun."

"The middle of nowhere is actually the back of a property overlooking a two-story mansion owned by a rich bastard I know." He pulled open the dishwasher and began stacking plates. "There'll be booze, friendly faces, and Penny. She looks forward to camp nights. It would be a good opportunity for you to speak with her while she's in a decent mood."

Maybe. Speaking to her cousin in a casual setting still seemed like the best way to approach the situation. But in general, it wasn't something she wanted to think about at all. She was shoving that carnage to the back of her mind until a later date.

"Will my friend Keenan be there?" She eyed the man in question and pressed her lips tight to fight a smile.

He inclined his head. Ever so slightly. He was almost dreamy in his unwavering hostility.

She leaned back against the counter, her arms crossed over her chest, and scrutinized him. She couldn't fathom his self-control. He was too calm, too composed, and entirely guarded. The need to taunt him until he cracked ate at her. Ate and ate and ate.

"Do *you* think I should go?"

His eyes narrowed and everything inside her stopped—her heart, her blood flow, her sense of self-preservation as she began to smile.

He nodded. Twice.

Holy shit. It was an unenthusiastic double nod, but a double nod no less.

"Whoa." She held up her hands. "Don't go getting excited, young man. I'll have to see what happens."

Dominic chuckled. "You're such a bitch."

She kept her focus on Keenan as her smile faded. Was she being a bitch? It wasn't her intent. Then again, just because she wanted to communicate and get inside the mind of the dark, handsome, and silent stranger, didn't mean he had a responsibility to give in. He obviously had a reason for being guarded.

"Sorry." She turned to the sink and rinsed off the remaining plates. "Once these are stacked, do you mind taking me back to the hotel?"

"Of course. Go say goodbye to Mom. I'll be finished by the time you return."

She nodded and kept her head low as she walked from the kitchen. Her aunt was still standing at the head of the table, smiling and enjoying the praise her cooking had inspired. Savannah came to her side and whispered in her ear, "I'm leaving now."

There were more hugs and kisses. A myriad of murmured words in her ear and pleas for her to come back as much as possible during her stay in Seattle.

"I will." She wasn't sure if it was a lie. Time would tell. But tonight had been fun. Kind of.

She waved goodbye to the guests still chatting at the table, and made her way back to the kitchen. Her steps slowed as she passed through the doorway and found Keenan and Dominic standing face to face, on opposite sides of the open dishwasher door. They both stiffened at the first click of her heels against the tile, and her cousin's harshly whispered words cut short.

"Did I interrupt something?"

Dominic shook his head and tried to appease her with a fake smile. "Is the princess ready to be escorted back to her tower?"

"Yeah." She tracked Keenan's movements as he stalked to the far side of the room and leaned against the wall. He didn't look at her this time. Didn't lift his focus from the lazy position on the floor. "It was nice to meet you, Keenan."

She measured her steps toward him and held out her hand. His chin lifted and she tensed when his eyes met hers. The soulful gray was intoxicating. Hypnotizing. A myriad of unspoken words drifted between them, but they were nonsensical, in another language. She yearned to understand him. To hear what his gaze implied. To comprehend what his harsh focus meant.

His fingers slid across her palm, rough and warm. There was no hesitation. No reluctance. She wanted to believe there was a flicker of seduction in his features. That the look he gave her was more than goodbye. He shook her hand, the slow rhythm in contrast to the hummingbird flutter in her chest.

"I might see you next weekend." She cleared her throat to cast away her embarrassingly husky tone and pulled back her arm.

He held tight, his unreadable expression not even flickering as he clutched her fingers. The connection was minute, a mere clench of his grip, yet the rush of fire it sent through her veins had her mouth opening and closing like a guppy.

Then he was gone. The brief withdrawal of his palm and slight jut of his chin toward Dominic done in the blink of an eye before he stalked from the room.

"Ready?" her cousin asked behind her.

No. "Yes."

She turned to Dominic, her mind a whirling mess of annoyance, curiosity, and the stinging bite of arousal. Keenan had cemented her fate for next weekend. She would be at the bonfire. With bells on. The tall, dark, and devilish stranger might be exactly what she needed. There was no way she could keep idle in her hotel suite when the perfect opportunity to move on from Spencer was passing her by.

"Come on." Dominic led the way from the kitchen. "I think we've had enough excitement for one night."

Five

Savannah spent the week smiling. A fake, torturous lift of her lips she didn't plan on replicating until Monday came back around.

Grandiosity's plan seemed crystal clear. They wanted to sweep out meager Rydel staff to replace them with their own bright and shiny set of minions. Whether or not they were trying to drive down the settlement was another issue. And both were in breach of the settlement agreement.

The list of staff resignations grew day by day—six housekeepers, one maintenance man, two receptionists, three kitchen hands, and a bartender. There were too many to remember, and Savannah had only had the charm to convince less than half of those to return.

The employees who had stuck by the company had made it clear they were only doing so because they had no other job to go to. They were scared, stressed, and wearing thin of all the bullshit. Rightly so, too.

Kelly, one of the three remaining receptionists, had a dying mother and excessive hospital bills to pay. Amanda, the event manager, had a wedding booked on the eve of Thanksgiving and less than enough staff to facilitate the life changing day for her happy couple. And Grant, the morning shift manager, had admitted to unhealthy anxiety issues and wasn't sure if he could medically remain working until settlement.

That was merely three of the items on her infinite list of waking nightmares. *Three out of a bazillion.* And her heart bled at each one. But the last thing she needed was emotional attachment. The weight of fixing this mess was enough for her shoulders to bear. She needed to remain detached, even when more than one employee had told her the insecurities started weeks ago when security footage showed Penny reserving a room under a fake name.

Her cousin then proceeded to intimidate every employee she came across until management had removed her from the premises forty-eight hours later. In a perfect world, she never should've been able to secure a suite, let alone manipulate everyone she came in contact with. Only the trickle of threats hadn't reached management ears until it was already too late, and staff had started to leave.

But all the manipulation and sabotage didn't currently matter, because it was Saturday night and Savannah was officially off the clock.

Dominic had texted her directions to the 'Rich Bastard's property,' and she was almost at her destination. A six-pack of wine spritzers sloshed from the passenger seat of her rental car. Blankets and pillows were stacked in the back. The road she drove along was bordered by tall trees and devoid of streetlights. It was the perfect setting for the start of a horror film.

She followed the curve of the road to the left, and the flicker of flames came into view. The bright orange glow illuminated tall hedges and the outline of a massive house consumed in darkness.

"How the hell do I get in?" Closed steel gates loomed at the entrance to the property, forcing her to look for an alternate entrance. There was no sign of life inside the house. No lights. No glow from a television.

She inched her foot off the accelerator and continued toward the end of the house, her eyes squinted. There was a barely visible open fence gate up ahead, the metal reflecting the moonlight. She stopped and peered along the wall of hedges separating the house yard from the stubbled grass of a barren field. There were cars parked in the distance, one lined after the other. All of them glowed in different shades from the fire.

This was it.

She turned the car onto the dirt road, the large hedge on her left, the massive house looming just behind the natural screen. People came into view, more vehicles, the massive bonfire. She pulled to a stop at the makeshift parking lot, reached for the bottles of alcohol, and then slid from her seat into the freezing night air.

"Savvy!" Dominic waved a beer bottle at her from the opposite side of the flames. "Come over here."

His intoxication became clearer the closer she approached. She could see the glaze in his eyes, the delirious smile that spoke of the liquid buzz running through his veins.

"I'm glad you made it." He slid his arm around her neck and yanked her in for a smothering hug.

"Yeah, me, too." She looked over his shoulder and her stomach took a nose-dive. She'd felt the same sensation throughout the week, whenever she had time to spare a thought on Keenan's intense eyes.

He stood alone in the shadows, leaning against a large tree trunk, a beer bottle in his hand as he stared at the flames. She feasted on the sight of him, her senses reigniting at what they'd been starved of all week.

She shouldn't be so quick to jump at the bark of her hungry hormones, not after the mistake of Spencer, but this man was different. He was cold and calculating. Mysterious and intense. Nothing near the deceptive perfection of Spencer.

Keenan's jaw still held the hint of dark stubble. His eyes were hooded yet fierce. He wore a thick brown jacket, the white woolen interior making his tanned skin seem darker. Almost olive. And his dark blue jeans were just as snug as the ones he wore last week.

"Did you find us easy enough?"

"Yeah," she lied and slid out of Dominic's clutches. "Have you got somewhere I can put these?" She held up the six pack of wine spritzers, determined not to let her attention wander back to the man standing on his lonesome.

"Give them here. I'll put them in the cooler." He yanked them from her hands, broke the cardboard packaging at one end, and handed her a bottle. "While I'm doing your bidding, why don't you go talk to him?"

"Who?" Her lips tilted as she feigned ignorance. She'd never been an accomplished liar.

Dominic scoffed and shook his head. He walked away, leaving her alone, vulnerable, and entirely susceptible to the dark gaze Keenan now gifted her.

"Shit." She couldn't control her heart rate. Not that she ever could.

His scrutiny made her feel like a bug under a microscope. He was learning her secrets with every glance, and she wanted the favor returned. To crack him open and see what hid beneath his tough exterior.

Hi. She mouthed the word, not wanting to cast her voice across the numerous feet separating them. He tilted his beer bottle at her and took a swig. Laid back. Without a care. There was less tension in his features tonight. He was still dark and devilish, but there was also a glimpse of humanity.

She strolled toward him, her chest thumping harder with each step. "Nice to see you again, Keenan." His name on her lips was far better than having it ring in her head for days on end.

He kept his position against the tree trunk, his attention raking over her as she approached. The appraisal was slow and deliberate. From her black ankle boots now covered in dust, to her tight jeans, her thick mauve coat, her matching scarf, all the way to her face.

He broke eye contact, and the corner of his lips quirked.

Something was funny.

She looked down at herself. Her fly wasn't undone. No cleavage was showing. Her clothes were casual. Maybe a little too laid back. She hadn't even bothered with make-up apart from mascara. But she looked hot. As hot as someone could get dressed like an Eskimo.

"You don't approve of what I'm wearing?" She withheld the frustration from her tone and gripped the cap of her wine spritzer, trying to twist it open without shredding her palm.

His face tilted, turning back to meet her. He lifted the beer bottle to his mouth, took a slow gulp, and never let his focus waver. The way his throat convulsed made her swallow. The moisture on his lips made her lick her own. There was no hope to control her rapid pulse.

She was lost.

Helpless.

She continued to twist at the bottle cap and winced at the sting of pain slicing through her skin. "Shit." She looked down at her palm and the imbedded red scratches. Right when she needed a drink, her girlie hands were betraying her.

Keenan shoved from the tree trunk and ate up the small space between them. He was frowning now, the lines on his forehead harsh as he snatched the bottle from her hands. With a deft flick of his wrist, he removed the cap and handed the bottle back to her.

"Thanks." Clearly, she hadn't been flustered enough, because now she had to deal with the heady scent of him making her dizzy.

He tipped his head and she stood frozen, waiting for his retreat. Waiting and waiting. He remained close. Too close to ignore how soft his lips appeared, or how badly she wanted to run her fingers over the harsh stubble of his jaw.

The tilt of his mouth returned, growing into a full grin.

Shit. She was staring, and now that he was actually smiling—a full, deliriously gorgeous smile—she couldn't bring herself to stop.

"Are you drunk?" That had to be the answer for his improved social skills. Or he was high. Probably both.

He shrugged and took another chug.

"How many have you had?"

His brows drew close as he pressed his lips together. He held up his hand and raised one finger, then another, and another, and another, and another. That beautiful smile of his increased, the harshness of his features evaporating as his chest convulsed with a silent chuckle. He shook his head, mouthed the word *two,* and held up the same amount of fingers.

Not drunk. Just a master of manipulating her libido.

"What a shame." She needed to regain the upper hand before she crumpled into a drooling mess. "I was starting to think you were reaching a level where I could take advantage of you."

His focus narrowed. His lips thinned. Then he spread his arms wide. *Come get me.*

Holy shit. Did she? Should she? It would only take a step. One slide of her feet and she would be upon him, able to wrap her hands around his neck. She could kiss him, a mere brush of lips, just enough connection to write home to Spencer about and prove she'd moved on.

He broke eye contact, focusing over her head with a determined frown. The seductive moment faded. Vanished. She turned and watched another car drive into the makeshift parking lot. She couldn't see the driver, not until the door opened and a slender woman stepped from the car, her long blonde locks falling over her shoulders.

She glanced at Keenan over her shoulder. He'd stepped back, placing space between them, making her chest hollow with disappointment.

"Who is th..." Her words trailed as she turned back to face the woman sauntering toward them, her long hair glistening, the deep V of her cleavage evident from the gap in her coat.

Penny?

Savannah took a long pull of her wine spritzer, fighting nausea as the sexy bombshell maneuvered through mingling drinkers. Her smile was wide—white, flawless teeth surrounded by sultry red lipstick.

Dominic appeared at Savannah's side. "Prepare for battle."

She released a nervous laugh and clung to the reassurance of the alcoholic beverage in her hands. Everything about the approaching woman daunted her—the sureness of her stride, the confidence in her straightened shoulders, the way she bit her lip as she focused on Keenan.

"*Brother.*" Penny shouldered past Dominic.

Savannah stood motionless, dumbstruck, as her cousin wrapped her arms around Keenan and placed a kiss on his cheek, her lipstick leaving a red stain in its wake. Penny played the role of a reunited lover, ignoring the world around her as she bent her knee and whispered words into Keenan's ear. Only his response skewed the image. He didn't return the affection. The harsh lines of his features returned. His mouth was thin. His jaw tight and nostrils flared.

"Hi, Penny." Savannah kept her baby blues on Keenan, hoping to increase his discomfort. Moments ago he was flirting with her. Now he had another woman draped over him.

Typical male.

Her cousin stiffened as she wrapped one arm around his waist and turned to face her.

"Savvy? I almost didn't recognize you." Penny's nose crinkled. "You look so old now."

Savannah smiled through the insult. The blatant cruelty announced loud and clear any communication—business or otherwise—was going to be a barrel-load of fun.

Their two-year age gap meant everything when they were children. Development and interests set them miles apart. Not now, though. Over time the divide disappeared.

"And I go by *Penelope* now, *not* Penny."

"Christ. Don't be such a bitch." Dominic shot Savannah a sympathetic look. "I'm going to get another drink."

He strolled away, leaving them in torturous silence. If this was what Savannah had to expect from her cousin in a good mood, she'd hate to see her during shark week.

"Sorry, *Penelope*." She kept her smile tight. "I actually hoped we'd catch up tonight so we could speak about the Grandiosity takeover. There's been staff—"

"Do you know how surprised I was to hear you were a part of the failing hotel chain?" Penny was glib. "The sale must be embarrassing for all of you."

Heat consumed Savannah's cheeks. There were no words. The assault hit too close to home. It *was* embarrassing. For everyone involved—local staff and head office management included.

Keenan cleared his throat and stepped to the side, extricating himself from Penny's touch. But it was too late. She couldn't separate them. They were one and the same. Two beautiful people capable of claiming the title for most accomplished assholes in the state of Washington.

"Would you look at that?" She raised the wine spritzer to her lips, chugged the remaining contents, and lowered it with a deep exhale. "I think I need another drink, too."

Screw Penny and her need to overcompensate for childhood issues.

They didn't have to get along. They didn't have to speak. As long as her cousin stayed out of Rydel business until settlement, Savannah wouldn't have to kick the prissy bitch's ass in the most non-literal way possible.

And screw Keenan for making her wonder if the seduction she sensed earlier was even real. Now she had to drown her libido in alcohol to ensure she flushed him out of her system.

Six

Savannah stood on her own, her back to the bonfire. She snuggled into her jacket and yanked up the collar to fight the lowering temperature. The heat on her legs was sublime. Almost painful. The slight burning took her mind off Penny, Keenan, and the growing need to pee.

There were no toilets out here. None. And now that she cradled her third wine spritzer, her bladder was determined not to let her forget.

"Hey, sweet thang," a male slurred from beside her.

She palmed the unopened bottle in her hand and shot him an unimpressed look. "Hey..."

"You single?"

She chuckled and went back to staring at the impressive hedge that separated them from the wealth of the house yard. "Who's asking?"

"They call me Fox."

Of course they did. "Well, Fox, you're extremely forthright."

"When I want something, I usually take it."

Unfortunately, her vagina wasn't on offer. To him, at least. Keenan, on the other hand, was an entirely different story. Even with the question of his relationship status hovering in the back of her mind, she still had to fight the need to turn and seek him out through the flames.

"You lookin' to get laid?"

She breathed through the need to snort and looked at him with sincerity. "Come on, Fox, you can do better than that. You need to woo me." She gripped the cap of her unopened wine spritzer and, yet again, tried in vain to twist it off.

A tingle ignited in her neck and she wiggled her shoulders, trying to brush away the sensation that someone was watching her. She knew it was her imagination. Her hormones, to be more specific. She wanted Keenan to be looking at her, his appraisal raking over her skin.

"Woo you?" Fox swayed from side to side and kicked the dust up at his feet. "How?"

A throat cleared behind her and she glanced over her shoulder to find Keenan. Right there. He was less than a foot away, his striking presence hovering over her. He reached out and gripped her wine spritzer. Time stopped as he brushed her hand away and twisted the cap.

"Thanks." She turned to face him, grateful that Fox took the hint and slinked away. "Ditched the girlfriend, did you?"

There was no response, only sterile silence. She lowered her attention to the ground. To his large brown boots, not wanting to break the ice between them. At some point he had to give her something, anything, to fracture the awkwardness.

But apparently that time wasn't now.

"Did you know there's no bathrooms around here?" She looked up through her lashes, thankful that the bitter bite of annoyance had left his eyes. "A guy at the cooler told me to squat behind a tree." There was almost humor in his gray depths.

"Squat," she continued. "Behind a freakin' tree." She was a city girl. If there weren't toilets, you didn't go to the bathroom. You held your bladder. Until you initiated kidney failure, if necessary. "I'm at the point where I either have to stop drinking to avoid the carnage, or become comfortable with a higher level of intoxication so it isn't mentally scarring when I drop my pants in public."

His lips lifted at one side, a lazy grin she wished she witnessed more often. He shot a quick glance over her head, past the bonfire, then grabbed her wrist and gently tugged.

"What?" She looked over her shoulder to find Penny with her back turned. "Are you hiding from her?" She wanted to add, "You big girl," but held her tongue.

Keenan tugged her again, regaining her focus as he began walking backward. He wanted her to follow, but where? A few feet away? To the shadows?

She stumbled after him, the heat of the fire leaving her body and an entirely different warmth enveloping her from the inside out. As darkness surrounded them, she chanced another look toward the partygoers and made eye contact with a glowering Dominic.

Yep, I'm disappearing with a stranger. Please come looking for me if I don't return. She smiled at him, ignoring his concern, and two-stepped to catch up with Keenan's confident stride.

"Where are we going?"

He didn't stop. His grip held tight on her wrist, never loosening, and she didn't want it to. The noise of the party faded and the sound of her boots crunching in the grass became clearer. So did the pounding in her chest. He led them to a gap in the head-high hedge and pulled her into seclusion.

"Keenan?"

He stopped and turned to face her, their breath fogging in the frigid night air. He didn't gift her with a wicked curve of his lips. No. He was far better than that. He simply stared at her, his interest brushing over her facial features until he paused at her mouth.

She couldn't help the reaction to lick her drying lips. It was instinctual. The same way her nipples hardened and her pussy tingled.

He raised her hand to chest level, his friendly grip around her wrist changing to something more when he brought them palm to palm and entwined their fingers. She didn't have time to cherish the rough texture of his skin, or concentrate on the way his thumb slowly brushed hers, because he started walking again, leading her along a stone path.

She tip-toed, well aware they were trespassing, but unwilling to pull her hand from his grasp. Perfectly trimmed knee-high hedges bordered their way forward, and the darkness grew the closer they approached the overbearing house. Large white pillars held up curved balconies with glass bannisters. Each window had the curtains pulled closed, not a glimpse of the inside visible.

"Isn't this private property?"

He didn't answer. Not in words or movements.

There were still no lights on inside, and the possibility that no one was home should've lessened the fear scorching her veins.

"Do you know who lives here?"

He tugged on her hand, making her realize she'd stopped in the middle of the path. She didn't want to move. At least not in a forward motion.

He tugged again, and her feet complied.

"Keenan," she hissed.

He stopped, huffed, and pulled her close, their feet bare inches apart. She swallowed over the restriction in her throat, and fell a little further under his spell from the glow of the moonlight on his skin.

"Do you know who lives here?" Her voice was so soft she could barely hear it.

He focused on her eyes and his nostrils flared. She didn't know what was happening. What they were doing. She only knew her body was overheating even though her breath fogged between them.

"Keenan." God, she loved the sound of her voice whispering his name. "Are they home?"

He raised a finger to her mouth, held it there, and made her yearn to lick it away with each second that ticked by. He bit his lower lip, still staring, still standing so close. Then she was left reeling when he turned back to the path and continued to lead her forward, not stopping until they reached the corner of the building.

"Okay." Enough was enough. "I'm all for breaking the rules every now and again, but breaking the law is a little different."

He tugged her toward a nearby door and crouched down, scouring the ground underneath a leafy shrub. There was another breathy huff, then he moved to the garden on the other side of the doorway and performed the same scavenging ritual. When he sat back on his haunches, the shiny silver key in his hand incited nausea to pool in her belly.

"You must know who lives here." He had to if he knew where the key was, right?

She couldn't do this. Couldn't enter someone's house without an invitation. What was that even called? They weren't breaking into anything, but they were entering without permission.

"Keenan."

He stood, brushed his hands together, and maneuvered behind her, leaving her to face the door.

Oh, hell no. "You know what?" she whispered. "You're hot, mysterious, and tempting as hell, but this is really pushing my boundaries."

His body sank into her back and he placed a hand over her mouth. She was nervous, scared, yet horribly, achingly aroused. Her heart was hammering, her pulse echoing in her ears, and all the while, the hardness of his chest resting against her was far too enjoyable for words.

She clung to his wrist that hovered near her face and moved with him as he leaned forward, inserting the key into the lock. There was a twist and a push, then the door was ajar, the pitch black of inside looming frighteningly close.

She shook her head. *Nope. Not going in there.*

The heat of his breath tickled her neck, and his scent filled her lungs. Her breathing grew heavier, faster, then his nose nuzzled gently below her ear and she was lost. Sensations overwhelmed her. Desire constricted her chest.

Her world was condensed to him and her. The two of them—the grip of his hand over her mouth, the hardness of an unmistakable erection against her ass, the palpitations of her heart as she fought not to turn in his arms.

His hips bucked and she stumbled over the threshold, the heavy clunk of her heels echoing loudly against the tiled floor.

She froze.

He froze.

He pressed his hand tighter over her mouth and she stopped breathing altogether. She was caught between the temptation of pleasure and the possibility of a criminal record. His fingers drifted away from her lips and his body heat descended, from her back to her ass then her legs. He crouched behind her, his palm sweeping over her calf, down to her ankle.

She closed her eyes and bit the inside of her mouth, tasting the coppery tang of blood. He gripped the back of her heel and yanked, dislodging her boot, then pulled it off completely. Her sock covered toes were guided to the tile before his hands fell upon her other leg, going through the same motions.

As he stood, he closed the door behind them, securing her fate. He wove a hand around her waist and kept the other on her hip, cocooning her in arousal. There was nowhere to go but where he desired. Nowhere to run if it meant she wouldn't be in his arms. She slid forward, measuring her steps, ensuring she didn't make a sound.

"I don't know where I'm going," she whispered so low she wasn't sure he could hear.

There were doors to her left, an archway to her right, every avenue leading into more darkness. Her surroundings slowly crept into her consciousness—the warmth of indoor heating, the high ceilings, the smooth tiles, and the total silence apart from their breathing.

Keenan tightened his grip around her waist, forcing a gasp from her throat as he directed her into a small alcove. Moonlight seeped in from an adjoining room. A bathroom. She looked around the space surrounding her, noticing a basin to her left, a hand towel on an elegant metal hook, and another door up ahead.

He gestured forward, toward the closed door. It felt like a trap, like wherever he was leading was a dead end. She twisted in his arms, facing him, trying to read his eyes. Her heart began to pound, throb, pulse in her ears with incessant force.

"Keenan…" She was an idiot. An overstimulated and sex starved idiot. "Please don't tell me you broke into a house just so I could use the bathroom."

His slowly building grin said it all. He was insane. Intriguing, arousing, and clearly mentally unstable. He stretched around her, the squeak of a turning doorknob making the lust dilute from her system.

She'd had this all wrong. She'd mistaken his psychotic interest as a prelude to sex.

Evidently, there would be no bumping of private parts...only a bathroom break. *Idiot.*

Her shoulders slumped as he straightened, the tiny glimmer of his grin still in place.

"I'll use the bathroom," she grumbled. "But I still don't appreciate that my first criminal act will involve urinating in an unauthorized area."

His silent laughter taunted her. She turned, her chest heavy with disappointment, and walked toward the small room. One step, two step, three step, fo— His arm slid around her waist and he swung her around to face him. He was upon her in a heartbeat, thigh to thigh, waist to waist.

He loomed over her, his eyes dark and menacing, his features tight.

Fear collided with the needy plea from every erogenous zone in her body. She wanted him more than she wanted a clean police record. More than her next breath. More than her sanity. Yet she knew nothing about him, and what she did know involved trespassing and what seemed to be a complicated relationship with Penny.

"You're a confusing man," she murmured.

There was a flash of a smile, a glimmer of a dimple, then his mouth was upon hers, stealing the oxygen from her lungs and replacing it with scorching flames. He was a puppeteer, pulling her strings with precision, his lips working hers in confident and entirely unapologetic strokes.

She whimpered, begging for more as she placed her hands on his shoulders and clung tight. Why had she ever wanted words from him? His kiss said it all. It answered all her questions and confirmed the mutual attraction.

Then just as quickly as pleasure engulfed her, he stepped back, breaking the connection with brutal force. They panted into the silence, their chests heaving, her palms sweating.

"Keenan—"

He placed a finger to his lips and quirked his head, listening as he focused over his shoulder.

"Is someone coming?"

He shook his head and met her gaze. *Lying.* There was something deceptive in his eyes, something completely devoid of the passion from moments before. He jerked his chin toward the door behind her and shooed her with his hand.

She couldn't hear a thing, only harsh exhalations and the pounding rhythm of her pulse. Her nausea returned, coalescing with her panic over being caught.

"Okay." She shouldn't trust him. Not his actions, his seduction, or his confidence. She really shouldn't. Yet she did.

She was a fool for being here. For turning her back, padding into the tiny room and closing the door between them. She'd known he was trouble the moment they met. Without a word, or a smile, the defiance in his eyes had yelled at her to walk away. But, God help her, she was more of a fool for succumbing to the falling sensation taking over her body.

She had to have him. At least a little more than a taste.

Seven

Savannah inched from the bathroom, unable to see or hear Keenan. As she'd used the facilities, the soft pad of his footsteps had disappeared down the hall. If he left her alone in this huge monstrosity of a house, she would track him down and slay him. No matter how enjoyably her lips still tingled from his kiss.

She tiptoed to the basin, gently squeezed the tap, and let the cold trickle of water wash her hands. An excited prickle of awareness buzzed at the base of her neck. His presence hummed against her skin, making her aware of him before she raised her chin and caught sight of him staring back at her from the mirror. His large frame loomed in the archway, one shoulder lazily resting against the wall.

"We should leave." The tremor in her voice spoke of fear. Only she wasn't scared of any physical injury from him. No. She feared for the pain he could emotionally inflict. Her thoughts were already incoherent around him, yet his eyes spoke of cold detachment. She was sure the weight of a million female heartbreaks rested on his shoulders, along with the scorn of a thousand ex-lovers. Another Spencer in disguise, but Keenan seemed far more accomplished.

He pushed to his full height and stalked toward her. One step. Two. He came up behind her, his gaze scrutinizing her in the mirror. She knew what he wanted. Even through the sterile disconnect, she could still sense his desire, could even see it in his unwavering focus.

His hip brushed hers and she sucked in a breath. Stiffened. He turned into her, his chest to her back, his pelvis to her ass, and enticed labored inhalations from her lungs. The rush of static in her ears was deafening and she was sure he could hear the coarse scratch of her throat as she swallowed.

There was no doubt where this would lead. No misconception. She craved whatever he had to give. The only thing nudging her conscience was the where, when, and why. She couldn't be caught trespassing, especially not when Penny was lurking outside. Her time in Seattle was meant for work. More bad publicity for the Rydel name would ensure a horrific occupancy rate and an end to her secure employment.

"I need to leave." She needed to run.

He wove an arm around her waist, bringing a silencing finger to her lips and a rush of adrenaline to her veins. With his free hand, he smoothed her hair back from her neck and placed his mouth below her ear. Her skin prickled beneath his lips, a thousand tiny sparks from heaven where their skin touched.

Her hips began to sway of their own accord, the gentle rock, rock, rock causing her ass to brush against something hard and unforgiving behind her.

His arousal.

His cock.

Her cheeks heated. She was far from chaste, yet she hadn't imagined a man like him would be as turned on as she was. Not when his movements were smooth and calculated. From his reflection in the mirror, his attention seemed almost lazy, absentminded in a completely attentive way.

Christ. She was going insane.

"Keenan..."

He trailed his lips lower, along her neck where it joined her shoulder. He devastated her nerves and made her shake. Every breath she took was filled with his spicy scent. She drew him deep into her lungs, holding it within her, savoring him. Any man in her future would have to smell this good to gain even a sliver of her respect, because every man preceding him already paled in comparison.

She didn't take her attention off their reflection in the mirror. It was like watching a movie. An out of body experience. Too captivating to be real.

She wanted more from him. Something that wasn't slow or deliberate. Something entirely unrestrained. She wanted to glimpse a replica of the delirious passion which pounded through every inch of her.

As his lips continued to devastate her, she sank her teeth into her lower lip, fighting delirium. She moved her hips in a rhythm now, harder than before, and ass rubbed with unapologetic strokes against his cock.

She thought she could hear him growl. That a deep, intoxicating vibration was seeping from his chest. She closed her eyes and sank into the fantasy, wondering what he would say if he could speak. How he would sound. How his words would make her feel.

He ground into her, their movements becoming a simulation of sex. The finger against her mouth delved deeper, parting her lips in an erotic gesture that had her opening her eyes to gain a visual.

He stared at her, their gazes mingling in a silent appreciation that tore a whimper from the back of her throat. He flashed a smile at her, pure seduction, and scraped his teeth from her shoulder to the sensitive skin below her ear.

She ached to hear something dirty whisper from his lips. *I'm dying to fuck you. To taste you.* But nothing came. Only harsh inhalations and the continued thrum of her pulse in her ears. She sucked his finger into her mouth, just the tip, and this time she was certain his growl wasn't a hallucination. It was deep and dark and devilishly sexy.

He kept his finger in place, while his free hand lowered to her waistband, tugging at her belt. The clink-clink of her buckle startled her, flushing some of the adrenaline from her system. Were they really going to have sex in the bathroom? In the dark? In a complete stranger's house?

"We should go somewhere else." Back to her hotel. Any hotel. Christ, the dampness in her panties announced she'd take him in the back seat of her rental if given the chance. She just didn't want to be here.

Short wisps of hair shimmied over his forehead with the authoritative shake of his head. The denial shouldn't have turned her on. Nope. Yet it did.

Everything he did was purely erotic. His undeniable control. His strength in the face of demanding arousal. She craved his discipline and wanted him to crack at the same time. Push, pull. Breathe, suffocate. Mindful, careless. She couldn't keep up with her own mixed messages.

She turned in his arms and placed a firm hand on his chest. "Keenan, we need to leave."

A smirk tilted his lips and he leaned in, brushing his mouth over hers. She couldn't deny his kiss. The sweep of his tongue was lethargic, as if he were savoring the taste of her, memorizing every second of her surrender.

His body pressed into her, pushing her ass against the counter and his cock to her pubic bone. It wouldn't take much. The lowering of a zipper, the yank of her jeans. Five seconds and he could be inside her, burying himself deep, taking away the ache and replacing it with euphoria.

Damn it.

She reluctantly tore her lips away and pushed harder against his chest. "It isn't right to stay here." Her voice was filled with indecision. Her mind, too. "I really should go."

He kissed the curve of her mouth, her cheek, the side of her jaw. She whimpered, defenseless against his A-grade seduction. He pushed the jacket off her shoulders and dragged it down to rest on the counter behind her, her hands still bound in the material of the sleeves.

She couldn't move, couldn't flee. At least that's what she told herself. He stole her strength and made her feeble. Weak and needy. This time when his mouth brushed hers, he was savage. He consumed her, his tongue dancing with hers, his lips stealing her breath.

The tension on her wrist loosened and she trembled at the grate of her descending zipper. Coarse fingers slid into her panties, over the slim patch of trimmed curls, and lower, across the smooth skin directly above her pussy.

She felt like the goddess of lightning. As if a gazillion volts of electricity were flowing through her veins, all of them on a collision course with one throbbing, aching part of her body. The need to stop him filtered in and out of her consciousness, but the necessity for an orgasm far outweighed any contemplation that they were breaking the law.

She was sure the owners of the narcissistic mansion would understand. The police would understand, too. Anyone with a set of eyes and a fully functioning libido would realize that passing up this opportunity with such an undeniable man would compare to spitting in the face of a winning race horse.

She leaned back, starved of oxygen, and released a faint cry as he guided his touch through her slick flesh. He held her gaze, those guarded eyes seeing into her soul as he inched deeper, breaching her sex.

Her name flittered through the air and she frowned, wondering if her ears were deceiving her. Keenan's lips hadn't moved. He hadn't flinched at all.

"Did you..."

She lost track of her thoughts as he pulsed his fingers inside her, his thumb deftly stroking her clit. Her panties were soaked, uncomfortably so, and her nipples beaded painfully hard, begging for his touch. The dull pulse of an impending orgasm clenched her core. He already had her strung tight.

"*Savvy.*"

There it was again, this time louder. Unmistakable. She straightened, standing to her full height, and yanked her arms from the confinement of the jacket. Her hands landed on his chest, firm, hard, and undeniable as she pushed him.

"Did you hear that?" She cocked her head, trying to listen.

Keenan's sigh was filled with annoyance as the faint call of her name drifted in from outside.

Dominic.

Her silent seducer didn't remove his hand from her flesh. His mind was still on the game and he was tallying major points for

46

perseverance, but Dominic's voice wasn't a soundtrack she could have sex to.

"I need to go."

His thumb continued to stroke her clit in a way that spoke of mass disappointment if she walked away. There was a promise of pleasure in his eyes. A solemn pledge of ecstasy in his sensuous lips. She couldn't move. Her legs wouldn't allow it.

She trailed her hands from his chest to his neck and dug her nails into his nape. "I don't want to leave."

The ferocity in his steely irises didn't change. He rubbed harder, enticing tiny gyrations from her hips. She fell into him, grazing her mouth over the stubble of his jaw.

"I don't want you to stop." Her whisper was almost poetic in pitch. Whimsical. Erotic. "But I think you should."

"*Savvy*." Dominic's yell echoed off the walls and doused her in a bucket of reality.

She lowered her hands from Keenan's neck and slid away from him. Her chest heaved as she backtracked. He didn't deny her retreat, he remained facing the mirror and leaned over, placing his fists on the counter. His stare was harsh, judging her and finding her lacking.

"I'm sorry," she murmured. Sorry for following him in there. Sorry for being unable to deny his kiss. And sorry for still wanting more.

He made no move to console her. Instead, he stole her voice with his scrutiny. Even though his expression was blank and his lips flat, his eyes crackled with denied pleasure. She wanted to believe that look was his way of begging her to stay. Wanted to believe it and had to deny it at the same time because the narrowed stare was too harsh to be kind.

With her heart pounding in her throat, she winced in apology, snatched her jacket out from in front of him, and rushed from the alcove, not allowing herself to look back.

Savannah tried to control her panted breaths as she ran on the tips of her toes to the back door. Her boots were still waiting for her, while her sanity was left somewhere inside the bathroom.

She flung her jacket over her left arm and clutched the footwear under her elbow. With the flick of her wrist she opened the door and snuck outside. Freezing air infiltrated her lungs as she rushed along the path in sock-covered feet. The smell of bonfire smoke flittered on the breeze, the brief wisps of white ascending into the sky above the head-high hedge she approached.

She increased her pace toward the drunken chatter, breaking into a run along a barely visible path. She was gasping by the time she reached the small break in the hedge and slammed straight into a chest that almost set her on her ass.

"Dominic." She clung to the arms of her cousin's jacket to stop from falling.

"Where the hell have you been?" He glowered at her, taking in her appearance and stopping at her socks.

Her toes were ice, mere seconds away from falling off. "Don't ask." She placed her boots on the ground and yanked on her jacket. Warmth slowly heated her veins, but it wasn't from the added layer of clothing. It was entirely from the images of Keenan in her mind. She'd followed him into that house, stumbling over her expanding libido along the way. He was the exact opposite of every business orientated, straight-laced man she'd ever slept with, and the favorable taste that still lingered on her tongue made it clear her previous appetite would no longer satisfy.

"Have you seen Keenan?" Dominic crossed his arms over his chest, annoyance personified.

"Um…" She leaned over, shoving her feet into her boots to buy time.

"Savvy?" His voice was a growl.

"Look, I'm sorry I disappeared." She fiddled with her socks, still unable to look at him. "But you don't need to worry about me."

"I don't care that you disappeared. But disappearing with Keenan is a bad idea."

She bristled. Straightened. "Because?"

"Because he's not the type of guy for you."

She opened her mouth, poised to retaliate, then snapped it closed again. Dealing with Penny and the stick up her ass was hard enough. She didn't want to argue with Dominic, too. He was her only ally. Her only friend in Seattle.

"I'm not trying to be an ass." He softened his tone. "I'm just looking out for you."

"Looking out for me?" She gave him a half-hearted smile and raised a brow. "Or maybe inserting yourself into something that isn't really your business."

He stared at her for a moment, the weight of thoughts heavy in his eyes, then turned to face the fire. "Women assume Keenan is different because of his lack of speech. They think it sets him apart from other guys, but it doesn't. He's the same fuck 'em and leave 'em type. He'll burn you, just like any other man would."

A derisive chuckle escaped her lips. He thought she was naïve? Well, she wasn't. Highly susceptible to charm, maybe, but she had no doubt Keenan wasn't a safe guy. Trouble flickered in the flecks of his blue-gray eyes, it was forged into his DNA, and she'd willingly followed his lead. She'd do it again, too. "I don't understand. I thought you said he was family. That he was good people."

"He is…"

"Then why are you concerned? You know I'm only here for a few months. I'm not in the market for commitment, I'm here to work." The crunch of heavy footsteps approached from behind and she lowered her voice. "What is this really about?"

Dominic turned to her, but his focus rested over her shoulder, past the hedge. "Keenan," he muttered, and she wasn't sure if it was an answer or a greeting.

An unforgettable scent tickled her nose and her spine tingled at the advancing footsteps. The man of the moment stopped beside her, his spiked hair teasing her periphery as she fought to keep a smitten smile from her lips.

"Fancy seeing you out here." Dominic didn't mimic her mood. Instead, he scowled.

She waited for a response, needing two seconds of silence to remind her that Keenan wouldn't fill the awkwardness.

"Penny is looking for you. She was wondering why you disappeared." Dominic spoke as if Savannah wasn't there. "You should go and explain where you were."

Discomfort crawled over her skin, shuddering over her in a wave from her fingers to her toes. She'd never been bad at math, but right now she refused to put two and two together. After what she'd experienced with Keenan, the equation that also involved Penny was impossible to acknowledge.

"Does Savvy know the two of you work together?"

Savannah snapped her lips shut and measured the breaths through her nose, calming herself before she chanced a proper look at Keenan. His jaw ticked and his eyes were narrowed. Everything about him, from his expression to his stiff posture, spoke of his fury.

"It didn't come up in conversation," she murmured, hoping her poor attempt at humor might derail the upcoming train wreck.

A burst of breath left Keenan's lips, the slightest laugh. He inched closer to her, right against her side, the strength and warmth of him making her solid. His gaze lowered, those haunted eyes reaching inside her to squeeze her lady bits. Pressure landed low on her back. His hand? She held her breath as he traced his palm down her jacket to her ass and slipped something into her pants pocket.

"That's hilarious, Savvy," Dominic muttered. "You should go and tell

Penny all about it. I'd love to see her reaction."

Keenan's lip curled in a snarl and he snapped his fierce glare back to Dominic. He may lack the ability to speak, but the way he mouthed *fuck you* was clearer than an announcer on a megaphone. They stared each other down while Savannah's chest thumped to the point of pain. Then Keenan strode away, heading toward the blonde goddess in question who was glaring at them, hands on hips, from the other side of the bonfire.

"For a man who lacks speech, he quite clearly made his feelings known." She smiled, hoping to hide the jealousy eating her from the inside out.

"This isn't a joke, Savvy. You're here to facilitate a smooth sale transition with Penny's company, right?"

She frowned. "Yes."

"Well, if she finds out you're fucking around with Keenan, she'll make your life a living hell."

The warmth from adrenaline and the growing bonfire didn't penetrate the chill invading her bones. "They're together?" She wished she could've hidden the resentment in her tone, but it was there, blaringly obvious. Along with the hint of disloyalty.

"I don't know for certain. They're close—physically and emotion-ally, but Keenan refuses to discuss my sister with me. What I can tell you, is that Penny has been in love with him for years, and seeing you anywhere near him will cause a shit storm you don't want to be involved in."

Discuss? With such a strong relationship, she would've thought her cousin had a better word to describe his communication with a man who remained silent. But focusing on specifics was only a diversion from the real issue—Penny was in love with the man who only moments earlier had his talented digits inside Savannah's hoo-ha.

Déjà vu, eat your heart out.

"He gave me no indication he wasn't single." She tracked Keenan's movements to Penny's side. Even now, with disappointment making her stomach heavy, she still couldn't see him as anything other than intensely gorgeous.

"Maybe he is. Maybe he isn't. But it won't matter to my sister. I've seen her fight for him before. It'll be worse now because you're already her rival."

Keenan stopped at Penny's side and turned his back to Savannah. It seemed almost deliberate. The emotional cut off that severed his connection to a mistress so he could devote his attention to his girlfriend. Had she really become the other woman? And if so, how much did she care?

"I don't owe Penny any favors." She met Dominic's gaze. "I kissed a guy she was infatuated with when we were teenagers. She hasn't had a nice word to say to me since. The guy didn't even like her. He thought she was a child. She *was* a—"

"She lost her virginity to that douche."

No. She shook her head. It wasn't possible. Penny had been a minor. She'd been so young. A child.

Dominic nodded. "I'm afraid it's true. We were always making her feel like a bratty little kid, and Mom blamed me, saying she only did it to try to prove herself. That she looked up to us and all that shit."

"Why didn't anyone tell me?"

"I probably would've told you at the next vacation, but it never happened."

No, that had been their last summer together. Dominic's father had passed away from a heart attack in the fall, and Savannah's had packed his bags and taken off, never to return. Both their families had been torn apart, and celebrating the summer had been the farthest thought from their minds.

"I'm sorry, Dominic, but I still don't believe it excuses her behavior." She wrapped her hands around herself, trying to ward off guilt from the past. "We were kids back then. We're adults now, and I knew nothing about her and Keenan."

It was a tiny lie. She'd witnessed the way Penny had greeted him. She'd known something was between them. And why was the blame on her, anyway? It was Keenan's responsibility to remain faithful if he was in a relationship. He hadn't given her the slightest impression he wasn't single. In fact, the way he glided his fingers into her pussy gave a vastly contrasting impression.

"I can apologize for the past, but what's happening now is all her doing. I'm not responsible for tonight's tension. She's the one who arrived with a pole-vault stick up her ass."

She took a step, heading God knew where. There was nobody else here for her to speak to. Unless she considered Fox a likely candidate, which she didn't.

"Please, Savvy." Dominic grabbed her jacket. "Be the bigger person. It's been too long since we've seen each other. I don't want this trip to end in an excuse not to see you for another ten years. Just leave and let tonight blow over."

"You want me to go?" He was kicking her out. Sending her home like a child.

"I'm trying to save you from the inevitable crash and burn that is my sister. We both know what she's capable of."

"I don't believe this." She shoved her hands in her jacket pockets and shook her head. "You're treating me like a whore."

"That's not my intention." His tone was unconvincing. "Whatever you do is your choice, Savvy. But whether you decide to leave or stay, you might want to think about re-buckling your pants so it doesn't look like you've been fucking Keenan in the bushes."

Blood drained from her face as he gave her one last knowing look and then strode away. The potency of humiliation made bile rise in her throat and she tugged the sides of her jacket together, hiding her lowered zipper from view. She'd never felt so cheap or worthless. Fury mingled, too.

She refused to take responsibility for what happened tonight. Yes, the past was her fault. She'd kissed a guy her much younger cousin had fallen for. She hadn't even apologized. But surely there had to be a time limit on holding a grudge over mistakes made by children. They'd been in school, for God's sake.

"I guess I'll see you around, then," she called after Dominic.

He paused, shot her an apologetic smile and then kept on walking. *Fuck.* This was humiliation at its finest. The unmistakable bite of rejection nipped at her heels.

She stormed to her car, her chin high, her shoulders straight. She yanked her car door open and sank into the driver's seat. After all these years, Penny was still a little brat. Nothing had changed. Not even Savannah's desire to kiss a man she knew her cousin was infatuated with. Which reminded her... She shoved a hand into her back pocket and grasped the piece of paper Keenan had placed there.

Meet me for dinner tomorrow at the Sated Palate. 8pm.

She stared at his messy scribble and couldn't pinpoint why her heart rate increased. Her feelings for this man she barely knew were crazy. Delirious. Unhinged. She felt tingly for the first time in years, but now those sensations were becoming clouded by guilt.

She glanced through the driver's window and found Keenan focused on her. The narrowed intensity of his gaze splashed her with a bucket of delight. She shuddered, from her shoulders to her toes, every inch of her skin restless because of those eyes that spoke of an unsettling future. He was fixated on her, not Penny at his side. He didn't even spare her cousin a glance as his severity rocked Savannah's foundations.

Come talk to me, she mouthed the words nonsensically.

Christ, what was she thinking? He wasn't the typical, everyday man. He was someone far more intricate. Someone who couldn't ease her discomfort with conversation.

She raised a hand, waved in farewell, and didn't wait for his reply as she jammed the keys into the ignition and brought the engine to life.

Maybe Dominic was right. Removing herself from the Keenan equation might be the best option. All she had to do was convince the pulsing parts of her body there couldn't be an encore tomorrow.

No matter how much body parts south of the equator protested at the thought.

Email Correspondence

Date: 20th December

Subject: Do you remember the first night we met?

Savannah,

I'm not poetic or romantic. I'm barely civil most days, but you nudged at those frozen parts of me and made me wonder what it would be like to be different.

From the first night we met, you captivated me with your non-bullshit attitude. You infuriated me, yet with equal ferocity, you intrigued me. I couldn't ignore you, no matter how much I wanted to. There was too much fire and enthusiasm in your hazel eyes.

Your infatuation was worse.

No other woman has looked at me like a puzzle strewn across the floor, waiting to be pieced together. I've always been seen as a completed picture—a skewed image that would forever be a shitty addition to a flawless collection. My faults make others feel better about themselves.

But not you. You never showed superiority over me. Not even at your worst. I only witnessed your affection and eventually your anger that hid the heartache.

I admit, the night of the bonfire wasn't my first mistake when it came to you, it just feels like one of my biggest. I was annoyed that you'd stayed on my mind all week. It was out of character for me to let a woman control any piece of me. Yet you did without even being present. Then you showed up in your rental car, completely impeccable in casual clothes and no make-up, and set the bar for beauty without even knowing it.

Leading you inside, kissing you, seducing you, it was impulsive. It was a mistake. If only I'd denied the carnality that always seemed to drag us under, things never would've become this complicated.

While you were in the bathroom, I escaped to the back door, grasped the handle, and contemplated leaving you to find your own way to the bonfire. It would've saved a lot of pain if I did. I knew there was no future for us. Nothing apart from gratification.

Only I couldn't deny wanting to taste every inch of you, touch every nerve, and inhale every one of those feminine gasps that made my cock pulse. I wanted to own you. To consume you the same way you were consuming me.

The fury was overwhelming as I held that door handle. I hated the effect you had on my libido. Worse was the response from more emotional parts of my body. I would've killed to come to your defense when Penelope insulted you. To be your knight in shining armor, as it were. But how? Through pantomime? That would've been fucking hilarious, right?

Instead, I tried to make it up to you through touch—the only thing I seemed to excel at when it came to us. I could've told you there was no need to be quiet. The house was vacant, but establishing a level playing field was an opportunity I couldn't deny. And what I had planned didn't require conversation. I wanted your body, not your words. Your acquiescence, not your intrigue. Most of all, I wanted you to experience passion from my perspective. To strip the sensations down to pure carnality. Devoid of placating dribble and nonsensical dialogue.

I wanted you and me and nothing else.

Only something happened to me that night. I didn't like it, nor did I want to allow it. You wove your delicate fingers around my consciousness and still haven't let go.

I need to see you. I need to explain. Please message me back and let me know you're receiving my messages.

Keenan

Nine

Savannah rested her elbows on the tiny suite desk and tried to pretend the bedside clock wasn't glaring at her from the other side of the room. Today was meant to be a day of rest. Instead, her Sunday had been filled with panicked phone calls from staff and impromptu meetings with management to discuss how to handle the latest Grandiosity bombshell.

Evidently, Penny *did* work on weekends.

Savannah spared one last glance over her shoulder at the bedside clock—7:25 p.m.—then sighed as she swung back around to re-read the email sitting unsent on her laptop.

> To all Seattle Rydel staff,
>
> Earlier this afternoon I became aware of concerns from employees regarding interview requests from Grandiosity. Please be advised this is a normal part of the changeover process.
>
> Although I wasn't informed that you would be contacted, it's your future employer's right and obligation to prepare you for the transition into their team. This should not be considered an interview to fight for your employment, no matter how the correspondence was worded. As previously discussed, the security of your job was promised in the sale of the

Rydel Seattle property.

I believe the interview is merely to establish a relationship between you and Grandiosity and to help pave the way to an informed future.

If you still have concerns, please feel free to contact me at any time.

Kind regards,
Savannah Hamilton

Her finger hovered over the send button, shaking. There was no doubt in her mind that Penny had sent the email in retaliation for last night. And it was entirely unacceptable. These employees had children and mortgages. They had bills to pay and family members to support. They also had guests depending on them to provide a hospitable environment.

Panic was expected. It was inevitable and exactly what Penny set out to achieve. All Savannah could do was work harder to soothe the uncertainty and hope her assurances wouldn't turn out to be lies.

As stated in the contract for sale, Grandiosity had to retain all incumbent staff. However, they would all be placed on a three month probation period. What happened during that period was out of Savannah's control.

She peeked over her shoulder again, still irked by the clock. 7:28 p.m. Last night, she decided meeting Keenan for dinner was a bad idea. It didn't matter that she could still feel his touch in the darkness as she tried to sleep. It didn't change her mind when she woke up from erotic dreams of him. And this morning, Penny's drama had cemented the reasons for not going.

Only now she was searching for excuses to go back on her decision.

His smirk haunted her every time she closed her eyes. When she licked her lips, they tingled with memories. She pictured him in the restaurant, alone, suave and dripping with confidence. The thought of disappointing him made her itch.

"Damn him."

She scrolled through her inbox, reading all the subject headings from terrified staff who feared for their future. It wasn't right. Penny shouldn't have this amount of control. And she certainly shouldn't use it to intimidate Savannah on a personal level.

"Damn her. Damn her. Damn her."

She pushed to her feet and faced the bed. The alarm clock changed before her eyes—7:32 p.m. She wasn't even dressed. Her hair was in a messy bun and she didn't have any make-up on. But if she met Keenan she could grill him for information on Grandiosity and Penny's authority as the CEO's assistant. The dinner could be used for business purposes. Meeting with him could give her insight to help smooth the sale transition.

It was in her employees' best interest for her to go...

"You're insane," she grated through clenched teeth and ran for the shoebox sized cupboard in the hall. She yanked a long-sleeved dress from a coat hanger, thigh-high stockings, a black jacket, and shiny pumps from the floor. By the time she was dressed it was 7:38 p.m.

Make-up took another ten minutes. She was going to be late. Really late.

She didn't bother with jewelry; she wasn't dressed to impress, anyway. It was business, after all. Business, business, business, even though the palpitations of her heart said otherwise. She tugged on her heels, snatched her clutch from the bedside table, and chanced another glimpse at the clock. 7:55 p.m.

"Damn it."

Keenan didn't seem the type to wait for anyone, let alone a woman he barely knew. She stalked from her room, ignored everyone in the reception area, and hailed a cab with the precision of a Playboy model.

Before she'd had a chance to properly consider what she was doing, she was outside Sated Palate, looking through the large floor to ceiling windows for a man she shouldn't be searching for.

Indecision kicked in. Or maybe it was common sense. He wouldn't have waited for her. Not for fifteen minutes.

She turned, prepared to hail another cab, and came face to face with temptation.

"Keenan," his name gasped from her lips.

The sight of him gave her vertigo. He was dressed in tailored pants that hugged his thighs and a collared, buttoned-up shirt which left little to the imagination of the muscled chest underneath. Even in the freezing cold his sleeves were folded above his wrists, giving him a kick of casual sophistication.

He raised a brow at her, wordlessly asking where she was going in such a hurry.

"I couldn't see you inside." Her mouth dried at the perfection of him, her body reacting to a rapid case of dehydration. "I thought you might have left already."

He smiled, a meager lift of beautiful lips before he began to leisurely take in her appearance, all the way to her feet. She could feel the trail of his stare. It skimmed every nerve along her skin, nudged all her erogenous zones one by one.

His eyes came back to meet hers and he mouthed, "*Stunning.*" Or at least she thought he did. He could've just as easily said *starving.*

She glanced at the cars behind him, at the sanctuary that would come from the inside of a cab. How was she going to communicate with him in a public restaurant? It was different last night. Their bodies had spoken for them.

He followed her gaze, searching for the truth she didn't want to give. She swallowed, unable to admit she was about to run. Anyone with a vagina would roll their eyes and groan at her desire to flee. Well, anyone apart from Penny.

But for the first time in Savannah's life she felt susceptible to exposure. She wasn't like most women. She didn't swoon over the thought of commitment or the possibility of marriage. Relationships didn't interest her, unless it revolved around phenomenal sex and no tightening strings.

So why did Keenan nudge her consciousness like no other man had before? He remained on her mind when she should be focused on work. He also intrigued her for reasons that didn't relate specifically to the bedroom.

It could be the whole want-what-you-can't-have scenario. She was only in Seattle temporarily, and the language barrier was a thrilling challenge. Her cousin's warning to stay away hadn't helped either. She'd regressed to her childhood when her mother would tell her not to say or do something. Of course she was going to disobey at the first given opportunity.

It was human nature.

Instinct.

A strong hand brushed her hip and he looked at her with a raised brow.

"I was..." She licked her bottom lip. "I shouldn't be here, Keenan. Dominic made it clear that I shouldn't spend time with you." *Christ.* She needed to keep her mouth shut.

His smile faded. The tiny increments of dissatisfaction stabbed at her sternum as his focus narrowed. He stepped into her, his lips tight, his eyes feral. The hand on her hip vanished and in its place came a delicate grip on her chin.

She swallowed hard, hearing everything he couldn't say in the possessive expression on his face. He didn't stop looking at her, didn't quit compelling her into mind-numbing confusion until his mouth pressed against hers, stealing her thoughts of fleeing.

He tugged her into his body and kissed her as if nobody was watching. As if nobody else existed. With deft flicks of his tongue and soulful movements of his lips, he made her toes curl and the most delicious sensation ignite in her belly.

When they broke apart, his attention was already fixed on the restaurant, denying her emotional attention to parallel all the sexual. With a jerk of his head, he coaxed her forward and held the restaurant door open for her.

"The table you requested is ready, sir." A young woman smiled at him and then led them through the bustling room to an intimate setting beside the window.

The building was contemporary. All dimly lit surfaces and quaint furnishings. It was neither upmarket nor shabby, which led her to believe he hadn't tried to impress her with the location. Not that she was hoping to be impressed.

Not at all.

Nope.

The atmosphere was casual yet still entirely appealing. Just like Keenan.

As Savannah approached the table, he grabbed her elbow, halting her. She opened her mouth in confusion, then closed it as he slid past her and graciously pulled out her chair. The gesture startled her. Confused her. She had him pegged as the bad-boy, mysterious type, yet here he was with impeccable manners and a pleased gleam in his eye.

"A gentleman?" She slid into her chair, loving the way his knuckles brushed the back of her jacket. "I never would've guessed."

He moved out from behind her, grabbed his own chair and repositioned it from the opposite side of the table, to the spot beside her. *Close, so close.* His leg brushed hers as he sat, and from the unaffected way he held his expression, she knew it was deliberate.

He wasn't startled by the connection that buzzed between them. He was probably immune. Too perfect to notice anything as meaningless as attraction. His gaze continued to focus on her. It didn't stop. They shared a conversation without words. A communication without speech.

"I'm sorry I was late." She shrugged off her jacket, needing to break the silence and sever the power of his stare. "I wasn't sure if I should come."

He gave a breath of a chuckle and grinned at the table as if he knew she hadn't planned on walking inside to find him.

"Did you have fun last night?" She should've stopped the question before it left her lips. He couldn't give her a definitive answer. Not without words. And she didn't want to second guess if an affirmative answer meant he'd gotten down and dirty with her cousin. "Forget I asked. I guess I'm not comfortable with silence."

She wished she would've spared a thought at the awkwardness of a shared meal. Maybe it would be different if she knew him like Dominic did. But a one-sided conversation in a bustling restaurant wasn't her idea of fun. The last thing she wanted to do was offend him, yet this situation was entirely out of her comfort zone, not only on a personal level, on a sexual one, too.

He frowned at her from under his lashes and opened his mouth as if to speak. She crept forward in her chair, poised to read his lips only to watch them press together again.

A menu was shoved toward her, his gruff movements announcing that she'd offended him with her 'uncomfortable with silence' comment.

"Thanks."

He didn't open his menu. Instead, he sat there, watching as she opened hers and then trailed an index finger over the list of food. She couldn't read a word. She was too busy stealing glances at him, wondering when or if the meal would become easier. The more he watched her, the more her nervousness built.

She wracked her brain trying to figure out what to say, what to do. He was relying on her to create a conversation and she was clueless when he couldn't reply. Apart from playing a one-sided game of twenty questions that only involved yes or no answers, she was stumped.

It wasn't like he was helping to soften the awkwardness. He could've pulled out his cell and texted her. Or maybe he didn't have a cell... Hell, a napkin and pen would've sufficed. But the hint of determination in his features seemed to imply his unwillingness to acknowledge his lack of speech.

She closed her eyes in defeat and internally chastised herself for meeting him. It was a bad idea. Dominic had already told her as much. She'd ignored the one cousin she trusted. All for what? A man who daunted her? A guy who didn't believe in fidelity?

The warmth of his touch slid over her knee and she opened her eyes to find steely gray irises focused on her. Breathing became hard, thinking even harder.

"Keenan." His fingers had a direct line to her sex. Each brush against her skin was like a swipe along her pussy. In the blink of an eye her apprehension flittered away and arousal descended like a monsoon.

She wanted him—his conversation, his attention, his body. Absolutely all the things she shouldn't want or couldn't have.

She shook her head, denying the pleasure taking over her senses. "I didn't come here because of us." She cringed at how presumptuous she sounded. There was no *us*. There were only stolen moments with his fingers in her cherry pie. "What I mean is, I didn't come here because of last night. I came because I hoped to get answers about Penny."

He straightened, the heavenly touch of his fingers sliding from her thigh to rest back on the table.

At least she had his attention.

"Dominic told me you work with her."

He nodded, the movement clipped, and grasped the glass of water in front of him. She watched as he drank, the clear liquid moistening deliciously full lips.

"Does that mean you work for Grandiosity?"

He inclined his head. She wanted to push for more information, to determine what role he played, but without pen and paper the guessing game could take hours. Grandiosity was more successful and had a larger scope of employees than Rydel. He could be anything from a graphic designer to a maintenance man. And she felt entirely guilty for assuming his position was low-level due to his limited ability to communicate.

No, it wasn't only his lack of speech.

He didn't boast an excessive bank balance. His attire so far hadn't included expensive suits. There wasn't a flash of an ostentatious watch or an offer to ride in his extravagant car. He'd taken her to an understated restaurant, spent time at family dinners and low-key bonfires. She'd spent enough time around men with deep pockets to know the signs.

She took a break from Keenan's scrutiny and focused on the far end of the restaurant. Business was no longer on the agenda. This was now about her body, the way it tingled, the way certain parts clenched when he stared, and most importantly, how she could get more. She had to spit it out. Get on with it. Confident the hell out of this discussion.

"Are you with her?" Her tone was authoritative. Fearless. Totally bad-ass.

He leaned back in his chair, crossed his arms over his chest, and shut her off to his suave affection. He didn't need money or power. That look alone sent her up in flames, exposing every nerve to his appealing confidence.

She glared, attempting to chink his superiority, and failed miserably. He was impenetrable. A stone-cold wall.

"You don't think I deserve to know?"

He appraised her with an impassive stare. There was no charm, no concern. He seemed like he didn't care for the conversation, or her in general anymore.

"Well, as informative and fun as this whole experience has been, I think it's best if I leave." She placed her hands on the edge of the table, preparing to push to her feet when his palm pressed down on her fingers.

"Are you ready to order?"

A waitress stepped into Savannah's periphery, a notepad in hand. Damn her and her impeccable timing.

Keenan turned his attention to the woman, his smile sly as he nodded.

"The usual?" the young, brunette asked.

Another nod. As the woman scribbled on her notepad, he raised a flat hand to his chin and then lowered it to expose his palm.

Sign language?

"No problem." The waitress turned her attention to Savannah. "How about you?"

"What is his usual?" It was probably something masculine and entirely caveman. Steak. Rare. Fries and definitely no salad or vegetables.

"He has the dipping breads as an appetizer, which is big enough to share." The woman shrugged. "Or you could order your own if you like..."

Keenan was already shaking his head, the gentle glide back and forth holding too much authority for her nipples not to take notice.

"No, I'm sure he'll let me have some of his." She grinned at him and then focused back on the waitress in a vain attempt to prove to him that he didn't hold all her attention.

"For the main meal, he has the twelve-ounce rib eye, cooked medium with pepper sauce and a side of potato wedges."

"That sounds perfect." She held in her laughter at her accurate assessment, not that it mattered. The sensation quickly faded. If she could pick his palate with ease, then she couldn't be far from wrong in her previous assumptions.

He wasn't about success and hard work like she was. But more distressing than that, he was trouble. Madness. He was going to cause her more days of unsettled thoughts and maybe a few gray hairs, and still she couldn't bring herself to leave. Not before she had her answer.

"The appetizers won't be long."

Savannah nodded as the waitress sauntered away. There was a beat of uncomfortable silence, one that settled discomfort at the top of her spine and slowly shimmied its way down.

"I need to know, Keenan." She couldn't let the conversation drop. "It's not like I'm going to run to Penny as soon as you divulge the truth. I just need to know for my own sake. To figure out if it's something I'm willing to get involved in."

She hadn't been sure. Not consciously. Being the other woman was a taboo, a severe slap in the face to the girl-code, yet she'd announced what her conscience had been trying to hide—she'd contemplated surrendering to this man, girlfriend or not. She'd contemplated it over and over and over again. Almost non-stop since the bonfire.

He leaned in close, so close their breath mingled as he shook his head. *No.*

"Are you sure?" Her voice was raspy, sex starved.

He came closer, gifting her with the seriousness in his eyes, before he swiped his mouth over hers in a firm press that had her thighs clenching together. When he pulled back, she felt like she'd disembarked from a speed boat race, and here he was, relaxed as if he'd just returned from a late night stroll in the park.

He remained there, *right* there, his nose rubbing against hers as he nodded.

"Do you know I'm only here for a few months?" Her throat was dry, making it harder to breathe. He nipped her lower lip, making her gasp. Everything he did was delicious. Why? Why, oh why had the heavens given one man so much power?

She pulled back, as far as her hungered libido would allow. "Is that the appeal? The foregone expiration date?"

He growled, the deep sound echoing between them. He ran a strong hand through her hair, holding her in place as he looked her in the eye. "*No,*" he mouthed with fervor.

"Oh, boy," she whispered, inspiring another of his jaw-dropping grins. "You're going to be a huge mistake, aren't you?"

His soundless chuckle brushed against her tongue and he nodded into her as he took possession of her mouth. He continued to hold her, his hand still in her hair, his lips firm and unyielding. He kissed her like they were seconds away from fucking, as if they weren't in a crowded room with a hundred witnesses to their carnality.

"Ahum." A throat cleared at their side. "The dipping breads."

She pulled back a hell of a lot quicker than someone who didn't have a problem with public displays of affection, and winced at the waitress.

The woman nudged the plate between them and placed it on the table. "Enjoy."

The waitress's sly smile announced she wasn't talking about the food.

Savannah giggled through the embarrassment and waited for the unease to disappear.

It didn't.

She was more nervous now than before the kiss. Before he blew her metaphorical socks off and out the door, never to be seen again. Because now they'd wordlessly acknowledged they were taking this thing between them a step further.

She was going to get to know him, at least physically, and if Penny found out it would put all the Rydel Seattle staff in jeopardy. More than they already were.

It was a lot of weight to place on Savannah's shoulders, all in the name of sex.

She gripped her cloth napkin and twisted it in her hands to remove the sweat from her palms. She didn't plan on advertising her involvement with him. Dominic already disapproved, and she didn't know anyone else in Seattle.

She could keep it discreet.

She totally could.

Her chest pounded in protest and she heaved out a breath to dislodge the ache. In slow motion, Keenan's hand glided over hers, squeezing a dose of support into her being. She met the question in his gaze and couldn't help the way her heart climbed into her throat at the sight of him.

He knew something was wrong.

"I'm nervous." Admitting the truth didn't alleviate the awkwardness. In fact, it increased it. "I'm worried what will happen if Penny finds out."

His brow furrowed. It wasn't in anger or resentment. There was a hint of regret to it. A softness that spoke of apology.

He turned her hand over and began to trail his fingers along the lines of her palm. Such a simple gesture, and yet the sensation ricocheted right through her. It tickled and titillated. Soothed and stung. Every single part of her was humming with life.

They sat in silence that was no longer uncomfortable. She took her time to appreciate all the little things she hadn't noticed before. Like the way his eyes told a tale. Those gray depths were descriptive, speaking louder than words. She could see how he was mesmerized with her. Intrigued. The same way she was with him.

And his mouth—oh, boy, his mouth. The way his tongue snaked out to moisten his lips, the slow, confident lethargy of the movement. And his smile. She sighed at the visual pleasure of him.

"You make me wonder what's going on in that mind of yours."

His gradually building smirk said it all. There were dirty things driving his thought process and she wanted to be involved in every single one of them.

She lowered her focus to the table and chuckled. "I wish you could tell me. It's frustrating not being able to have a con...ver..." Her gaze snapped to his as she realized what she was about to say. "I'm sorry. I wasn't thinking." Dread settled over her, along with shame that heated her cheeks.

Her apology came too late, he'd already stiffened, his shoulders broad, his chin stubbornly high as he pulled his hand from hers.

She hadn't meant what she said... On second thought, she had. It was frustrating being unable to hold a conversation with him when her mind wanted to hear all his secrets at once. Only she hadn't realized how ignorant and insensitive her insult was until it echoed in her ears. "I just mean, I'd love to be able to talk with you."

The narrowed disgust of his eyes stabbed through her. She'd done it again, adding more heartless fuel to the blazing fire.

"It's not criticism." Okay, that's exactly what it was. It was rude and harsh and entirely unforgiving. Word by word, she was digging a hole and burying herself. "I'm sorry."

His smile was feral as a scoff fell from his lips. He stood, his chair abruptly screeching against the tile. She sat in shock as he pulled his wallet from the back pocket of his pants and dumped cash on the table.

"Keenan." He couldn't be serious. They hadn't even touched their bread, the main meal was still to be cooked. He couldn't leave. He had to give her a chance to make it right. Or was he really that sensitive? "*Please*, sit down."

They were gaining an audience. People were looking, judging her, but nowhere near as harshly as Keenan was with the sneer curling his lip. He flipped the black leather closed and shoved his chair under the table. He didn't meet her gaze again and she was thankful. She didn't want those powerful eyes sending her to hell and back with one glance.

"Please forgive me," she whispered.

He heard her, it was visible in the way his jaw ticked, and he walked away nonetheless, taking any respect she had for herself along with him.

Date: 21st December

Subject: The sated palate

Dear Savannah,

So many weeks later and the thought of that night still makes me fucking crazy. If only you knew how many times I had to clench my fists from the need to speak to you. I would've given anything to say your name, to whisper it in your ear, to make you shiver with the beauty of that one word.

I've told you before that you saw more in me than anyone else, yet you also stoked to life insecurities that I haven't felt since childhood. You made me want to be someone else. You made me wish for a perfection I wasn't capable of.

How did you do that?

Without even asking for anything, I want to give you the world. I would've given anything to be able to smile back at you that night and brush off the disappointment of your comment. Anything, Savannah.

I could've explained the possibility of communicating with sign language. I could've taken out my cell and messaged you words that would distract you from my defects. If only you hadn't knocked my legs out from beneath me.

You know me now, Savannah. You know we can communicate

without the need to speak. Please come back to me so we can work this out.

Keenan

Ten

Days passed without communication from anyone apart from the employees in the hotel Savannah currently inhabited. There was no sign of Penny, no emails from Mr. Rydel, no calls from Dominic, and definitely no word from Keenan. She'd even spent an entire day calling recruitment agencies to fill the holes in their current staff levels to ensure the upcoming wedding didn't go to hell, but she was still waiting for even one reply.

She'd become ostracized, cocooned in her own little world. Her friends back home were busy with work and their upcoming plans for Thanksgiving. Spencer was the only one going out of his way to connect with her, and she was trying to dodge his calls as best as possible.

The positive result was her workload being up to date. She'd found a semblance of routine in her work hours, and staff even began to smile at her in greeting. They trusted her, and she was devoted to strengthening that trust through continuous conversations and responding to unending emails of concern.

But the nights were lonely. She'd spent five evenings alone in the bath, a gossip magazine clutched between her fingers, and now the luxury had worn off. Evidently, relaxation wasn't her thing. Even the frangipani salts the concierge had bought her hadn't increased the enjoyment of tonight's soaking.

It didn't leave her optimistic for the rest of her stay in Seattle, either. It was only Friday night—a mere two weeks since she'd arrived, and there were still so many desolate nights ahead of her. If only Dominic would call. He was her only hope for a social life. She couldn't even risk contacting her Aunt Michelle regarding another dinner invitation in case Penny or Keenan showed up, too.

She'd successfully backed herself into isolation and the feeling wasn't welcome.

Resting her head against the edge of the bath, she closed her eyes and willed Dominic to call. She was even prepared to admit he'd been right about Keenan. Not that the sexy, silent man had been the problem. It had been her. But she'd take the blame if it meant having a conversation with someone that didn't involve Rydel and the upcoming sale.

She shimmied lower under the water and her eyes snapped open at the vibration of her silenced cell against the tile floor. "No way." She sat up straight and wiped the moisture from her hands onto her dry arm before picking up the device.

She expected her imagination to have had the better of her, but no, the light in the top corner flashed with a notification. A message. The number was unfamiliar. The text equally puzzling.

Unknown: *I apologize for my behavior. It was uncalled for.*

She had Dominic's number stored so it couldn't be him. Maybe it was Penny. Hell, the apology could've come from any number of irate employees she'd had to talk down this week. Even Spencer, who had a list of things he could apologize for. But her heart kick-started at the possibility of it being someone else. Someone dark, mysterious, and deadly silent.

Savannah: *Who is this?*

She brought her knees to her chest, suddenly chilled in the warm water.

Unknown: *How many people owe you an apology? I'm not sure if that makes me feel like more of an asshole for my behavior, or better because I fit in with the crowd.*

She bit her lip, determined to calm her excitement. She wanted it to be Keenan. Her body hadn't been able to let go of the intimate moments at the bonfire. Or the kiss at the restaurant. She craved him, even though she'd done her best to forget him.

> *Savannah: I have high standards. Most people don't even know they're on my shit list.*

She placed her thumb between her teeth and began biting her nail.

> *Unknown: I deserve to be on that list.*

Damn it. She was dying.

> *Unknown: It's Keenan.*

Everything inside her shifted. Her heart fell to her stomach, her stomach to her feet, then they all climbed back up again in a rush of euphoria.

> *Savannah: How did you get my number?*

She didn't care, didn't even want to know, but her brain lacked the clarity to find another sentence to continue the conversation. He was speaking to her. These were the first words they'd shared apart from his scribbled message to meet her at the Sated Palate.

> *Keenan: I'm silent, mysterious, sexy, AND resourceful. Accept my apology?*

She smiled at the echo of what she said at the bonfire and pretended her chest wasn't about to explode.

> *Savannah: There's no need to apologize. I'm the one who should beg for your forgiveness. I was insensitive and I'm sorry.*

Every time she relived last Sunday night she shuddered. Her comments had been heartless. They were unintentional insults, but insults all the same.

> *Keenan: I guess both of us were out of our element. But I*

have a better excuse for being flustered. I acted like an A-grade ass because I'm completely enamored by you.

Her trembling fingers threatened to drop her cell into the bath. She frowned, questioning the legitimacy of his message, questioning whether it was really him texting at all. She even questioned if this was all a dream and she was about to drown in a pool of frangipani scented water.

Keenan: Savannah?

How could she reply? There was no response, only internal giggling like a schoolgirl. He'd turned her into someone she didn't recognize, again, in the space of seconds. She didn't know how or why. If anything, her time with him was constantly awkward. Yet she wanted more.

Savannah: Have you been drinking?

It was a legitimate question. It had been days since he walked out on her. Alcohol or drugs had to have played a part in his desire to make contact.

Keenan: Can't when I have to drive home soon.

Ah, so this was a spontaneous conversation.

Savannah: Are you at work?

She tried to picture what he did in his day-to-day life and made sure her mind didn't stray to menial tasks in a position that lacked authority. He deserved a powerful position. He'd brought her to her knees, after all.

Keenan: No. I'm on the street outside your building.

Her heart stopped.

There was a second of surging blood through her ears. Then another before she scrambled from the bathtub and pulled a heavy white robe over her soaked skin. She rushed to the window and pulled the curtain aside. She didn't need to search to find him. He was near the curb, leaning against a lamp post. Everything about him spoke of casual indifference. He was dressed in dark jeans and a cream jacket, his ankles crossed at a GQ cover model angle.

"So damn fine." Even from three floors above, he was suave. Dark stubble lined his face and his penetrating eyes peered up in search of her window.

Savannah: I'm not dressed for visitors.

She pressed send and enjoyed the resulting smile that crossed his face. No man had ever been more appealing, yet all he did was lean against that lamp post like he owned it and tapped something back into his phone.

Keenan: I'm not asking for an invitation. Although I wouldn't protest being beside you right now, staying down here is a better option.

After nights spent tossing and turning, all for the sake of hearing his words, talking seemed overrated now. She was beyond the need for conversation. She wanted that smirk right in front of her, and those hands that were always controlled.

Savannah: And why is that? You don't think you can keep your hands off me?

It was an off the cuff joke, but as soon as she pressed send, she was dying to read his reply.

Keenan: No thinking necessary. My hands would be all over you. You'd be incapable of stopping them.

She shuddered, head to toe, totally digging the underlying threat. She didn't even have a chance to reply before her phone beeped again.

Keenan: But you need to know all those wishes you had in the restaurant will never come true. I'll never be able to hold a face-to-face conversation with you. I'll never be able to murmur in your ear and tell you how fucking sexy you are, no matter how much I want to. I don't like being this way, Savannah, but it's who I am.

He gazed up at the building, his focus catching hers. She would've liked to believe his lips quirked at the image of her, but in honesty, she couldn't tell.

Savannah: I'm sorry. I never should've said what I did. I didn't mean it.

It wasn't a lie. Not in hindsight. He was enough without his speech. In fact, she wasn't sure if she would like him any other way. The slow progression to get to know him without conversation was a thrill.

Keenan: You did mean it and that's okay. Most people aren't comfortable with my silence. But if we spend time together again, we'll do it someplace private so I can show you how I like to communicate.

His message had a hair-trigger on her shudder reflex. Everything he said had an underlying edge of sexiness. He probably didn't mean it that way. It was her own mind leading her astray.

Savannah: If we spend time together again?

She didn't want there to be any question of if. They *would* spend time together again. And they would do it soon.

Keenan: That's up to you.

Was he kidding? Of course she wanted to. She was practically falling over her salivating tongue to grasp the opportunity.

Keenan: Savannah?

She nodded and held his stare.

Savannah: I want to see you again, Keenan.

He typed again.

Keenan: Name the time and place and I'll try to make it happen.

Her fingers trembled as she looked down at herself. She had no makeup on. No suitable clothing either. All she wore was a white hotel bathrobe.

Savannah: *Here. Now.*

She held her breath and squinted to catch his expression. A smirk tilted his lips, a devilish, pussy-fluttering smirk she wanted to taste.

Keenan: *Are you sure?*

"Ha." Her sanity had the same question, but her body had a mind of its own.

Savannah: *Yes.*

She opened the curtain wider, letting him see her, *properly* see her. Robe and all.

Keenan: *Be certain, Savannah. We both know I won't be coming up there to talk.*

Oh, Christ. He was giving her an out and there was no way she could take it. She was already lost to anticipation. Her mouth was watering, her nipples hardening. She wanted to be taken by him, to drown under the command of his touch and become a slave to sensation.

Savannah: *I'm in room 305.*

She watched as he read her message. There was no sly gesture or cocky arrogance at her reply. He merely settled his cell into his jeans pocket and continued to stare up at her.

For long minutes they held the connection. No words. No movements. Just eye contact that grazed every inch of her skin. It was foreplay. Successful foreplay, to say the least. She was already burning for him. Shaking, too.

He pushed from the lamppost, his gaze still locked on her, and strode for the hotel.

Eleven

Within seconds Savannah was on the phone, insuring reception gave Keenan a card to gain access to the elevator. They weren't going to mess things up this time. They would see this through. There would be no interruptions from meddling cousins, no misunderstandings. She would have him. No words, no doubts, just no-strings, high-cardio sex that she could shove back in Spencer's face.

"Oh, shit."

Her heart rate increased from excitement to horror. She was naked under the robe, her face was probably a smudged mess of mascara and foundation, and she wasn't even sure if her legs needed a decent shave.

"Oh, fuck."

Breathe. Relax. She'd just bathed, her body parts should be prime frangipani goodness. But her hair... She ran to the hall mirror and the air left her lungs in relief at her reflection. Her mascara was tight, her cheeks flushed, and her hair pulled up in the butterfly clip had a messy, damsel in distress vibe going that didn't look all that unappealing.

It would have to do. She wasn't going to pull out the girlie card and leave him standing at the door so she had a few more minutes to impress him. Yeah, he was sexy. Yeah, he was mysterious as all hell. But she wasn't going to hyperventilate over imperfection. Not any more than she already had.

She turned back to the room, skimming her vision over the

perfectly made bed, the messy table with her laptop and notes scattered everywhere, and finally rested her glare on the disaster that was her suitcase.

A knock sounded on the door behind her, loud and authoritative. The noise ricocheted through the room, her chest, and settled in her heart. *Thump thump, thump thump.*

She padded down the short hall, an extra sway to her hips, and opened the door. She stood tall, barefoot, and surrounded in fluffy, white material, while he held an air of cool, calm, and collected. His hands were in his pockets, short wisps of his hair falling over his forehead as he peered up under his thick lashes at her.

"Hi." She tried to clear the arousal from her throat. Tried and failed. His eyes were intense. Dark silver depths holding her against her will.

"I...um..."

He raised a lazy finger to his mouth, demanding silence in the simplest of actions. He stalked forward, once, twice, and even though she didn't want to retreat, the pure confidence ebbing off him had her sliding from reach. His presence frightened her. It also invigorated. The mere sight of him placed her on a roller coaster rife with sharp bends and terrifying dips.

She'd never been nervous around men, yet Keenan wasn't merely a man. He was above and beyond. He was one in a million, someone unique and fascinating.

The door drifted shut as he continued to stalk her into the middle of the room, the bed to her right, the television to her left. She was running out of space. Running out of oxygen.

She planted her feet, raised her chin, and swallowed over the palpable chemistry flittering through the air between them. He stopped, too, mere inches from her. His gaze raked her body like a feather, deliciously soft, gliding over her skin, lingering on places she wanted him to touch. To taste.

His hand rose, the calloused palm moving to cup her cheek and steal her breath. There had never been a moment in her life when she'd wanted to be controlled. Not at work. Not in previous relationships. But in this moment, every part of her ached for his mastery. She wanted to be commanded by his eyes alone. To be manipulated by the strength in his grip and the fierceness in his expression. She didn't need his endearments or his compliments. She didn't need words at all.

He glided his fingers to the back of her hair and released the clip. Strands fell to her shoulders and tickled her neck as he placed the hair piece on the television stand, his focus never leaving her.

She had no power to look away. No strength. She was at his mercy.

Willingly.

Wholeheartedly.

He cherished every part of her face with his scrutiny, taking in her appearance like she was a puzzle he wanted to not only complete, but immortalize. With each breath he inched closer—his legs, his chest, his lips.

Time quickened with the rapid pulse of blood in her ears, and the outside world ceased to exist. There was no Rydel or Grandiosity. No Penny or Dominic. There was only Keenan and the chilling, steel eyes she would never forget.

The heat of his exhalations brushed her lips. It was an excruciating tease, a caress of awareness that lasted a lifetime before his mouth descended, taking hers in a kiss so gentle and soft she whimpered in sensation overload.

She closed her eyes at his expertise and placed her palms inside the opening of his jacket to rest on the hard planes of his chest. He parted her lips with his tongue, deepening the connection, manipulating her emotions. They were one, their bodies fused with anticipation, their mouths molded in passion.

It was just a kiss, not unlike any other in physical form, yet everything inside her was different. Her heart was rampant, her lips tingled.

She wanted more.

She *needed* more.

There would never be enough.

His fingers continued to hold her, his grip tightening in her hair. The palm of his free hand came to rest on her waist and slowly descended. She could feel the trail it made as if he were burning her beneath the robe. From her hip, then slowly to her ass. He palmed her flesh in his grasp and ground into her, making her moan at the distinct hardness of his erection at her abdomen.

She'd never desired a man so much it hurt. But there was pain now, an ache low in her belly she couldn't ignore. It wasn't mere arousal or the hunger of a starved libido. It was emotional and physical. She just didn't understand why or how. Keenan had her wrapped around his finger and it hadn't even taken a syllable.

He pulled back and left her gasping for air. Her arms fell to her sides and her heart fell with them. He stared back at her, his smile nowhere to be seen. There was no warmth in his features. Only ferocity. Pure lust.

She didn't want to break the silence. Her mouth wouldn't work even if she wanted it to. If he couldn't speak, neither would she, but the pressure to fill the void irked her. She never knew how much she relied on words to self-soothe until she met Keenan. They eased discomfort and dissolved nerves.

Now there was only instinct and intuition.

He held her focus as he shucked his jacket and threw it on the end of the bed. She wasn't going to swallow. Nope. No matter how dry her throat or how wet her pussy, she refused to give him any more power. He already had enough. She was weak—her knees, her arms, her restraint.

Her fingers twitched, wishing he would hurry as he grasped the top of his shirt and manipulated the first button through the hole. One by one, he exposed more skin to her periphery, yet she fought not to break his gaze. He was the first to look at her with such raw savagery; he could very well be the last. Each second of the connection was like a drug she wished to save for later. She was hoarding his passion, memorizing it, storing it in a safe place at the back of her mind to bring out whenever the need arose.

Her palms itched to touch him, and instead of listening to the meek voice inside telling her to be careful, she reached out and made contact. Her skin collided with muscle and the fine dusting of coarse hair on his pecs and still, their eyes danced.

INARTICULATE

She couldn't stop looking at him.

Wouldn't stop.

Refused.

She slid her hands higher and guided the shirt off his shoulders, down his arms, to his wrists and let it drop to the floor. Swallow after swallow, she tried to soothe the dryness of her throat, but nothing in her body wanted to comply with her demands. Everything inside her was attuned to his frequency.

He grabbed her hips and a breath shuddered from her lips as he guided her backward to sit on the small desk. Large hands gripped the tie of her robe, the soft tug, tug, tug of the knot coming undone, along with her control. Her heart was fluttering in her throat. Her stomach had become an Olympic rhythmic gymnast.

Would she hold enough appeal to satisfy his desire? Would she be enough?

The forefront of her mind told her his opinion didn't matter. He could love her body or strut his sexy ass to the door. But in the back of her thoughts was a constant drone of unease. A man this alluring, this intoxicating, wouldn't be affected by mediocrity.

She wanted to impress him. To make his eyes narrow in lust or widen in appreciation. She needed that hit of undiluted emotion that washed away the need for words. She needed to see the fascination he couldn't announce and feel the praise in his touch.

The front of the material separated, the trim settling on the inside of her breasts. She remained still as Keenan stole his focus from her eyes and tracked his full attention down her body. Her skin tingled under his scrutiny, from her lips to her throat, her sternum to her stomach, all the way to the trimmed patch of curls at the apex of her thighs.

His nostrils flared. His fingers twitched at his sides. She sucked in a breath, deep and empowering. Her nervousness vanished. How could she hold on to doubt when he looked at her with such hunger? With one look, *that* look, he transformed her into a supermodel. She was flawless beneath his appraisal.

She gripped the edge of the desk, her movements spreading the material further, and let him look his fill.

His attention backtracked, from her pussy, to her belly button, her sternum. Every inch made her heart rate increase.

He met her gaze, briefly, so briefly, before he decimated the space between them in one step and took her mouth with his own. She didn't have time to think, to gasp. He was all over her, one arm sliding around her naked waist, his other hand circling the back of her neck.

This kiss was the evil twin to its predecessor. *This* kiss was rough and punishing, vicious and feral. Their tongues clashed in harsh strokes, their teeth clinked. She scrambled for his shoulders and tugged him as she dug her fingers into his skin.

He growled, a deep rumble of sound that emanated from his throat. It was beyond sexy. It was animalistic. Hedonistic.

It made her stop. Think. Reevaluate.

"You can growl?" She pushed at his chest, her cheeks flushed with the excitement of the heady vibration. She'd heard that sound from him before, but she couldn't ignore it now. It was too wondrous.

"That was sexy as hell." She was panting, trying to calm her breathing when he seemed to be entirely under control.

His gaze became guarded. His pleasure fading.

"I mean it."

He ignored the compliment like it was a thinly veiled criticism and leaned into her, this time taking his lips to her neck. She had no time to ponder. He nipped along her carotid and gifted her with his sound again. The deep rumble sank into her chest and made every rib tingle. She arched her neck and fought for control.

She couldn't wait to have more of him. The thought wasn't whimsy or wishful thinking. She *could not* wait to have more of him. It was an impossibility.

"I'm done with waiting," she whispered and cascaded her hands from his shoulders, down his chest, over his muscled stomach, to the waistband of his jeans.

He pulled back and met her gaze, silently giving her permission to go further.

"You're just going to watch?"

He didn't move, didn't even change his expression. All she received was a lazy blink of those gunmetal eyes.

"Fine. Be a spectator. I'll unwrap my present by myself."

She lowered her attention to his waistband as his chest convulsed with laughter. Starving her, *tormenting* her, wasn't nice. He'd soon learn from his mistakes.

The clink of his belt mingled with the sound of labored breathing. She undid the button at the top of his jeans, lowered the zipper, and froze.

"Holy..." He didn't wear underwear. At least not today. The bulge he'd been hiding stood proud, staring at her. Her throat dried to the point of pain. Her desire for him grew uncontrollable. It had to be pheromones or poor air ventilation.

Something.

Anything.

The delirious need wasn't normal. Not for her.

She tugged his pants in a frantic rush, her robe gaping before him, and left his waistband to stand in the middle of his muscled thighs. There wasn't a hair, freckle or scar on this man that wasn't perfectly situated. He was flawless. A picture of masculine perfection.

If only he could...

She shook away the selfish thought and peered up at him. His eyes were dark and full of male pride as he leaned to the side and grabbed a condom from his lowered pocket. He didn't readjust his pants, didn't even move them an inch from where she left them. He kept himself on display, his cock standing proud, the thick veins pulsing along his shaft.

He sheathed himself with an unshaking grip. She knew he was watching her, seeing her fascination and desire, and still she couldn't drag her gaze away from his hands and the way he worked his length.

The men she'd slept with had never been so blatant. They didn't protest if she was in a frumpy mood and asked for the lights to be switched off. They weren't proud of their bodies like Keenan was confident with his. This man made sex seem like a natural progression for two strangers. There was no shame or trepidation. It was logical.

Even essential.

She bit her lip at the unfamiliar reassurance and felt her pussy clench, preparing itself for the necessary stretch of muscles needed to accommodate him.

He glanced over his shoulder, eyed the bed, then looked back at her in question.

No. She shook her head. She wanted him here, on the desk, with her fingers in his hair and his hands palming her ass.

He inched closer, his legs pressing into hers, and nudged her thighs apart with his knee. His steely focus peered down at her as his rough hands gripped her hips and lifted, placing the curve of her bottom on the flimsy wood.

He was close, his cock almost brushing her entrance, when his palm came to land on her sternum. He seared her, branding her flesh as he trailed his touch through her cleavage, to one shoulder, then the other, pushing her robe off.

The fluffy material pooled at her back, comforting her in her nudity. There was still no shame. There couldn't be. Not when he cherished her with the appreciation in his eyes.

He gripped the base of his shaft and when he lowered his focus, she was compelled to follow, all the way down to where the head of his cock was poised at her pussy. He trailed himself back and forth, back and forth, sliding himself through the slickness of her arousal.

Every nerve inside her was thrumming. Every heartbeat was labored. He knew what he was doing by making her wait. He was well aware she was delirious with need, and when she was sane again she'd repay the favor. But until then, she'd continue to pant into the silence and pray for the sweet bliss of orgasm.

He rested the tip of his cock inside her and grabbed her hip tight.

She was poised at the top of the rollercoaster, holding her breath for the steep descent. He gripped her chin in his free hand, and stared deep into her eyes. There was a wealth of communication between them. She didn't need his voice; she could already hear it in her mind. His desire was screaming at her, and his passion whispered in a delirious chant.

Then he plunged deep inside and took her lips in a harsh kiss, shattering her with sensory overload. Whimpers pulled from the back of her throat. She wanted to give him silence, but there was no control over the needy sounds. She was a victim of passion. A prisoner to mindlessness.

She wrapped her arms around his neck and held tight. With each thrust, he devoured her mouth, kissing the oxygen from her lungs. Still, she couldn't get enough. She doubted she ever would. He was too much—too much passion, too much confidence. He enslaved her with a mere glance and she never wanted to be set free.

She encircled his waist with her legs and groaned at how he sank deeper. His growl returned, the carnal sound making her shudder. He pulled back and watched the way he plunged inside her. She couldn't follow his focus this time. Her pussy was already tightening with the prelude to orgasm and she wasn't ready for this to end yet.

Instead, she closed her eyes, let her head fall back, and relaxed into his supremacy. He kissed her neck, her shoulder, her breasts. Every inch of her skin was tattooed by his lips.

"Keenan..."

He increased the pace of his thrusts and the ferocity of his lips. She was helpless to stop her body taking over. She straightened as her core began to spasm and she gripped his chin, forcing his mouth to hers.

They nipped and licked, their tongues tangling and colliding as they came undone together. With each pulse of orgasm she gripped him tighter and jolted with the pounding of his hips. Over and over she toppled into euphoria, her gasps slicing the air between them.

He didn't slow until her pleasure had faded and she was drooped against him, devoid of strength. The exhilaration dissipated from her veins as her breathing calmed and her mind cleared. She straightened and stared up at him, not knowing what to say or what to do. She was the only one who could fill the silence and yet her tongue was tied.

Bliss left the room in a vacuum and awkwardness took its place. He stood there, his chest pounding as he looked at her in expectation, waiting for something profound when she couldn't even remember her own name.

"Thanks."

That muscled chest of his began to convulse in laughter, turning her cheeks to flame.

"*No,*" he mouthed and raised his hand to his chin, cementing her embarrassment as he repeated the gesture of appreciation he'd given the waitress at the restaurant. "*Thank you.*"

Twelve

Savannah began to sulk as Keenan pressed a firm, chuckling kiss on her lips and then sauntered his sexy, jean-covered ass to the bathroom.

There wasn't a definition in the Oxford dictionary to explain her humiliation. It was too profound for words.

"Don't mind me," she muttered and grabbed the robe nestled behind her bottom. "I'm just ruining that perfect moment, one breath at a time."

She shrugged her arms into the heavy material and secured the tie around her waist. A rush of water sounded from the bathroom and the faucet was quickly turned off again, followed by the unmistakable grate of an ascending zipper.

He strolled back into the room, the ends of his hair dripping with water, his face glistening and his expression set with determination. He didn't stop his progression until he was upon her, kissing the humiliation from her system.

His lips defied comprehension. They took away her thoughts and cognitive skills.

He lifted her, cradling her body in his arms as he circled to the bed and placed her on the coverings.

She remained quiet, unwilling to risk embarrassing herself again as he lay on his side next to her, peering down at her in whimsy or maybe thoughtfulness. It was a look he hadn't gifted upon her before.

"Why are you staring at me like that?" she whispered.

She felt like a princess under his gaze. A goddess. Someone worthy of worship.

Respect had always been a companion in her career. People admired her professional skills and business mind. But this wasn't comparable. The way he revered her was unlike anything she'd experienced. It was too powerful to be real.

He pursed his lips, a silent *shh* drifting between them as he slowly untied her robe with one hand. The lapels fell open, exposing her belly, and lower, all the way down to her toes. With teasing fingers, he trailed his touch over her skin, back and forth, over and under. The exploration wasn't sexual, it was far more meaningful than that.

He treasured her with his fingertips and made the casual act of what they just shared into something with depth. Something she wasn't prepared for.

"Stop."

His focus gradually lifted to her eyes, but he didn't comply, he didn't quit moving his fingers in a nonsensical trail that made blood rush through her ears at a painful pace.

"I want to know you."

His gaze didn't change, didn't even flicker. He looked at her like he knew all her secrets, yet she didn't even know his full name. "What makes you tick, Keenan?"

He didn't respond. He simply kept drowning her in his touch. Rough skin against soft flesh.

"Come on. Give me something. Do you have any siblings?"

He grinned, shook his head in exasperation and pulled his cell from his pocket. Her stomach flittered with excitement. She was finally going to get some answers. She wasn't even disappointed when he furthered the distance between them to rest his back against the headboard.

He typed into the device in his hands and flashed the screen at her. *I'm an only child. You?*

"I'm the same." She rolled onto her stomach, her lips too damn close to the muscles surrounding his ribs, and looked up at him. "What about work? What do you do?"

His brows pulled together as he typed. *With Grandiosity and Rydel being a point of contention, can we skip the career talk?*

"Sure." She tried to ignore the pity welling inside her and failed. It was clear his position in the company inspired contempt, and she hoped it wasn't because he was comparing his career to hers. "What's your favorite memory?"

He smirked as he turned his focus to his cell and tap, tap, tapped. *Almost two weeks ago when an unbelievably sexy woman accused me of being an asshole for not talking to her.*

She snorted. "You could've warned me. It's not like it's impossible for you to communicate."

I know. But you were too much fun.

"Fun?"

You were devastated that you didn't have confirmation that I was succumbing to your charms. You were frustrated to the point of ogling my package to gain my attention. Your persistence was refreshing.

"Refreshing?" she parroted him again, unable to stop her lips from spreading wide. "You're cruel."

He typed quickly, his fingers flying over his cell screen. *I feel the same about you. Your smile does things to me that should be illegal.*

Her lips pulled tighter, her cheeks lifting of their own accord. Something other than lust made her heart tippy-tap and she leaned over to playfully nip at his ribs. "Well, your smile has no effect on me whatsoever."

Liar. Bite me again and see where it gets you.

She opened her mouth and poised her teeth over his skin. She was tempted, so damn tempted, but she was already overcome with feelings for him and she didn't want to lose herself to whatever this was.

She was in Seattle to work. Outside complications needed to be kept to a minimum.

She snapped her mouth shut millimeters from his skin. "Fine. We can go back to basics. What's your favorite color?"

Colors, really?

"Why not?" She shrugged.

Fine, but why restrict myself to one? He waggled his brows. *What is the point? The world is filled with profound hues, all of them at my disposal. I choose not to pin myself down.*

"Are we still talking about the same thing?" She turned toward him with a raised brow. "Or are you one of those guys who can only talk about women and sex?" Another Spencer.

The implication should've caused revulsion. Too bad she was already lost to delirium.

Sex is always a preferred topic.

She laughed and he followed suit. His chest convulsed, his muscles flexed, and she couldn't stop herself from placing her hand over his sternum to feel it. It was a strange sensation—sharing someone's laughter for the first time. It stripped her of all pettiness and made her fall for him a fraction more. She wanted to experience all his responses, from the ones he made in pleasure, and also the ones in pain.

His humor faded as he pressed his hand over the top of hers, telling her with his gaze alone that he knew how important this moment was. It was more than sex and seduction. It wasn't just pleasure and gratification.

They'd just paid the price of attachment.

Email Correspondence

Date: 22nd December

Subject: Speak To Me

Dear Savannah,

I know you look back on our time together and relive it through tainted eyes. I'd do the same. You believe everything we shared was clouded with deception, but that's far from the truth.

I had to keep things from you. I had to hide the parts of myself that I wasn't proud of, otherwise there never would've been a chance for us to begin with.

Before the night in your suite, sex had never held an emotional connection for me. Not even with past relationships, not that there were many. The act had always been a physical release and nothing more. It was sport, and I was always the winner.

Until you.

You took away the game. There was no champion. No score. You tied me to the bed with invisible strings and made me yearn for emotion I never thought I'd wanted.

Can't you see how profound that is?

Now that you're gone, I wish I could go back and change everything. I'd beg for any sort of different outcome. Maybe I should've informed you of the truth from the start. Or I could've stayed away from you entirely, never having experienced any of those moments in time.

I would never give up what we shared, but I'd do anything to spare you the hurt.

Anything, Savannah.

If I knew back then what I know now, I never would've let the lies fester. But hindsight is a marvelous thing, and unfortunately, I don't have the liberty to go back and change my mistakes.

Please let me make up for them instead.

Give me another chance.

Keenan

Thirteen

Savannah awoke the next morning to the sound of her suite door clicking shut. The bed was empty beside her. Keenan had left.

She could've run after him and asked if he wanted to share breakfast with her, but the non-existent farewell was better. She'd become blindsided last night. He'd hooked her, distracting her with pleasure and enamoring her with affection.

More than twice.

The man may be silent but he made up for it with virility and enthusiasm.

She hadn't wanted to encourage feelings for him. This was only sex with an expiration date. But as she'd watched him sleep during the early hours, her chest had done an uncomfortable throbby thing that announced she had no control over any of this.

She was too intrigued by the hidden parts of him and too ravenous for his touch.

With a groan, she rolled onto her stomach and reached for her cell on the bedside table. Two missed calls and a message.

> **Dominic:** *Mom called to warn me that Penny is on the warpath this morning. Apparently, she was trying to contact Keenan at home and suspects he spent the night with you. I hope she's wrong. He's a great guy, Savvy, but you'll only get hurt.*

No, she wouldn't. Penny's pathetic existence was the only one in the firing line. If the woman didn't back off on her own, Savannah would do something to ensure she did.

Savannah: *Don't worry about me. I'm staying out of trouble.*

It wasn't a lie. She knew where things stood with Keenan. There was no future, no commitment, no exclusivity. She had erected clear emotional boundaries... Well, she would. It was on the top of her to-do list—emotionally detach yourself from silent and mysterious lover.

They both knew where they stood. Keenan hadn't left a note or text message to say goodbye because it wasn't necessary. They were two adults with heightened attraction issues they were trying to get out of their system.

Nothing more. Nothing less.

Unfortunately, she spent the next twenty-four hours with her head in the clouds anyway. While floating on a euphoric high, she convinced two more employees to rescind their resignation and return to work. The short Internet promotional campaign she'd organized with marketing had increased occupation rates until settlement and Mr. Rydel was openly pleased with her success.

She began chatting with staff on a personal level, gaining their friendship. For the first time on her Seattle excursion, it wasn't all work and no play. She was in control, and damn, it felt good.

The next morning she skipped her room-service breakfast and sat at one of the many vacant tables in the hotel restaurant.

"Morning, Ms. Hamilton. What can I get for you?"

Savannah met the blue eyes of the young waitress and tried to remember her name. The woman was a single mother with a fifteen-month-old son. She still lived with her parents and last week had openly shed tears over the threat of losing her job.

The more time Savannah spent learning the individual stories of each employee, the more adamant she was to create a smooth transition into settlement. Penny be damned. "Please, call me Savannah."

The woman inclined her head and flipped to a new page on her notepad, her pen poised to take an order.

"I'd love a fruit salad and a coffee with cream, no sugar."

"Certainly. The kitchen will have it prepared right away."

Yes, the kitchen certainly wouldn't take long. Not when the restaurant was practically empty when it should've been the busiest morning period.

"Thank you."

The woman walked away as Savannah reached for her cell on the side of the table and opened her email application. Her position here was to facilitate the settlement and extinguish the spot fires that continued to spark to life. It wasn't her job to continuously speak to marketing to develop strategies to bring the hotel into the black for the few remaining weeks. That was in the hands of hotel management, and she outlined a quick email telling them as much.

"Here's your coffee."

Savannah didn't look up as the liquid gold was pushed across the table. "Thanks." She kept her focus on her emails, writing a mental list of all the things that needed to get done today. Only, it didn't matter how busy she became, her thoughts always traveled back to her bedroom and the man who left the intoxicating scent of his cologne on her sheets.

She wondered if he had to sit through an inquisition from Penny on his whereabouts from the other night. She wondered way too much about him—where he was, what he was doing. Did he think about her?

"Savannah, can I have a word?"

She placed her cell back on the table and met the concern of the hotel shift manager. "Sure, what's wrong?"

Grant stood over her table in an immaculate business suit and slicked back hair. He was around her age and didn't have a relaxed bone in his body. Now wasn't an exception. In fact, his anxiety seemed worse than normal as he picked at the quick of his nails and dodged his gaze around the room.

"You look stressed." She pushed out the chair opposite her with her foot and took a sip of coffee. Her cell buzzed between them and she looked down to see Keenan's name on the screen.

Keenan: *Meet me tonight.*

She schooled her expression, trying to dissuade the grin threatening to explode across her face. Where was the question mark? The arrogant bastard was dictating rendezvous with the assumption that she would snap at his command. And maybe she would, but there was no need to be overtly cocky.

She flipped over her cell to hide the screen and cleared her throat. "Take a seat, Grant."

"Um…" He rubbed the back of his neck.

"Sit," she ordered. "Did you just get my email about increasing numbers in the restaurant?"

"Yes, but that isn't why I'm here." He pulled the spare seat out further and sat. "I need to talk to you about something."

"That's what I'm here for." She pasted on an expression filled with managerial comfort and waited for him to elaborate. Normally, she had the patience of a nun with a lifetime of service, but there was an unanswered message on her phone and she wanted nothing more than to put Keenan in his self-righteous place before she confirmed a time and date for their next tryst.

"I had to fire one of the housekeeping staff this morning."

"You what?" All thoughts of pleasure vanished as she grasped at her coffee mug to hide her frustration. Deep breaths. Calm down. "I'm fighting to convince the staff who have already left to return. Why would you make my job harder?"

He looked away, the tops of his cheeks flushed as the waitress came toward them with a bowl in her hand.

"Sorry to interrupt." She placed the fruit salad in front of Savannah and straightened. "Can I get anything for you, Grant?"

"No." He dismissed her without a glance and remained silent until they were alone. "There was gossip."

"And?" She tried to remain calm by forking a piece of strawberry into her mouth. "I hope there's more to it than that." She chewed, fought to swallow, then forked another piece of fruit.

"There is." He ran an anxious hand over his mouth. "Can we chat in the office?"

Fucking hell. "No." The restaurant was barely functioning. There was no threat of being heard. "Just tell me."

"But..." He was fidgeting now, playing with the edge of the tablecloth.

"Look, it can't be that bad. I've solved ninety-nine problems so far. I'll be able to fix this one, too."

He met her gaze head on, his lips thin. "I overheard her sharing private information about a guest's room."

"What kind of information?"

"*Private* information."

She sighed and dabbed at her lips with a cloth napkin. "Is this really something that required her to lose her job?"

"It was your room, Savannah."

Okay, so maybe it could be *that bad.*

"What do you mean by 'private'? Did she read my business emails?"

Savannah didn't have anything to hide, and although a reprimand was unavoidable for this type of situation, she did understand how frantic staff were for information. She'd already witnessed many times how the loss of job security could make people do uncharacteristic things. "If that's your concern, I appreciate it, but it's unwarranted. I haven't hidden anything from you or anyone else regarding the settlement. I've been open and honest about how it will go ahead."

"No." He shook his head. "This was entirely personal."

Her stomach clenched. All she could do was look at him and raise a brow. Her underwear wasn't anything to gossip about. She hadn't packed silk lingerie. She hadn't even packed a vibrator.

"She found numerous used condoms."

Her mouth fell open at the same time her face blazed with the heat of a furnace.

"Apparently," he lowered his voice, "she found them while changing the trash bin."

"W-who did she tell?"

He cringed and she held up her hand, no longer wanting clarification.

"Why?" she asked. "Why is this even newsworthy? Do they think I'm shirking my responsibilities while I'm here?" Or did they know she was in bed with a Grandiosity employee? Was her integrity being questioned?

"No. Not at all. It was childish gossip. I think the majority of staff think you're doing a fantastic job."

And now the minority would have something to hang over her head at a later date.

"My sex life is my business—"

"I know," he added with conviction.

"Who I take to my room in my own time—"

"I know, Savannah. I'm not judging you. That's why I took care of it on my own." There was comfort in his eyes and for the first time he wasn't fidgeting. "I just wanted you to be aware of what happened so you don't mistakenly contact her thinking she left because of the Grandiosity changeover."

She placed her fork beside her bowl, her appetite non-existent. "Thank you for letting me know."

She wasn't sure what to do. If she addressed the entire Rydel Seattle team, people who weren't previously exposed would now know the gossip. Yet she couldn't let it go. She wouldn't be manipulated or made fun of for having sex. It was the twenty-first century, for Christ's sake.

"I approve of how you handled the situation. I would've done the same." She swallowed down the bile rising in her throat and squared her shoulders.

He nodded and pushed out his chair.

"Wait." She pinned him with a look so scathing it gave herself goosebumps. "I don't want to exacerbate the situation, but I'd appreciate if you could tell those involved that they'll be out the door without a second thought if I hear any more news of this."

He inclined his head.

"I'm not finished," she seethed. "If I hear one word, even a whisper, or a laugh at my expense, I will make sure they pay. Not just with their jobs. I'll take it further if I have to."

INARTICULATE

She pushed from the table before he could blink. She would *not* be fucked with. Not by Penny, not by Spencer, and definitely not by Rydel staff that she had lost sleep over trying to save.

They were on their own. And now, so was she.

Fourteen

"**Spencer, you need to click on the specific parameters for the** report I wrote in my instructions. Otherwise, it will automatically include all of them and print out a mass of unnecessary pages." Savannah held the conference room phone to her ear in one hand and cradled her forehead in the other.

"Quit with the tone. Your writing is far from legible."

"My writing isn't the problem," she grated. "Can't you ask Rebecca to help you tomorrow?"

It was already past seven and she hadn't left the conference room for more than a toilet break all day. She wasn't even sure she could muster the enthusiasm to put one foot in front of the other in an effort to get to her room. The path through the lobby to the elevators seemed like a journey far too adventurous for her tired muscles, and the conference table, lined with plates and coffee mugs, was beginning to look like a suitable alternative to her bed.

"Your assistant shouldn't even have access to these reports, let alone be able to run them. This is classified information."

Savannah rolled her eyes. "Classified? Really?" She started massaging her forehead in an effort to steady her pulse. The gilded stick up Spencer's ass was starting to test her anger management. "Look, all you have to do is go through the data input process slower. Read over each section. Make sure you place the right date, the right properties, and the individual income classifications. If you can't get it right next time, I'll do them myself tomorrow."

The tapping of a keyboard sounded through the phone, then a whimsical, almost taunting sigh. "No need. I was just messing with you. I already finished the reporting hours ago."

She straightened, her free hand falling helplessly to smack against the conference table. "Are you serious? You already have the report?"

"Yes, my sweet. I figured it out on the first attempt. I just wanted an excuse to speak to you."

"You're such a *dick*, Spencer."

Apart from waking with the memory of satisfying dreams, this had been a day spawned from the deepest pits of hell. She couldn't even admit to herself that she'd hidden in the conference room all day, unable to meet the knowing looks from employees.

She had sex.

So what?

She was allowed to bang the greater Seattle population if she wanted to. It was outside business hours. It was consensual. There were no animalistic slaughters or cult-like chants of any kind.

She was a grown woman who considered the act of gossip deplorable. But the height of her annoyance stemmed from a dark place in her chest that she wished would go away.

It wasn't the assumption of her loose morals that irked her. It was the possibility of staff exposing her bedmate. She had already been nervous that Keenan worked for a rival company, but the enemies to lovers situation wasn't the peak of her concern. It was vanity that weighed her down. The man she had slept with was mute, and her powers of deduction had pinned him down to working in a low-level position within Grandiosity.

They came from different worlds with vastly differing income brackets. She had read the shame in his features when they discussed his employment, just like she'd started to successfully read all his other emotions.

And she hated herself for being conceited. Hated and hated and hated.

"That's it?" Spencer shoved himself into her musings. "I wasted twenty minutes of your life and all you're going to do is call me a dick?"

"I'm in Seattle. I can't really spike your coffee with laxatives again."

"Again?"

"I like to help keep you regular, Spence. I'm surprised you haven't noticed."

He chuckled, but the tone was sinister. "It sounds as though you're not dealing with the stress of the settlement. Maybe I should catch the first flight tomorrow and oversee what you're doing."

"*No.*" God, no. "I can handle it myself. It's under control." Kind of. Sort of. Maybe not. The upcoming wedding was a constant nightmare in the back of her mind, and the mere thought of Penny made her shudder. There were numerous other things, too, but she wasn't going to give Spencer the excuse to fly to Seattle and try to rekindle something that was dead and buried.

Her cell beeped with an incoming text from across the conference table and she reached over to grab it.

"I've actually made a lot of progress." She opened the message and couldn't control her heart as it fluttered at the sight of Keenan's name.

> **Keenan:** *With my inability to communicate clearly, I'd appreciate if you met me in the lobby so I don't have to Marcel Marceau my way through a charade with your receptionist.*

"Oh, shit." She pushed to her feet, the conference phone sliding toward her with the movement.

"Everything all right?" Spencer's voice was distant, a fading whisper being drowned by the whoosh of blood in her ears.

"I've gotta go." She didn't want staff to put a face to the owner of the used condoms from her room. "I'll speak to you tomorrow."

She slammed the receiver down and rushed to the lobby on the toes of her pumps. Her focus caught him immediately. His formidable frame was near the hotel entry, his gorgeous face impassive as their gazes collided.

She continued toward him and chanced a cautious glance at the receptionist. Kelly was on the phone, her face bowed, her attention occupied. Apart from a couple seated on the leather sofa, engaged in conversation with suitcases at their sides, there was no one else in the lobby.

She was thankfully flying under the radar, even though her heels sent a deafening tap through the room with each step.

Please go. She implored Keenan with a look of dismay and shooed him with a hand movement. His brows knitted together, the sting of dismissal hitting his features before he could school his expression. He turned toward the entrance, keeping a steady pace as she came to his side and they walked into the cold night air together.

"Why are you here?" She continued down the steps leading to the sidewalk and didn't stop until a hand clasped hers and pulled her up short. She turned to him, her gaze flicking from the lobby to his penetrating eyes as she breathed fog between them.

He pulled out his cell from the inside pocket of his jacket and showed her the messaged he'd sent earlier.

"Shit." She placed a hand over her mouth and fought to control a shiver over the vastly differing temperature from inside. "I forgot to reply."

His eyes raked her in concern, bringing with it a dose of overwhelming exhaustion far greater than what she'd already been experiencing. The only thing prepared for excessive exercise was her heart which beat at a lust-starved pace.

"Today has been a nightmare." She hung her head and massaged the bridge of her nose. All she wanted to do was go home to San Fran and sleep in her own bed. She was sick of drama, tired of playing Whack-A-Mole with all the staff problems, and the buzz of delirious energy he'd left her with the day before seemed to have transformed her into a clump of nonsensical putty.

His hands slid up her arm, over her elbows, to grip her shoulders. He stepped into her, the white wisps of his breath drifting between them in the freezing air. She tilted her mouth toward his, so close, so tempting.

She needed to tell him to leave, the words were already poised on the tip of her tongue, yet her lips parted with other movements in mind. This close she was senseless with the need to kiss him. To taste him.

"I can't be seen with you." She was trying to convince herself, attempting to break the spellbinding way his eyes seduced her.

His brow furrowed in confusion, but he didn't loosen his grip. They remained toe to toe, thigh to thigh.

"One of the housekeeping staff went through my trash," she said breathlessly. "Apparently, the number of times I got laid the other night was hot gossip."

His hands fell. His face, too. Fury took the place of his concern and he glanced back at the hotel with a narrowed stare.

"The shift manager fired the housekeeper in question, but my sex life is still the topic of conversation." She placed her hand on his stomach, stealing back his attention. "It's not the type of scrutiny I can afford. Especially when I don't know what position you hold within the company."

She was digging for information to appease her vanity, but the jut of his chin and the thinning of those sensuous lips said she wouldn't receive what she was searching for. He was ashamed of his job, and she was even more ashamed for repeatedly bringing it up.

"I don't know what to do," she admitted.

He scoffed as he tapped into his cell screen and then turned it to face her. *It sounds like you're looking for excuses to stop seeing me.*

"I already have numerous." She stepped back, needing space from the palpable annoyance ebbing from him. "But when I'm with you, the reasons are hard to remember."

He wasn't convinced. His chin remained high, his jaw tight. He typed into his screen again and held it up between them. *When you figure it out, let me know.*

He lowered the device and slid away. Each foot of distance he placed between them made her heart ache. It wasn't right. She didn't ask for this. It was meant to be sex, and she'd stupidly tripped over the line of passion and stumbled into something unfamiliar that seemed a lot like infatuation.

INARTICULATE

"Keenan, wait."

He didn't pause. Those rugged shoulders of his kept drifting further away.

"Keenan." She took off after him in a huff.

She should be running in the opposite direction, endeavoring to place more space between them. Only, the need to have him stare at her in appreciation was killing her. The desire for it was a living, breathing thing, clawing up her throat and cutting off her breath.

She reached his side, the streetlight bathing them in a warm glow, and gripped the crook of his arm. He swung around and peered down at her with disdain.

"Don't look at me like that."

He did as she requested, turning his focus away to glare at the world.

"I want to spend more time with you." The only problem was that she needed to be discreet. Oh, so discreet. She had to move on from Spencer slowly. He couldn't find out she was with an employee of their competitor. He'd be furious, and his father would lose faith in her work ethic.

Keenan's inability to speak would also be held against her. Spencer would try to humiliate her to save face. Worse, he would inevitably try to humiliate Keenan.

Christ. It was such a mess. So why couldn't she take the easy option and watch him walk away?

"We need to keep this quiet."

His nostrils flared and he nodded.

"Is it worth it?" Her question was meek and needy, the fragility demanding reassurance.

He pinned her with his glare, but this time was different. This time his ferocity said *hell yes, of course it is.* He stepped into her, his large physique overbearing.

Her throat tightened with his proximity and she swallowed over the need to kiss the anger from his features. He grabbed her hand and tugged her out from underneath the streetlight, his long stride taking her to a shadowed position beside a neck-high shrub.

She'd never been with a man who had less than an executive role in a company. Not unless you included high school. But when he looked at her, when he touched her, none of it mattered, not his job or his lack of speech. Not even her cousins warning her away.

"How are we going to do this?"

He pressed into her, thigh to thigh, and grasped her hips. She struggled for air, the deep breaths she'd been inhaling now coming out in puffs of short, sharp white fog.

She was overwhelmed with a sensation she'd never experienced before. Lust was no longer the only facet to the attraction between them. Other things were weaving their way in. Emotional things. Needy things.

It was wrong. Yet while she stood against him, it felt entirely right.

Her career didn't matter. Her cousins didn't exist. Even the hardship of restricted communication didn't stand a chance against the insanity of her emotions. She wanted a repeat of the other night. A continuous loop of lust and passion, for days on end. It was vital that she acquire everything he had to offer.

He tugged her into a one-armed hug and she went willingly. His scent comforted her. Crisp and clean. Sexy and inviting. He typed with his thumb, never releasing her, and held the screen between them.

I can keep my mouth shut if you can.

She closed her eyes and laughed at his self-deprecation. They shouldn't joke about this. It wasn't a game.

"Hiding seems childish."

He squeezed her, demanding she look at his cell. *We don't need to hide. We'll just be careful.*

Careful? They were far beyond that. Careful meant not following him into the private property of a darkened mansion. Careful wasn't sitting beside him at a local restaurant or inviting him into her suite.

You're tense.

"Yeah," she admitted and turned her gaze to his.

His ferocity was gone. Now the familiar man from her dreams was at the forefront. He slid his palm around her neck and leaned in slowly, giving her a chance to protest before his mouth grazed hers. She sank into him, placing her hands on the hardness of his chest as his tongue snaked across her lips.

Desire warred with self-preservation. She tried to pull away, but he held her neck tight, hypnotizing her with a kiss that couldn't be denied. *Shouldn't* be denied. Her fingers tangled with the material of his shirt, their noses brushed. He ground his hips into her, and the unmistakable erection nestled between them doused her in a bucket of crystal clarity.

She shoved from his grip and gasped for breath. "Not here."

He inclined his head, his lips kiss-darkened, and he stepped back to use both hands on his cell. *Go get changed. I'm taking you out.*

"No." She backtracked, distancing herself from whatever pheromone-induced stupor he'd pulled her into. "I should lay low for a while."

A lot lower than kissing behind a shrub out in front of her hotel.

Why? His forehead crinkled in the cutest look of desperation. *You'll be gone soon enough.*

He reached out his free hand and she stepped back, fearful of her weakness. A smirk tilted his lips and the glint in his eye said he knew exactly why she was fleeing.

"The best thing for me is an early night."

His smirk remained in place. Teasing. Taunting. He stared at her, unblinking, and began hypnotizing her into submission.

"Keenan..."

He raised a brow, feigning ignorance of his appeal.

"Stop using that smirk on me."

"*What?*" he mouthed, innocent as sin.

His confidence was her Achilles heel. But he was right. She was only here for mere weeks. Not nearly long enough to get to know him like her body demanded.

"You're manipulative."

His focus didn't waiver, the smirk didn't falter.

"Fine," she huffed. "I'll go get changed. But you need to wait out here and cool off a little."

He gave an almost indecipherable nod, sealing her fate, banging the gavel and resigning her to another ride on the emotional Keenan roller coaster.

Email Correspondence

Date: 23rd December

Subject: That night.

Savannah,

Do you remember the night you made me stand in the shadows of your hotel while you went inside to change your clothes? Can you imagine the thoughts that went through my mind while you undressed in your room?

Five minutes is a long time for a man to wait in the cold. But I never felt the chill. Around you, I lacked normal sensation. I lacked control and foresight. And everything else that I'd grown to rely on.

The night our movie plans were ruined is evidence of that.

I don't chase tail, Savannah. I don't run after women or heel when lovers come running after me. But I'd happily go to the ends of the earth if it meant you'd come back to me.

Will you? Will you ever come back? Will you ever return my emails?

Keenan

Keenan was leaning against the lamp post when Savannah returned. He stood in the same GQ fashion as the other night, his casual sophistication making every erogenous zone on her body take notice.

He straightened on her approach, but she didn't acknowledge him. She turned onto the sidewalk and continued toward the corner, her head low, her coat tight around her waist. It was time to start being careful, no matter how intensely her body tingled with the need to be near him.

His footsteps grew louder, the thump of his boots sending a constant shiver up her spine. When she reached the end of the block, she took a cautious look for oncoming traffic even though her mind was stuck in daydreams instead of the real world.

A deep, masculine throat cleared behind her, *right* behind her, and she sucked in an anxious breath. She could see him in her periphery, his muscled build a looming temptation. He brushed into her, his shoulder against hers, and trailed his hand into her already occupied pocket.

Her veins tingled as his palm glided over hers and he entwined their fingers in the sanctuary of the material. She didn't look at him, and he was facing straight ahead, too. They were merely two strangers, walking side-by-side, with their hands inadvertently tangled.

No biggie.

They continued across the street, toward the sanctuary of upcoming businesses that would hide them from all possible view of the Rydel hotel. Each step increased the rampant beat in her chest and her lungs began to labor.

As soon as they reached the corner of the first building, her shoulders relaxed and she chanced a look in his direction. He was peering down at her, his focus trained on her eyes. All calm fled, her footsteps faltered, and the world faded to black.

"Keenan…" She knew that look. She knew what it would bring.

He grabbed her around the waist with his free arm, lifting her feet off the ground and backtracked her into the wall. The cold bricks infiltrated her clothing, but the warmth of his body had her melting. Liquefying.

She clung to his forearms through the thick material of his coat and glimpsed a flash of his fierce gaze as he leaned into her.

"Don't," she whispered against his mouth, making him pause. "Not here."

Anywhere but here.

They needed privacy.

They promised to be careful.

He nudged closer, their noses brushing, his bottom lip sweeping hers ever so gently. If he kissed her, she'd be lost. He knew it. She knew it. And he did it anyway, his mouth manipulating hers in a dance so exquisitely soft and sweet that she whimpered from the pleasure of it.

She kissed the lethargy from her system. She tangled her tongue with his in a sparring match to alleviate the frustration of the day. All the earlier irritation from work poured into him and he took it. He grasped it all, strengthening her. Invigorating her.

When he pulled back, she kept her lids closed and bit into her lower lip to savor the throb. The man sure knew how to kiss. He knew how to do a lot of things unlike any other man she knew.

"That wasn't unpleasant." A smile broke free and she blinked her eyes open.

Intensity was no longer a viable word to describe what stared back at her. It was more than ferocity, deeper than pleasure. It was severe and harsh and feral. It was passion and seduction and lust. All the warring emotions rolled into one deliriously sexy shade of silver.

"We should go and do something productive."

Luscious lips quirked before her eyes.

"Not reproductive," she clarified and nudged at his chest. "Come on."

They strolled along the sidewalk amongst the foot traffic of passing people, hand in hand, fingers entwined. The darkness of night placated her, making her feel like they were hiding comfortably in plain sight.

"How about here?" She stopped and peered up at the cinema display board. "Do you feel like watching a movie?"

He shrugged, then gave her an approving nod.

"What do you—" Pressure shoved into her back, a cement-like shoulder propelling her forward. She gasped and Keenan's strong hands caught her waist, stabilizing her.

"Jesus." She turned in his arms and caught the disdain from a man looking over his shoulder as he trudged amongst the foot traffic. "He could've walked around me."

Keenan's hold dropped from her waist and he lunged, gripping the crook of the man's arm to spin him around.

"What the fuck do you think you're doing?" the guy spat.

"Keenan," she warned. "Let it go."

The muscles in his neck tensed and his focus narrowed to pinpoints.

The man yanked his arm from Keenan's grip. "Well? What are you looking at?" His expression turned smug, the caustic grin taunting. "Next time tell your bitch to stay out of the way."

"Let's keep walking." She inched forward and Keenan did, too, raising his chin in the man's face. He was ready to fight. For her.

"What?" The man laughed. "Cat got your tongue?"

"Oh, shit," she whispered.

Keenan clenched his fist and pushed the man's chest with his free hand.

"Stop it." Savannah slid in front of him and placed her palm on his sternum. "Ignore him." He didn't quit glaring over her shoulder. "Please, Keenan. You don't need to prove yourself to him."

"Yeah, Keenan," the man mocked. "You don't need to prove yourself."

The asshole had no idea what he was up against. Couldn't he see the threat of violence in Keenan's eyes? God knew she couldn't ignore it.

"Keenan?" She nudged his chest again. "Look at me."

His jaw ticked, the vein in his neck pulsed, and long seconds flittered by before his focus met hers, steely and determined. The man scoffed from behind her, his presence leaving moments later.

"That wasn't necessary," she murmured and cupped his cheek. "You're better than him." It was the truth. If anything, it was an understatement. But he grunted anyway and glared into the distance.

She could see the damage to his pride. The destruction was like a flare in the night, a brutal wound on otherwise unmarred skin. He couldn't handle assaults aimed toward his lack of speech. He may have mastered the skill to silently communicate, but his ability to reject insults was non-existent.

"Let's get out of here." Her tone held delicious meaning, only he didn't reciprocate the desire. "Please, Keenan."

His lower jaw flexed under her palm and his harsh inhalations pained her. She reached on the tips of her toes and pressed her lips to his, feeling nothing but the sterile rigidity of his mouth. It was useless. She couldn't soothe him.

She fell back on her heels. "We should call it a night."

Wrath was drowning the beauty of his irises. He gripped her chin, making her gasp as he held her in place.

She knew what he wanted. She could see it in his eyes. He needed to be in control of something. Anything. He needed to feel like he mattered. And he did. He already mattered so much to her.

He plastered his mouth against hers, painfully hard, and swept his tongue into her mouth. There was no sweetness shared, only anger, and she liked it. She enjoyed being the one to take his ire.

She could take a whole lot more, too.

He yanked his head back, panting, his chest rising and falling in quick succession.

"I love when you do that."

He frowned in question.

"You hold me, controlling me like you think I'm going to flee." She shook her head. "I'm not going anywhere. Not unless that's what you want." She'd made up her mind. There were still weeks until she left Seattle, and she wanted to spend them with him.

"I'm yours to do with what you will until I fly home."

She couldn't read the message in his eyes. Right now she couldn't tell what he was thinking at all. He released her chin, his hand falling down between them to grip her wrist. He strode away, leading her along the sidewalk, not once stopping to glance over his shoulder.

"Where are we going?"

From his profile, she could see a sinister grin. That was her only answer—devilish focus.

He tugged her around corners, down an alley, and onto another street. She was glad she wore her flats, otherwise her feet wouldn't have made the distance.

He pulled her to the left, down a wide pathway before a menacing tower. Her attention raked over the mass of gleaming windows toward the twinkling sign above the front doors.

Grandiosity.

"Oh, no." She shuddered at the egotistical phallus symbol. An elaborate chandelier glistened in the foyer, the bright twinkle almost blinding. Everything was shiny, refined, and pretentious.

"Are they overcompensating for much?" she drawled.

Keenan's gaze landed on her, and she met his raised brow.

"I'm sorry. I didn't mean to offend your employer."

His brow raised higher.

She chuckled. "Okay. It was clearly meant in offense. But everything here is so..." Arrogant? Imperious? Narcissistic? "...over the top."

He ignored her and tugged on her hand.

"No." She planted her feet and pulled her arm back. "I can't be seen in there."

He pressed his lips together, shrugged, and then walked toward the entrance to the building. She remained in place, watching as a middle-aged doorman descended the steps to greet him with a strong clap to his upper arm.

"Keenan, my man. What can I do for you tonight?"

Keenan pointed a lone finger to the sky with a raised brow.

"What the hell are you doing?" she hissed and turned her back to him. So much for being careful. This was stupidity at its finest.

She raised her collar, lowered her chin like she was some sort of secret agent, and swiveled back to the men.

Keenan had pulled out his wallet and was handing over a stack of bills.

What the hell? "No." She raised her voice, unwilling to let him waste his money on her. "What are you doing?"

Keenan ignored her as she came forward. The door man couldn't take his eyes off the cash, his tongue working his bottom lip in hunger as he eyed the money.

"Let me see what I can do." The guy jogged back up the stairs and pushed into the building to head for the reception desk manned by a lone woman.

"What's going on?" She couldn't help the accusation in her tone. The money he'd handed over wasn't pocket change. It was a substantial amount of bills. Something she couldn't allow him to give away. Not on her account.

He waggled his brows and grasped her hand to raise it to his lips. He placed a long, lingering kiss on her knuckles, almost succeeding in making her forget where they were and what they were doing.

"We agreed we were going to be careful." She waved an arm at the building. "*This* isn't careful."

The door swished open behind her and she stiffened at the approaching footfalls.

"You've got until nine." The doorman handed Keenan a room card.

Nine? She stared at Keenan, but he was ignoring her again, nodding at the other man.

"I've organized the usual."

"The usual?" Savannah murmured.

"But remember, be out by nine or my ass is on the line."

As the men shook hands in farewell, Savannah retrieved her cell from her pants pocket to check the time. It was almost eight. Whatever they had planned would only last an hour. Sixty minutes of potential exposure.

The doorman walked away and Keenan stepped into her, his fingers finding her chin, his grip tightening.

"That dreamy hold isn't going to work on me." She lifted her lashes and met his steely stare.

He leaned in, his gorgeous mouth approaching.

"Nope." She snapped her fingers up to cover his lips. "That won't work either."

He quirked a brow of disbelief.

"What are we doing here?" she whispered.

He raised the room card, taunting her with the promise of seclusion and pleasure.

"Why am I even contemplating this?" It was only sex. Only a mingling of limbs and lips and private parts. Yet something so simple and entirely physical had a hold on her like a steel trap around her ankles.

"I can't be seen in there." She pleaded with her eyes, hoping he would be the lighthouse in the storm of rushing hormones.

Instead, he yanked at her jacket collar, pulling it higher to cover her jawline, then trailed his hand down her arm to link their fingers.

He stepped away, taking the first approach toward temptation. She kept her feet planted, their arms outstretching between them as her body filled with the freezing night air. This was one of those moments when she knew what she was doing was wrong. It was stupid. It was careless. And still her feet stumbled forward of their own accord.

She followed where he led—up the stairs, past the front doors, and through the lobby. She kept her head low, hiding under her collar while Keenan's thumb stroked her hand, back and forth, back and forth.

She focused on the trail of tingles his touch ignited, not once looking up until they were in the sanctuary of the elevator hall. A relieved sigh left her lips and she leaned against the wall, waiting for one of the four doors to open to her rescue.

"What do we have until nine, Keenan?"

She chanced a glance to her side, but her vision bypassed the gorgeous man and became hooked on the security camera in the corner of the roof. *Shit.* She ducked her head and snuggled closer into him.

"I shouldn't be here," she muttered.

Keenan squeezed her hand and spun her to the far elevator behind them, its doors now open wide. She shuffled to keep at his side, hiding behind the wall of his shoulders as they entered the small space.

"Where to now?"

He ignored her and slid the room card into the security panel before pressing the button for the top floor.

"Keenan?"

The doors closed and he stared at the numbers that increased the higher they ascended. Three... Eight... Ten... Her heart rate climbed, too. Fifteen... Twenty... Twenty-five... Thirty. *Ding.*

Inch by inch, a view of immaculate tiles and a crystal chandelier opened before her. She stepped out of the elevator and into the opulence, immersing herself in the overbearing beauty of highly priced wall art.

Keenan's palm pressed into her back as he led her to the penthouse door.

"I really shouldn't be here." But it was only for an hour. What trouble could they get into in sixty minutes?

He opened the lock with a press of the room card against the small black panel on the frame and ushered her inside. Her mouth was open wide as she entered the hall. The vast difference between Grandiosity and Rydel were laid before her in sparkling colors.

He slid his palm into hers, and the tingle of his touch accompanied her into the main room.

"Oh... Wow..." More pompous narcissism bombarded her, but it was beautiful. Oh, so beautiful. The black of night pressed against the floor to ceiling windows, and the reflection of glistening tiles and stainless steel appliances beamed back at her. Everything was immaculate, just as you'd expect from a room which probably cost her healthy monthly salary for one night within the sacred walls.

"It's magnificent." Keenan made to step away, but she clung to his hand and pulled him back. "It's magnificent... But we should leave."

The nudge of guilt entered her mind. Not only was she in a competitor's building, she was in the penthouse, fantasizing about one of their employees and all the naughty things they could do under their roof.

He tugged her toward him, into his chest, and kissed her. He seduced a whimper from her throat and compliance from her body. It was confounding—his power. She shouldn't be this malleable to a man, and yet all her heart thrummed to do was to please him. To make him smile. To make him growl.

He broke their connection slowly, his gaze staring down at her, saying silent words she deciphered like a mastermind code cracker. He wanted her, too. Not just a kiss or a caress. The need flowing through her veins was equally as potent in his. But there was more. She could see mindlessness staring back at her. He knew they shouldn't be here, he knew all the risks and how careless this was. She could also see something bigger, something that added a spark of vulnerability. Did he want more than gratification? Was he aiming to steal her heart?

He turned toward the glass doors leading outside and opened them wide. The freezing air didn't stop her from following after him, onto a balcony bigger than her San Francisco apartment. She blinked away the clouded fog in her mind and focused on the glistening shimmer of the illuminated pool. The surface seeped with mist, the warmth of the water fighting back against the cold of night.

The sound of rustling clothes came from beside her, and she glanced over to find Keenan throwing his jacket to a nearby lounger.

"What are you doing?"

He shot her a sly look and toed off his shoes.

"You're going swimming?"

He unbuckled his belt and shucked his pants, leaving them in a pile on the tile floor. His shirt was next, exposing a mass of muscled skin covered with gooseflesh. One by one, he took off the remainder of his clothes, leaving only his boxer briefs behind.

He outstretched a hand, offering her an invitation to his insanity.

"Oh, no. I'm not getting in there with you." He had no concept of what it took to be careful—not when it came to this connection between them, and definitely not where hypothermia was concerned. "You can't be serious."

The bulge pressing against the crotch of his boxer briefs announced that he, in fact, was dead serious. He padded barefoot to the far end of the pool and bent over, preparing to dive. Back and forth he swayed his arms, giving her a self-satisfied look that made her want to shake him and fuck him at the same time.

Then he was moving, gliding through the air, penetrating the fog and plunging deep. He swam underwater, effortlessly progressing until he reached the opposite end of the pool and broke the surface.

Liquid shone on his skin, the droplets falling from his hair and down the muscles of his back. He glanced over his shoulder and jerked his chin for her to come forward.

"Nope." She couldn't be eloquent at a time like this. Not that she ever was. But with a Greek god on display, his body ripe for her touch and her teeth, she couldn't even form a string of syllables.

He dived to his left, swam toward her side of the pool, and gripped the edge in one hand. He worked her with that sneaky smirk, commanding all her nerves to heightened sensitivity before crooking a finger at her.

"No. I'll watch." She shook her head and crossed her arms over her chest, hiding her hands inside the jacket to keep warm. "We only have an hour. I plan on using my time wisely." For example, memorizing every inch of his profound body while it was at her visual mercy.

He frowned. "*Not one,*" he mouthed. His hand breached the water's surface and he flashed his fingers once, twice, then held up three on their own.

"We've got thirteen hours?"

He didn't answer in movement. Only the gleam in his eyes announced they had more than brief minutes at their disposal. They had an entire night. In the penthouse. In their own private pool.

"Nope. I'm still not getting in there."

He splashed her, the wave of water penetrating her shoes and pants.

She squealed and jumped back. "It's freezing out!"

He shot her a look that spoke of undeniable heat. A look so captivating it made her forget it was ten-thousand degrees below the desired temperature to be swimming. She eyed her surroundings in apprehension. The balcony was bathed in darkness, the pool lights were dim, but the penthouse was a backdrop of illumination. She wondered if the few neighboring skyscrapers would be a platform for their peepshow. The distant buildings could house a plethora of voyeurs.

She turned back to him, immediately pinned by the weight of his stare. There shouldn't be any question that this was a bad idea. She was professional, mature, and independent. Yet all those attributes died under the weight of his grin.

He was unbelievable. Undeniable.

"You know you've got me wrapped around your little finger, don't you?"

The curve of his lips increased.

"Smug bastard," she murmured under her breath and toed off her shoes. There was no conclusion to this night that wouldn't end in a runny nose and shattering chest cough. And still she continued to undress, albeit faster and with less seduction than Keenan had. She threw off her jacket, ditched her long-sleeve top, shucked her jeans, and yanked off her socks.

The tile was ice beneath her feet. The air around them cold enough to freeze Santa's balls. She tiptoed to the pool stairs, dipped her foot into the water, and was surprised by the warmth heating her tiny toes.

Keenan approached her in the shallow end, his strokes effortless, his muscles taut. He stood to his full height, his chest exposed to the elements as she descended to the first step.

"We're going to catch pneumonia when we get out."

He laughed silently and lunged for her. His wet arms sailed around her waist to lift her off her feet. She squealed as he dragged her against his chest and into neck-high water.

"I hate you. I hate you. I hate you." Her teeth chattered even though she wasn't cold. It was his hold that made her shiver. His touch that confused her senses.

His mouth took over hers as they glided through the warmth. She circled his waist with her legs, his neck with her arms, entwining them as one. There was no need for air, only more of him. She held him tight, tighter than she'd ever held any man before, and tried to kiss the desire out of her system. Each stroke of tongues inspired more need, each clink of teeth made her fingers clench for more. There was no end in sight. No relief within her grasp.

He held her as if his life depended on it. One arm was around her waist, strong and protective. The other curled around her back, along her spine so his fingers mingled with her hair. The hard length of his erection nudged her pubic bone and she pulled back to clear her head. They couldn't have sex here. Not in plain sight. Not when they were illuminated by the underwater lights.

"We need to stop."

She nuzzled her cheek against his, letting the rough stubble scratch her skin. She kissed the side of his jaw, his earlobe, his neck. She wanted to kiss him everywhere, and would've if she wasn't desperately clinging to the last vestiges of her control.

The first time they met was intriguing. The night of the bonfire was thrilling. When they slept together, he'd won over her body. But tonight she worried he was winning over her heart. Worse, she feared he'd see it if she looked into his eyes. There was no way her feelings weren't written all over her face.

She released her arms from his neck, her legs from his waist, and leaned backward, swimming away. He stalked her with his eyes, watching her swim as if his focus was glued to her with an invisible string. He didn't come after her, which made it worse. There was no rejection, only a slowly building determination.

Soon, he would pounce. He would dash after her, making her scream, making her squirm. His lips kicked, plaguing her with painful arrhythmia. She didn't like anticipation, not when it came from a confident man like Keenan. No. She loved it. She thrived on it. She wanted to breathe deep of his cockiness and never forget how it made her feel.

A clatter of sound came from behind her, and Keenan's attention darted to the penthouse. She froze, the hairs on the back of her neck lifting in a wave of panic. He was focused on something, or someone, and she chanced a glance over her shoulder to see two people inside.

Oh, shit. Her gaze cut to Keenan and he held up a hand to calm her, casual yet authoritative. She shot another look inside, taking in details. The two men were dressed in a uniform. Hotel staff. Room service. They were laying out plates along the dining table.

Keenan approached. One of his hands wove around her waist, the other gripped her jaw and brought her face back to meet his. There was understanding in his eyes, a steely determination that said he knew she was petrified and he wouldn't let anything happen to her.

"If I'm caught here—"

He leaned in, his lips brushing hers, careful and delicate. Each sweep was a placation, every swipe of his tongue told her that he would protect her. When they broke apart, she chanced another glance over her shoulder, to find the main area of the penthouse abandoned.

"They're gone?" She turned back to those gorgeous eyes and measured her relieved sigh when he nodded. "Good." Now she could breathe.

Almost.

His lips took command again, sweeping her up in relief and morphing it into lust. A rough palm grazed down her back, underneath her waistband and around her bottom. She stiffened, knowing it wasn't right, not when they were outside, exposed. But it was a battle her common sense couldn't win. She was defeated by hunger, unable to think straight through her unquenchable appetite.

She whimpered, clinging to his shoulders to gain control. "We need to go inside."

He walked her backward and leaned her into the pool wall. His touch descended, that naughty hand in her panties reaching further to brush right where she wanted him to.

She squeezed her eyes shut at the rush of blood that drained from her face and settled between her thighs. His stubble grazed her jaw, his lips skimmed her neck. He inched closer, chest to chest, and his fingertips breached her entrance, the teasing, torturous touch increasing her desire and frustration in equal measure.

"How do you do it?" she whispered. "How do you continue to wordlessly convince me to do things I know I shouldn't be doing?"

She ground into him, her clit against his erection. His fingers sank deeper, twisting, pulsing. She gasped, over and over, her nails digging into his skin. His other hand skimmed the curve of her breast. He lifted the cup of her bra, molding the flesh in his hand, and tweaked her nipple with his thumb.

She'd been born for this moment. The world existed for the pleasure he gave her. There was no rhyme or reason... Well, the reason was his deliriously good looks and skilled hands. But what she felt for him went above and beyond that. There was so much emotion building inside her.

"What are you doing to me?" she whispered.

Her core clamped down on his fingers and she froze as her orgasm hit. She mewled into his neck, losing the battle to remain quiet, and sank her teeth into his flesh.

She was *that* woman now. The one who put sensation before sanity. The one who thought with her body instead of her mind. He'd rewired her circuits and transformed her into someone unrecognizable.

And she couldn't think of one good reason to ever return to normal.

Sixteen

Keenan pushed from the pool, a wave of water seeping over his flawless skin. He reached for his pants, pulled something from his pocket, and then turned to face her with a dictating finger pointed her way. "*Wait.*"

Savannah bristled at the command and shuddered at the same time. She watched his sexy, naked ass disappear into the opulence of the penthouse. Moments later he returned draped in a fluffy white robe with another hanging over his forearm. He crooked a finger at her. Another silent command. She was losing her sanity to those gestures.

It was the demand, the silent mandate that sang to her.

She wanted to disobey him, to refuse his request and see his reaction. But not this time. She was too addicted to his look of approval, the tiny gleam in his eye that spoke of satisfaction.

She swam to the edge of the pool and he leaned over to offer her a hand, pulling her from the water. His appreciative gaze raked the full length of her as they came face to face. Even in the harshest winter, that look would've burned.

He placed the robe around her, engulfing her in the thickest, softest material known to man before placing a hand on the low of her back to urge her inside.

"What about my underwear?" She glanced back at the water and spied the two pieces of clothing now seated at the bottom of the pool.

He responded with a firm press of his hand. There would be no going back. Not tonight.

"I guess I'll scoop them out later." She followed him to the doors, the soles of her feet stinging from the chill, and stepped into bliss. The air inside was warm with the heavenly aroma of mouth-watering food. Shiny, silver domes were scattered over the coffee table. At least eight of them of varying sizes. The placement was strategic. Where the meals could've been shared on the large expanse of the dining table, they'd instead been seated in front of the intimacy of the sofa.

There was even a silver bucket holding a bottle of wine and two glasses.

"This is the usual?" She wondered how many times it took to make something a remembered ritual. How many women had he shared this with? How many lovers?

He strolled forward to sit on the sofa. His robe stretched wide, gifting her with the expanse of his muscled chest as he spread his arms along the backrest.

"How many women, Keenan?" she purred, pretending like she wasn't entirely invested in receiving his answer.

He leaned forward and lifted one of the domes, exposing a bowl of strawberries dribbled with white and milk chocolate. He threw one in his mouth, his jaw working over the fruit in a devilish rhythm that made her ovaries want to dance.

"You're not enjoying my line of questioning?" She sauntered toward him, meeting his raised brow with a seductive grin. "How many, stud?"

She wanted to know the number of women she had to erase from his mind. Was the total achievable? Did she stand a chance?

He turned his focus back to the coffee table and reached for another strawberry.

Fine. He was a stubborn bastard. But more potent than her desire for answers was her thirst for his attention. She wanted those eyes focused on her, his visual embrace caressing every nerve ending.

She stopped before him, their feet brushing. She placed one knee on the sofa beside his thigh and licked her lips in a blatant provocation as she straddled his lap.

If he wouldn't gift her with his focus, she'd take it instead.

"How many?" she whispered against his mouth.

He met her gaze, reading her, his mental feelers getting to the heart of her question.

"*No*," he mouthed.

The scent of his strawberry breath tickled her nose, but it wasn't tempting enough to dislodge the vulnerability that prickled her skin.

She was struggling to bat away the emotional baggage piling at her feet. Their time together was about sex. It was merely physical. Entirely casual. Yet it seemed like they'd passed into something tangible a long time ago. At least she had.

"Lost count, huh?" She leaned into his shoulder and ran her lips along his neck to hide her face. "I guess I'll have to try extra hard to make a lasting impression."

He gripped her waist and pushed her back so suddenly that it tore a gasp from her throat.

"*No*," he mouthed and this time it was with anger. He pointed at his chest, jabbing his finger against his skin in harsh movements. "*I do*."

"You have to make an impression?" Her lips curved, her pleasure visible for him to see. "You already did that long ago. I've become obsessed with the unique thrill of you." She still knew very little about the man who had tangled her heart in his grasp. But everything apart from the here and now seemed inconsequential. Background noise.

"You're a guilty indulgence, do you know that?"

His focus remained harsh as his arm sailed around her back, holding her, controlling her, as he leaned forward to snatch another strawberry. This time he didn't bring it to his sensuous lips, he touched it to hers, teasing, tempting.

She opened her mouth for a taste and he retreated to trail a path of chocolate along the side of her jaw, then her collarbone. His eyes tracked the journey, and the arm holding her disappeared to roughly tug the lapels of her robe apart. He swiped the fruit down her cleavage, over the top of her breast, and then grazed it over her nipple. Back and forth he moved, tightening the flesh to a painful peak.

"Care for a taste?" she teased.

She didn't have a chance to pause for breath before his mouth was on her, his tongue licking the chocolate off her nipple like he was starved of sustenance. He was rough, ravenous, as he retraced the path from her breast to her cleavage, her collarbone and then her jaw.

She ground into him, succumbing to her body's demand for friction. All she could see was him—those eyes, delicious lips, smooth, flawless skin. Then he took her mouth, licking the chocolate from her lips before delving deeper with his tongue. They became a mass of tangled arms that fought for supremacy and nails that dug into skin. There was no finesse. No control. It was all jerky movements and grinding hips.

He pulled back in a harsh withdrawal and panted into the air between them. He was shaking, his chest convulsing in a defenseless movement that sprinkled her confidence with magical fairy dust.

"Am I too much for you?" She bit at his lower lip, sinking her teeth deep.

He growled, low and devilishly sexy. She smiled into the vibration and then gasped when he gripped her hips and stood. She clung to him, her arms and legs holding him tight as he marched them toward an open door at the far end of the room.

She peered over her shoulder, her heart skipping a beat at the king-size bed. It was darker in here, the lights of the city and the glow from the main room of the penthouse their only illumination. He placed her down on the covers and dug into his robe pocket to pull out a condom.

He sheathed his length before she could reposition herself on the mattress, then he was back between her thighs, the head of his shaft finding right where it needed to be.

His focus was riveted on her, more forceful than the throbbing cock nestled at her entrance. There was no voice, no sound, yet boundless communication flittered between them. They weren't limited because of his lack of speech. They weren't inhibited at all.

She could see his lust in the clench of his jaw and the narrowed savagery in his eyes. Emotion flowed from him in waves as he sank into her in a violent plunge, so deep the skin on her arms shivered.

The sex was a blur, an emotionally drunk collision of delirium and euphoria. They were animalistic in their carnality. She clawed and bit and licked. He tugged and squeezed and growled. For the first time, sex was a sparring match. They battled for supremacy, pushing and tugging, teasing and tormenting as they rolled from one side of the bed to the other.

"You're killing me." Her legs were burning from fatigue, her lungs struggling under the need for oxygen.

He slowed his rhythmic grind beneath her, his hands becoming gentle on her hips. He completely obliterated their fast tempo, replacing it with something smooth and romantic.

The fight became too much. She grew overwhelmed in the confusion of how perfect they were. How undeniably matched they seemed in the bedroom. It had to be a dream.

She closed her eyes and ground her hips, making the undulations longer, grating her clit over his pubic bone. She straightened and cupped her breasts, tiny whimpers escaping her lips as she became lost to sensation. There wasn't a part of her that wasn't affected by him. There wasn't a thought, or a nerve, or a heartbeat that didn't comply with the delicious feel of this man.

When she opened her eyes, she froze. Keenan was staring at her. No, not merely staring, he was in awe, his lips slightly parted, his attention riveted. He mouthed something, maybe it was *beautiful*, maybe it wasn't. But the affection reflected in his eyes made her pussy pulse with a new wave of tingles.

She kept one hand on her breast and moved the other to his chest as she rode him harder. She continued to melt into the sea of dark gray and crashed under the waves of his scrutiny as her core clamped down and began to spasm.

A gasp parted her lips with the first pulse of orgasm. Then another and another.

He matched her, his gyrations becoming harder as he jerked into her, each time becoming harsher than the last. She watched him come undone, and the sight was exhilarating. Such a strong, confident man at his most vulnerable.

She'd never forget that sight. Not tomorrow, and definitely not once she left Seattle.

"You're not going to get a thank you this time." She quirked her brows and tumbled to lie beside him. "You've completely obliterated my focus." She rested a hand over her eyes and breathed deep to slow the rapid rise and fall of her chest.

His hand came to rest on her side, his touch a delicate balm. He twirled his fingers over her flesh, back and forth, up and down. She could've almost fallen asleep at the perfection of his attention, until he broke the silence with a harsh clearing of his throat.

Her eyes snapped open as she lowered her arm to look at him. *Shit.* He'd been trying to get her attention. "Sorry."

He pinched his fingers together and bobbed them toward his mouth. "*Hungry?*"

She shook her head and sank into the pillows. "Sleepy."

He smirked, the twitch of his lips announcing he was proud to cause her exhaustion.

"Go on." She shooed him with a lazy wave of her hand and relaxed into the coverings. "Eat."

She nestled her face into the pillow to hide her look of smitten devastation. He was under her skin in a big way and she couldn't even tell anyone about it. Not Dominic, who wouldn't approve. Not Penny, who would start sharpening her knife collection. And definitely not her mother. who would immediately call Aunt Michelle to gossip.

She was on her own with this, and her body didn't mind one little bit.

Seventeen

Savannah woke up alone, again, this time surrounded by decadence and cocooned in silence. The heavy curtains were drawn together and barely a slice of morning light was seeping through.

"Keenan?" She clutched the sheet to her naked chest and sat up. He wasn't here. There was no movement in the expanse of the penthouse. No rustle of sound. No clink of cutlery.

She flung back the covers and swiveled to place her feet on the thick pile carpet. Her concentration narrowed to a piece of folded paper on the bedside table, her name barely visible on the front due to the dim light. She flicked on the lamp and lunged for the note with starvation. She couldn't get enough of him, not after a night of sex and not after weeks of his dreamy stare in her mind.

She flipped open the paper and devoured the note word for word— *I have commitments tonight, but I want to see you on Friday.*

A smile tugged at her lips as she refolded the page. Tomorrow seemed an eternity away, but she'd take it. She'd take any sliver of his time, especially if it involved leaving her body in this same dreamy, lethargic state. She could barely clench her thighs. Each muscle ached in a different way—her arms, her legs—even her back felt different.

She stood, stretched, and noticed her clothes piled on the end of his side of the bed. He'd placed them there neatly, one sitting on top of the other, perfectly folded. She wished he would've stayed, or at least woken her. Her skin was sticky from sweat and the lingering hint of chocolate. They could've showered together. He could've scrubbed her clean. Instead, she'd have to do it on her own, letting the shower wash away parts of him that she wasn't ready to lose.

Blinking her dreary eyes, she dragged her feet to the end of the bed. She was still half asleep, her mind in a blissful plane, until the red numbers of the alarm clock beamed at her from Keenan's bedside table.

She blinked harder. Faster. Again and again.

The numbers didn't change. 8:56 kept staring back at her.

"Holy shit!" She had to be out of here by nine. *Nine!*

She lunged for her clothes, riffling through the items—her pants, her long-sleeve top, her jacket. Where the hell was her underwear? "Damn it."

She yanked a robe off the floor, shoved her arms into the sleeves, and made for the balcony doors. The cold air greeted her like a slap in the face as she ran for the pool in search of her bra and panties.

Thick mist wafted toward her from the water, the entire top of the surface blanketed in fluffy white.

"*Shit.*" She spun in a circle, looking for a scoop, a rake, anything that could possibly assist in retrieving her intimate apparel and help avoid a scandal.

Nothing was there. Absolutely nothing. There was only two options—dive in or run.

"Fuck it." She chose the latter and sprinted back to the penthouse bedroom on the tips of her freezing toes.

She shimmied out of the robe like an electrocuted belly-dancer and then pulled on the available layers of clothing, sans underwear. The material adhered to her skin, the sticky chocolate and abrasive material working together to increase her annoyance.

Once she was in the vicinity of suitably-dressed, she checked her pockets for her belongings and ran for the front door, finger combing her hair along the way. The hall was empty, the thick silence increasing her paranoia as she waited for the elevator.

Minutes ticked by. Hours. Then the *ding* of her arriving chariot filled her ears.

She checked her teeth in the elevator mirror and tried to bring conformity to her unruly hair. As the bell dinged her ground level destination, she looked at the tiled floor and kept her focus there until she was outside the hotel doors. There was no way she was making eye contact with anyone.

A walk of shame was always painful. Sneaking out of a rival penthouse without your underwear was excruciating. But even though the embarrassment was aggressively potent, a grin still curved her lips. There was an added energy to her step, a bigger bounce that came from the way her body still hummed from Keenan's touch.

She wasn't in first grade anymore. Her panties didn't have her name clearly written on the tag. There would be no lost property announcement or search for the owner.

There was no need to panic.

The sunshine beamed extra bright as she walked through the Seattle streets, sipping a takeaway coffee and reliving the night before like it was her first trip to Disneyland. Nothing could've wiped the smile exercising her cheeks, nothing except Penny, who stood at the bottom of the stairs leading to the Rydel front doors, her arms crossed as she glared.

"Have fun last night?" her cousin greeted.

Savannah tried not to wither as the overdose of orgasmic bliss flushed from her system in an immediate detox. "What do you want, Penny?" She stopped in front of her cousin, sipped her coffee, and pretended as though she wasn't currently doing the walk of shame without panties.

"I want to ask you nicely to stay away from him."

"From who?" she drawled.

"Don't play coy. It doesn't suit you."

Savannah rolled her eyes. "Then don't pretend to be nice, because that doesn't suit you either."

Penny dropped her hands to her sides and raised her chin. "Keenan didn't go home last night and you didn't answer my calls when the receptionist buzzed your room. It's safe to assume the two of you were together."

"Assumptions lead to false accusations, Penny. You should learn to be more professional than that."

"Just stay away from him, okay?"

Savannah didn't enjoy thinly veiled threats, especially when they came from someone who had just snatched her morning high with the finesse of a Brazilian wax. The two of them were never going to get along. It was clear. Crystal. So there was no point in deflecting drama. She needed to face it head on. To gobble it up with a voracious smile on her face to ensure Penny knew she wasn't interested in playing games.

Savannah lowered the coffee cup from her lips and calmed her expression. This could be handled with civility, right? "If you feel threatened by me, maybe you should take it up with this man of yours."

"Or I could take it out on your staff?" she sneered. "Interviews start soon. It would be a shame if I was too angry to judge Rydel staff fairly."

Or maybe civility was a stretch. A long stretch.

"Do that and we're going to have a lot of problems."

"I think we already do."

True. They were embroiled in a mess that started years ago, and now it was morphing into something bigger, something nastier.

"Look, I've asked repeatedly and have been assured that the man I'm spending my time with is single." She wasn't going to doubt Keenan again. She had no reason not to trust him, and until he did something that made her question her judgement, she would ignore her cousin's attempt to cause drama.

"Ha." Penny shook her head in disgust. "Keenan is always single, yet you'll never see him without a woman on his arm or me in his bed."

"Well, you weren't there last night." Savannah snapped her mouth shut, wishing she could take back the taunt. Silence engulfed them. The sound of traffic grew distant. The presence of pedestrians walking to work disappeared.

Penny's face fell and paleness creeped into her features. "No, but I bet you won't be tonight."

No, she wouldn't be. Keenan had already left her a note telling her as much.

Savannah bit her tongue and breathed deep through her nose. They were in a boxing ring, landing invisible blows that still packed a physical punch. It would go on forever unless she put a stop to it. She sipped her coffee, taking the additional seconds to regroup, then met Penny's scowl head on. "All this is beside the point," she continued. "Because I'm not sleeping with Keenan."

If Penny could lie, so could she. They were done with this. She was moving on. She took the first step toward her hotel and ignored the sound of callous laughter that sent a shiver down her spine.

"Are you really going to stick with that load of bullshit?"

Savannah took the first step, and the second, not slowing her stride. "What I'm going to do is extricate myself from this childish situation and pretend like you were never here."

There was a beat of silence, one slow, blurred glimpse of the light at the end of the tunnel before, "Dominic said he told you about what happened on our last summer vacation."

Savannah paused on the top step, this time out of respect for the mistakes of her past. "Yes, he did."

"And you have nothing to say?"

She kept her gaze straight ahead. The reflection of Penny in the lobby windows was enough to test her composure. "If you told me years ago, I would've apologized profusely. As it stands, I still feel horrible. But we were kids, and I refuse to let you drag the past into the present. That summer is over and we've both grown up." She took the last step. "At least I have."

"You're such a bitch, Savannah. You always thought you were better than me," Penny raised her voice. "I'll destroy the lives of all those employees. One by one. And I'll make sure they know you're to blame."

Savannah continued walking, her head high, her shoulders straight. She wouldn't show fear, no matter how excruciatingly tight her chest became. "Goodbye, Penny."

"It's *Penelope*," her cousin snapped.

Savannah pushed open the hotel door and glanced over her shoulder. "I don't care."

Eighteen

Savannah wasted yesterday trying to deny she was hiding from staff over the condom scandal. Today, she refused to acknowledge that she felt threatened by her cousin. Neither day was spent in the skin of a woman who was confident and calculated. She was beginning to see a stranger staring back at her from the mirror. A stranger who had left her underwear in the bottom of the Grandiosity Penthouse pool.

Through phone calls to the San Francisco office, emails to local staff, and numerous coffee breaks, she struggled to concentrate. She spent hours working in her hotel room without a second unmarred by thoughts of Penny. Her mind couldn't focus on work. Instead, she fought with herself not to question Keenan's motives or honesty.

The easiest option was to extricate herself from the situation and kiss goodbye to a phenomenal yet temporary sex life. But she didn't think she could. Keenan had edged himself into her life, and even though she would eventually go back to San Fran and leave him behind, she couldn't bring herself to cut him off prematurely.

She pushed from her tiny hotel desk and dragged her feet to the window. She could still see him leaning against the light post, his confidence beaming back at her. Not a second passed without his remembered touch on her skin.

Eight months with Spencer didn't equate to one night with Keenan. Her ex wasn't even in the same ballpark. Who would've thought that a wealthy, articulate man like Spencer with his pretty-boy looks and his

CEO inheritance would be no match for a guy as rough and gruff as Keenan?

The man she was falling for didn't have an army of seductive words at his disposal. He didn't have a portfolio of assets or a gushing bank account. There was only the man himself—pure sex appeal with no added distractions.

She settled her hand against the cool glass of the window and wished he was still down there, his devouring stare peering up at her. She wasn't sure how long she stood there daydreaming. It could've been seconds. It could've been days. And when her suite phone trilled, she was torn from her fantasies hard enough to wrench a gasp from her throat.

She pushed away the curtains, stepped past the desk chair and around the bed to pick up the receiver. "Hello?"

"Savannah, it's Kelly at reception, I'm sorry to bother you—"

"It's no problem."

"A package has arrived for you. Would you like me to arrange for someone to bring it up?"

A package? Her heart sank. There was no excitement over the delivery, only a slowly dawning dread working its way from her feet to her chest. Life was becoming ridiculous when your initial reaction was to envisage your cousin sending a severed cow's head or sheep's heart in the mail. "No. I can come and get it. Do you know who it's from?"

"It doesn't say on the box, but there's a card. Want me to open it?"

"No, it's okay. I'll be there in a minute." She hung up the receiver and pulled on her shoes before leaving her room. When she entered the lobby, Grant and Kelly were on the customer side of the reception desk, both peering down at the counter that held a silver box adorned with ribbon. The package was at least a foot long, marginally shorter in width and around eight inches in height.

Too small for a severed head. Too big for a sheep's heart. *Winner.*

"Is this it?" she asked as she approached.

"Yep. It was delivered by courier." Kelly greeted her with a smile. "And it sure looks pretty."

"Thanks." She lifted the box, surprised at the light weight. "I'll be back down later to get a coffee and check the occupancy reports."

"You're not going to open it here?" Grant asked.

She eyed the package. "No, I didn't plan on it."

"Come on." There was no nervousness in his features, no twitch to his hands. "We need something to brighten our day."

"I'm not sure the contents of this box will help with that." She shook the package and nothing clunked. Whatever lay inside was soft. Come to think of it, it was probably a box full of bubble-wrap, with compliments from Spencer who liked to waste her time and the company's money on stupid shit like this.

"Just open it," he chastised.

"Pushy much?" She glared and placed the box back on the counter. Kelly and Grant encroached, both hovering over her shoulders as she pulled at the pink ribbon and lifted the lid an inch. Silver tissue paper stared back at her, the contents hidden from view.

"Here, let me hold that." Kelly snatched the lid away.

"Slow down." Savannah looked at them in turn. "With the settlement being temperamental, I don't want to rush into opening unmarked packages."

Kelly took a step back. "What do you think is in there?"

"I don't know." She slid her hand under the layers of tissue paper and relaxed at the soft texture under her fingertips. She grasped something that felt like lace and lifted. Bright purple material came into view. Black stitching was woven around the edges, more and more of it becoming visible as she slowly raised her hand.

"Is that..." Grant's voice drifted off.

Oh, shit. Scorching heat flooded her cheeks. She shoved the tiny sliver of underwear back into the box and snatched the lid from Kelly's grip. "I think it's best if I open this in private." She slid the package off the counter and clutched it to her chest. "The card?"

Kelly scooted around the desk and lifted a white envelope from her keyboard. "Was that lingerie?"

"I don't know." *Liar, liar, libido on fire.* "But it's definitely not work related, so I'll take this back to my room."

She ignored the twitch of Grant's lips and swiveled toward the elevator. She ignored their laughter, too, and walked at a clipped pace, fleeing the lobby and ascending to her room with adrenaline flowing through her veins.

She pushed her front door open with her hip and ran for her bed, dropping the box down immediately and throwing away the lid. She unfolded the tissue paper and stared in shock at the numerous pieces of matching lingerie.

One by one, she lifted the items—red satin bra and matching panties, purple lace bra and matching G-string, bright pink, see-through camisole with a tiny string of material that could not be described as underwear.

She checked the tags, all of them displaying the same name of an expensive women's lingerie company along with the notification of her size. *Her* size. The size that nobody else in the world should know except her.

She reached for the envelope, tore the side, and pulled out a pearl white piece of cardboard.

Rumor has it that you left a souvenir in the penthouse pool. I hope these make up for your loss.

Keenan.

That overwhelming heat flooded her cheeks again, and a torturous, undeniable double-tap thumped in her chest. She pivoted, snatched her cell from the small desk and began typing with fingers that were overdosing on adrenaline.

> **Savannah:** *Thank you for the inappropriate and outrageously beautiful gift. I assure you I didn't plan on leaving a souvenir, however, I was rudely left to awaken alone and in enemy territory moments before the troops were scheduled to attack. I think my nights of sleeping naked are well and truly over.*

She clicked send and threw her cell onto the bed. She was buzzing—her limbs, her heart, her thoughts. Whenever she thought his seductive appeal was unable to reach new heights, he surprised her all over again, weaving his web of infatuation tighter and tighter.

"You're killing me," she murmured to the empty room.

She backtracked into the small desk, clutched the wood, and scrutinized the package from a safe distance. The contents were masterful in their appeal. He'd purchased items to make her think of sex, *their sex*—last night and in the future—and she'd already been overdosing on the topic.

Her cell vibrated and she practically lunged for the device, sweeping it off the mattress in a lithe swoop as she casually dropped against the end of the bed.

> *Keenan: A woman of your outrageous beauty should never sleep with clothes on. Especially in my bed. I will endeavor to make sure that disservice to the world never happens on my watch.*

She stared at the message. Couldn't stop. Her focus was stuck on two words—outrageous beauty. Yes, they were her words repeated back to her with alluring perfection, but it was much more than letters and syllables.

She actually felt beautiful in his presence. It was probably why her brain was a mass of fog and giddy contemplation. He made her feel gorgeous. Adored. Revered wasn't a stretch.

What so many men before him couldn't articulate, he did without voice. He transformed her into a goddess whenever they were together. His presence, his dominance, even the possession in his eyes, it all wordlessly danced together to wrap her in a confidence unlike what she experienced in the professional world.

Her cell vibrated in her grip.

> *Keenan: I expect a fashion parade tomorrow night.*

Tomorrow. Not tonight.

The giddiness faded and in its place came a vision of Penny. The reminder of her cousin's taunts made all happiness dissipate and an unhealthy amount of determination ignite.

> *Savannah: How about tonight? I can wait up for you.*

She started packing the orgasm-inducing lingerie into the box, taking her time to admire each item. She could pretend his reply wasn't as important as her next breath. Yep. She could pretend the shit out of that.

> **Keenan:** *My commitments aren't in the city and I'm not sure when I'll be finished. I promise to make it up to you on Friday.*

And there it was, the ball sailing gracefully into Penny's side of the court.

Savannah fell back onto the mattress and stared at the ceiling. Her options were narrowing. She could either trust a man she barely knew or give credit to someone she was beginning to loathe. Neither made her heart flutter with joy. In fact, both options kind of felt like a knife to her kidneys.

Penny's claws were gripping tighter around her throat. The woman was winning. At the very least, her manipulation was starting to dent Savannah's thin layer of professionalism because all she wanted to do was forehead slap her cousin and tell her to wake up to herself.

Should she tell him about the confrontation with her cousin? She'd held off all day, not wanting to make a big deal out of it. But now that she had his attention, she didn't want to let the opportunity slide.

> **Savannah:** *Penny was waiting for me when I arrived at my hotel this morning.*

She picked up the purple bra and twirled it on her finger, waiting for her cell to buzz.

It didn't.

She pulled all the lingerie out, inspected them, replaced them back into their box, and still there was no reply. Her body reacted as if starved of oxygen. Her heart rate increased, her lungs threatened to explode. There was so much angst waiting for one message. A few words.

Was it really worth it?

She closed her eyes and was immediately greeted with Keenan's grin. She could feel his touch on her neck—his fingertips, his lips. She could sense the warmth from his strong arm wrapped around her waist, and her heart began to do that tippy tappy thing.

The phenomenal sex may not be worth the jealousy and anger Penny inspired. But Keenan's attention, his affection, made the negative side-effects less harsh. Yes, the risk was great. Huge. Only there were so many other reasons to negate those bad thoughts. Seattle was lonely. She needed stress relief, and she needed to prove, not only to herself, but to Spencer, that she could move on.

The familiar vibration of her cell startled the silence, and the pressure in her chest lessened.

Keenan: *What did she want?*

She began typing instantly. *Penny threatened me to stay away from you...* No, that was too dramatic. She deleted the words and then started again.

Savannah: *She wanted to talk about you.*

This time the response came within seconds.

Keenan: *What about me?*

There were numerous paths to take. The dramatic, dump-Penny-in-trouble route or the let's-not-make-a-big-deal-out-of-this avenue.

Savannah: *She told me to stay away from you.*

Once the wait for a reply ticked into minutes, she began to pace. She should get back to work. At least show her face in the lobby so Kelly and Grant didn't think she was up here playing with lingerie instead of doing her job.

She palmed her cell, staring down at the device that had begun to run her life. Mr. Rydel wouldn't approve. Spencer, Dominic, Penny, and even her mother would feel the same.

She should spend her spare time sightseeing. Doing whatever Seattle people did for fun, instead of becoming obsessed with her experiences between the sheets that seemed to act like an addictive drug.

The screen brightened and another message beamed up at her.

Keenan: Do you plan on listening to her?

She sucked in a breath.

Savannah: Should I?

Keenan: Probably.

She waited for more. At least an explanation.
Nothing came.

Savannah: Is that what you want?

Her stomach flipped as she pressed send. She wasn't sure how she would react to an affirmative response. She didn't want anything other than a glowing indication that she wasn't the only one ignoring the wishes of the world.

Keenan: You know it's not.

Maybe, but a girl deserved confirmation.

Keenan: Nobody has ever affected me the way you do. Nobody. Ever. I leave you and within seconds I have to push myself not to turn back and go in search of you again. It might be a normal feeling for others, but for me it's a first. And although I don't have the experience to back it up, I think this uncomfortable, clingy sensation might be something normal people consider a good thing.

What she wouldn't give to see him right now. This very second. She had a million plans that involved kissing, licking, sucking. She'd assure him this was a good thing. She'd make him goddamn sure he knew the difference.

Keenan: Too much?

Never, she wanted to reply.

Savannah: That's a good enough reason for me.

She pressed send again and this time her stomach flipped in excitement. They weren't going to let her cousin ruin this. In fact, she wouldn't let her cousin get away with it.

> **Savannah:** *I think I should speak to Grandiosity about Penny. I can't risk her causing more trouble for my employees.*

There was no delay this time; his reply came in seconds.

> **Keenan:** *Let me talk to her. She'll listen to me.*

Of course Penny would. They were close.

A dull ache impeded every heartbeat, bringing with it a sixth sense of apprehension, and yes, jealousy, too.

> **Keenan:** *Savannah? Let me talk to her, okay? I can smooth this over without involving more people.*

She re-read his messages, hating that it was the most logical strategy when her anger demanded blood. Trust was going to have to play a role in this thing between them. Anyway, it already did. Her reputation was in his hands, and at the moment, she was content to allow it.

> **Savannah:** *Okay.*

She would step back and give him the opportunity to pull Penny into line. It was the best move for her, seeing as her position was already under scrutiny due to the condom heist and now the lingerie display.

Distancing herself was the best option. She had to play it cool. Be careful. And most of all, she needed to trust that he wouldn't be sharing a bed with Penny tonight, no matter how much her cousin's taunts were currently haunting her.

Email Correspondence

Date: 24th December

Subject: How did the lingerie look?

Dear Savannah,

I'm not the type of man to be intimidated when walking into a lingerie store. In fact, the morning I picked out those items for you was akin to foreplay at its finest. I imagined stripping you of every item I passed. I could've spent my life savings in one purchase just knowing that the skimpy material would adorn your skin.

I still wonder what you would've looked like in the items I bought for you. I wish I would've had the opportunity to see you in them before you shoved the package back in my face.

You deserved to keep them. You also deserved not to go through the heartbreak that caused you to give them back.

I want you to be aware of something, though. Do you remember the day I sent you that package? Do you remember the messages you sent back? One of them was a chastisement for leaving you to wake up alone. Do you ever wonder why I did that? Do you ever think back and see how I was trying to protect myself from you?

The first night in your hotel suite, I left as soon as you began to wake. I hadn't noticed how much time I'd spent lying there watching you. I memorized the way your features changed as you dreamed. The way your lips twitched. The way your breathing hitched.

INARTICULATE

I was even more careless the night in the penthouse. I slept peacefully beside you until morning. I woke up with the scent of your hair in my lungs and the softness of your body against mine. I awakened to an extra beat in my chest that I already knew I wanted to keep.

I didn't want to let you go. I suppose it's clear I still don't.

When you told me about your argument with Penelope, I knew it was the beginning of the end. Hope vanished as if it was never there, and I became frantic for the briefest of moments with you.

I'm not an optimistic man. I'm a realist. And the devastating reality of what Penelope could do with your feelings for me made me panic. She held all the power. She held our relationship in her hands.

It wasn't easy speaking to her. Penelope is extremely protective of our past, present, and even the future. But the realistic part of me had thought our discussion had sunk in. I told myself you were only in Seattle temporarily, and the measures I'd taken with Penelope were sure to work for that amount of time.

It could've worked out. It could've remained perfect.

I guess I became complacent, too blind with thoughts of you that I didn't notice how truly wrong I was. It's a weak excuse, but I told myself that I hadn't lied to you.

How could I, when I'd never said a word?

But now we both know I was deceiving you with every breath. Every touch. Every kiss.

I'm sorry. I'll forever be sorry.

Please, let me show you how sorry I am.

Keenan

Nineteen

Savannah entered the lobby the next morning to find a group of staff hovering around the reception desk. They spoke in hushed whispers, around eight or nine of them hunched together like a mob of angry villagers, only the occasional sentence being raised to a level where she could hear the caustic tone.

"Good morning." The cluster stiffened at her voice. One by one they looked her way and muttered greetings before disbanding to a smaller group of Kelly, Grant, and Amanda.

"I guess it's not a good morning?" she addressed Kelly, who stood on the working side of the reception desk, one elbow resting against the top counter. "Did I miss the memo for the staff meeting?"

"No." Kelly sank into the chair behind her computer screen and tapped buttons on her keyboard. "Just more bullshit from Grandiosity."

The printer burred to life, spitting out page after page.

"More bullshit?" Savannah had actually had an uninterrupted seven hours sleep. She was energized, pumped, even overly enthusiastic about Keenan kicking some Penny ass.

"It's probably nothing," Grant offered, skirting the counter to stand beside the printer. He grasped the spat out pages, separated the top sheet from the rest, and handed them to her one by one. "This is your usual occupancy report. Nothing new there. But this..." He handed over the other piece of paper. An email header lined the top of the page, with two paragraphs of text below and an ominous business signature from Penelope Augustine at the bottom. "This is the latest correspondence from the evil queen."

"What has she done now?" She skimmed the Times New Roman text.

> Dear future Grandiosity staff,
>
> By the end of business today, you will receive an individual email notifying you of the time and date allocated for your interview with someone in our management team. Due to the large number of interviews necessary, we are unable to facilitate changes to the schedule.
>
> We appreciate your understanding on this matter and would like to reiterate that attending your interview at your allocated time is imperative in securing your position in the new Grandiosity hotel.
>
> Penelope Augustine

"Is this what everyone was discussing?"

"It's nothing, really." Grant's expression said otherwise. "We could all be reading too much into it."

Amanda scoffed. "Discussing is probably an understatement. Everyone is pissed."

"That email is only half of it." Kelly made a shooing motion with her hand and the three of them straightened on the other side of the reception desk at the approach of a young family.

As Kelly checked the guests into their room, Savannah flicked through the pages of the occupancy report. It wasn't anything new. She already had access to the numbers from her laptop and had a notification installed if a sudden influx of cancellations occurred.

Only her problem now wasn't the probable influx of cancellations, but the rush of resignations she sensed approaching. Without staff, the unlikelihood of turning away guests would become a reality. And the wedding... *Jesus Christ.* If more of the Rydel team found new employment, or walked regardless, Savannah would have to stand beside Amanda as she told the bride and groom they couldn't have their special day.

It was a lawsuit waiting to happen. A disaster that would gush more money from the company.

"*Fuck*," she muttered and then winced as the family of four eyed her on their way to the elevators.

Kelly stifled a snort and Grant looked at his toes, a sheepish grin tilting his lips. They remained silent until they were alone—a receptionist, a shift manager, the event manager, and Savannah, the person who was meant to fix a mess she couldn't fully fathom.

"You said the email was only half of it," she started.

"Yeah." Kelly leaned on the armrest of her chair. "Some of us already have our allocated times. I'm booked in to see them during the middle of visiting hours at the hospital. I won't get to see my mother that day."

Savannah winced.

"Sue in the restaurant is scheduled for her only day off and doesn't know how she will find a sitter for her daughter. And Terry in maintenance is scheduled during one of his shifts. He's already covering the work of two other people. Even if he did have permission to leave, he isn't sure it's feasible because the jobs he already has logged are too much for him to handle." Kelly released a defeated sigh. "The entire hotel is going to hell in a handbasket."

Savannah nodded. Nodded and nodded and nodded. "Right."

She could fix this. Everything was fixable. "We'll all work together. I'm a chameleon when it comes to this type of thing. I can work reception, albeit temporarily. I can help out in the restaurant and assist with cleaning rooms, if necessary. If we all work together we'll be fine. I don't mind if Sue needs to bring her daughter here for me to babysit."

She didn't know the first thing about children, but she'd learn. Penny wasn't going to defeat her.

"That's what I said," Grant added. "I'm happy to work extra hours and cover where I can."

"I wish I could say the same." Amanda's face was a mask of distress. "This wedding is going to be the death of me. I'm already working three to four extra hours a day. I don't think my kids recognize me anymore." She ran her hands down her cheeks. "I'm not like everyone else here. I don't need this job. My husband is making enough money off shore for the both of us. But I can't shirk my responsibilities. I can't let this bride down. It will kill me if I do."

"We're not going to let anyone down. Especially not your mother." She met Kelly's gaze. "Can you open a new email for me?"

The receptionist nodded and focused on her computer screen.

"Write the following: *Dear Rydel Seattle staff. Please notify me immediately if you are unable to make your interview appointment with Grandiosity. I will be on stand-by, covering positions where possible, to make sure you can leave during work hours. If you are unable to attend due to personal reasons, please rest assured that you will also be catered for.*"

Kelly's fingers pattered like tiny tap dancers.

"Then sign it off from me," Savannah added. "Include my email address and cell number. I want to make sure everyone feels comfortable calling me with any concerns instead of forming an angry mob in the lobby."

"So, we're just going to try and make this work?" Grant picked at the quick of his nails, his anxiety evident. "How are you going to work around those with personal issues?"

"I'm not, but Grandiosity will." Savannah pulled her cell from her suit pants pocket and double checked her credit card was still stored in the case.

"How?" Grant's voice rose. "What are you going to do?"

"Something I should've done when I first arrived." She gave them a salute in farewell and strode toward the lobby doors. It would've been best to grab a coat, or at least taken a few moments to calm down, but anger would keep her thoughts sharp and hypothermia at bay.

It was only a short cab ride to the building that housed the Grandiosity head office. Short, yet enough time to let her annoyance fester and determination solidify. She glanced up at all the reflective glass and shiny metal and swallowed against the churning in her stomach.

Keenan had his opportunity to dissolve the situation with Penny, and he failed. It was her turn now.

She didn't care if he was trying to protect a long-term friendship, or whatever relationship he had with the Augustines. Savannah's responsibilities were far more important. She had a long list of employees who deserved security. They were owed the right not to fear for their future. Especially when the holidays were upon them.

He'd understand. He had to. Right? Or should she warn him?

She palmed her cell, unlocked the screen and opened a new message. The curser blinked at her in deafening silence. Yes, no. Yes, no.

"Forget it." She placed the device back into her pocket and sucked in a calming breath. For now, she needed to forget him. Forget Dominic and her aunt, too. This was business.

She held her head high as she entered the immaculately polished lobby, scanned the directory for the correct floor, and then stalked into the awaiting elevator. There was no prepared speech, no inkling of how the conversation would unravel, and it didn't bother her in the slightest. This was her job and she was going to forgo all thoughts of Keenan to ensure it was done to the best of her ability.

The elevator doors re-opened on the Grandiosity floor and she stepped into an office environment dripping with over-indulgence. The space was akin to their Seattle hotel. A chandelier hung from the roof, sparkling its glow over the shiny black walls. Elaborate floral arrangements scented the air with sweet perfection, and the receptionist beamed a smile at her from her position behind the speckled marble of a high counter.

"Can I help you?"

"Yes, please." Savannah approached the woman. "I need to speak to Patrick Black."

The slightest glimpse of a wrinkle marred the receptionist's brow. "Is he expecting you? I don't have anyone booked into his schedule at this time."

"No, he isn't. But my name is Savannah Hamilton and I'm from the Rydel head office. It's imperative that I see him to discuss the upcoming settlement."

The woman gave a faux smile. "I understand. He's on a conference call at the moment, so I'll send his computer a message to make him aware that you're here."

"Thank you."

Savannah turned in a half circle and headed for the white leather sofa. She crumpled into its firmness and mentally batted away the barrage of thoughts about Keenan. He had no place here. There was no room to falter due to her feelings. But guilt began to niggle. It crept up her spine and settled itself on her shoulders, pressing harder and harder the longer she waited.

She wished she could deny that her decision had even the slightest tinge of jealousy woven into her reasoning. It was only minute, the tiniest gleam of the green-eyed devil, but it was there nonetheless.

Keenan kept shielding her cousin. He stood proud at Penny's side at the bonfire. He protected her when Savannah was ready to draw battle lines over the vicious emails. Their connection was something more than friendship, and yes, Savannah now had the balls to admit she didn't like it. The bond between the two nipped at her insecurities, taunting her every waking moment no matter how she tried to ignore it.

Her heart began to thump, the growing echo throbbing in her ears. She reached for a magazine on the coffee table and mindlessly flicked through the pages. The pictures swam past her vision, not one of them sinking in. It was useless. She threw the publication down, pulled out her cell, and began typing.

> **Savannah:** *I'm sorry, but I couldn't wait for you to handle the Penny situation. She's upset more employees this morning, and I'm now waiting to discuss the matter with the CEO of Grandiosity. I hope you understand.*

"Ms. Hamilton?"

Savannah glanced at the receptionist as her finger hovered over the send button. "Yes?"

"Patrick will see you now."

"Thank you." She pushed to her feet as she sent the message. *Done.* There was no turning back. She switched her cell to vibrate, placed it back in her pocket, and made her way to the receptionist who stood waiting.

"I'll escort you to his office."

The click of heels were the only sound as they walked down the long hall. Offices were on either side of them, each open door giving view to polished wood tables and floor to ceiling windows.

"This is his office." The woman stopped in front of a set of double doors and knocked twice before turning the handle. "Patrick, this is Savannah Hamilton from the Rydel Group."

The woman held the door wide and indicated for Savannah to proceed into the pits of hell.

"Thank you." She stepped over the threshold and smiled at the man behind the desk. Not unlike Mr. Rydel, Patrick had to be in his late fifties with black hair tinged with gray. He sat leisurely in his high-back leather chair, appraising her with a lazy gaze before pushing to his feet.

"Welcome, Savannah." He greeted her at the front of his desk with an outstretched hand. "I'm pleased to meet you." The handshake was brief, a mere graze of palms that spoke volumes about his lack of respect for her position. "What can I do for you?"

The question was fake. It would've been more truthful if he'd asked—What can I do to get you out of my office? But she smiled anyway, playing the same game.

"I wanted to inform you of some concerns I have about the upcoming settlement."

"Concerns?" His brows knit tight. "I was under the impression that the transition was going ahead smoothly."

"Unfortunately, that's not the case from my perspective. The communication between parts of your management team and my staff have come across as confronting, and at times almost threatening. I appreciate that it may be a misunderstanding due to the sterility of emails, but I also wanted to ensure Grandiosity wasn't striving to lower our occupancy rates."

Patrick leaned back in his chair and sucked in a long, slow breath, his chest expanding wide with the inhalation. "That's quite an assumption."

Her cell vibrated in her back pocket, short and sharp. A message from Keenan, no doubt. A warning not to do what she was doing. A sign to pull back on the reins.

"Yes, it is." She dropped the smile and raised her chin. "I'm sorry to be blunt, but these employees don't deserve to be fearful of their future. They have families and responsibilities. They're hard-working—"

"Obviously, they don't work hard enough to maintain a profitable business."

Shock made her stiffen and she rallied to contain her anger. Then her cell vibrated again, splitting her thoughts into two different disastrous categories. She should've expected the taunt, it was natural, but instead her mind was only half on the game, with the other half tangled in all things Keenan.

"I think we can both agree that a lot of aspects are at play when a hotel fails to remain profitable." She refused to throw her staff under the bus. Neither would she announce that the responsibility lay at her feet, or anyone else higher up the food chain. "Alienating future employees won't help to increase productivity."

"No, but it would certainly weed out those who aren't determined and willing to fight. We want strong staff, Savannah. We go through a rigorous employment process for every member of our team, from maintenance to management. Your people get to bypass those hoops. They should be thankful for that and eager to do whatever necessary."

She ignored another buzz from her cell, and tried to silence everything—her thoughts, her feelings, her anxiety—to concentrate on the man's expression. She had to give him credit. He'd done well not to admit the obvious intentions of Grandiosity while also backhanding her with an insult.

"I see." She should've come prepared. This was stupidity on her behalf. Ridiculousness. She'd lost focus due to her surging libido, and now she was paying the price of pleasure. "I guess we're done here."

She inched forward in her seat, preparing to stand. "I'll make sure to send you a copy of the information I intend to forward to our legal team. I'm certain they'll be interested to hear what's been going on, especially when the communication from your company has resulted in resignations that are costing us money. I wouldn't be surprised if there's cause to claim compensation."

Seconds ticked by, maybe minutes, with no response from Patrick. Then slowly, almost unperceptively, a sly grin spread across his lips.

"You've got balls, Savannah—"

"Actually, I don't." She squared her shoulders, preparing for round two. "I just have a lack of tolerance for bullshit."

He chuckled, long and low. "Well, whatever it is, I find it admirable."

She relaxed, marginally, and sank back into the chair. "I appreciate the admiration and hope your honesty comes with it."

His smile didn't falter, nor did the position of his eyes. He remained still, composed. The only sign of his discomfort came from the lack of genuine friendliness staring back at her.

"I'll admit I've had very little to do with the upcoming changeover. I've been occupied with the development of another property in Chicago and entrusted the new Seattle property in what I thought were capable hands. But I'll speak to my team and clear things up. I want to ensure any future communication is welcoming."

"Thank you." Savannah released a silent sigh of relief. "Can I ask one more thing? Is it possible for your interview team to be more flexible with their schedule? I know most of the staff will be able to make their appointments, but I do have a few people who will have problems attending. Specifically, a woman who has an interview booked during the only time she can see her dying mother in hospital."

"Of course. That should go without saying."

"Actually, the email we received implied the opposite." She waited for him to ask for clarification.

He didn't.

"I assure you, anyone unable to attend will be accommodated." He leaned forward, as if to stand and mark the end of their conversation. "Was that all?"

She measured her breath while revenge and commonsense warred inside her chest. The ability to open her mouth and blame all of this on Penny was a simple sentence away. She could take her cousin down. Make her pay. Only, the moral high road was a bigger and brighter path. It was shiny and filled with gushing amounts of good karma.

Stupid karma.

"Yes, that was all." Patrick would respect her more if she kept it short and sweet and simple. He didn't want to know the intricacies of every badly worded email or who they came from. "Thank you for sparing the time to see me."

"Not a problem." He stood and offered his hand. "It was nice to meet you, Savannah."

"You, too." She raised to her feet and grasped his offering. "We should do it more often."

He chuckled and shook his head. He was like Mr. Rydel in so many ways, and she'd won him over just as quickly.

"Goodbye, Mr. Black." She dropped her hold and turned toward the door.

"Wait a minute."

She paused and glanced over her shoulder as he opened his desk drawer and pulled out a business card. "If you have any concerns in the future, please feel free to contact my son. I'll make sure he sorts it out personally."

She grasped the card and the thick, formal font glowered back at her.

Keenan Black

Director of Operations

An invisible hold grabbed her around the neck and tightened. The world crumpled to ash and memory after memory after memory flashed in her mind. Each thought was consumed with one man and a past that now seemed like a bad re-run of a B-grade horror movie.

"Keenan." She cleared her throat to dislodge the fist caught in her windpipe. "That's an uncommon name."

"Yes. My son is quite unique," he muttered, announcing an annoyance with his offspring that she currently reciprocated.

"I bet he is." She ran her finger over the embossed lettering and tried to deny the betrayal staring back at her. Keenan hadn't held contempt for his position. He didn't have a low-level job. He was the pomp and circumstance behind her competitor's hotel chain. He was the charm and the arrogance.

He was Grandiosity.

"You'll need to send any concerns via email," he continued. "My son doesn't have the best communication skills and refuses to answer his phone."

No shit.

"On second thought..." He reached for his drawer again and handed her another card. "Penelope is probably the best person to speak to. The two of them are joined at the hip. Practically husband and wife. If you have any concerns that need urgent attention, call her and she can convey the problem to Keenan."

Her head bobbed of its own accord. *Husband and wife.* That little fucker.

"Thank you again for your time." She cast him one last glance and wished the family resemblance hadn't escaped her until now. He had Keenan's stormy eyes. And that smirk. *Christ.* She should've noticed the picture perfect curve of lips the moment he shot that look her way.

She measured her steps to the door, making sure she didn't falter, or worse, run, no matter how much her rampant heart rate demanded it.

She couldn't deny Keenan was good. He was so damn good. He'd fucked her physically and professionally at the same time, which disputed the lifelong myth that men couldn't do two things at once.

He'd never worn a suit in front of her or anything expensive to tie him to his obvious wealth. He'd given her the impression he lived in the suburbs, for heaven's sake. And how convenient that he could use the unfavorable competition between Rydel and Grandiosity as a scapegoat to never discuss his position.

But why? Was he hoping he'd screw sensitive information out of her? Had he, without her noticing? Or was he helping Penny get revenge?

Disgust crawled under her nails and crept along her skin like termites on a rampage. The overreaction must be due to the Seattle air. Or the stress of the settlement. She hadn't experienced even a tenth of the overwhelming buzz of fractured emotions that currently overwhelmed her when the months with Spencer had ended.

Jealousy made the muscles in her legs burn, which was pathetic in itself. She should be focused on the betrayal and lies. Instead, she stormed into the reception area, livid at how badly she'd underestimated his relationship with Penny.

"Do you have something I could write with?" She suppressed a wince as her cell buzzed in her back pocket like a beaver trying to burrow its way into her ass.

The receptionist held up a shiny silver pen.

"Paper, too?"

She needed to do something, anything, to get this humiliation off her back. Maybe other women would cry and blubber about the betrayal, but she preferred retribution. Unfortunately, she'd never had to achieve it while restrained by professional guidelines.

If this was on a completely personal level, she'd like to think she could walk right up to Keenan, smile, and knee him in his perfectly proportioned cock. She hadn't even envisaged that when Spencer had cheated on her.

"Here you go." The woman slid a sheet of paper along the countertop.

Great. Now what was she supposed to do?

Savannah stared down at the page, wishing she had the right mix of wit and spite to leave a perfect message for Keenan.

Nothing came.

She was blank and unable to leave, not without making her own strike. She needed him to be aware she wasn't hurt. That her heart wasn't a pulverized mess in her chest. It was all about perception. If nobody knew she was devastated, then it wasn't real, was it?

The elevator doors dinged from behind her and she bristled. Call it a sixth sense, or the uncanny remembrance of the sound of his footsteps, but she knew he was approaching her. And the tap, tap, tap of heels belonged to Penny.

"On second thought, I don't need these." She slid the pen and paper toward the receptionist and turned to face her enemies with a beaming smile. "Morning."

"Morning." Penny beamed back.

Savannah wished she lacked the self-preservation stopping her from slapping the look off her cousin's face. "You know what? Your boss is right. You do look like husband and wife. I guess I never pictured it because I was unaware that the two of you worked side-by-side all day long."

"You didn't know?" Penny snickered. "That's hilarious."

It probably was. Unfortunately, Savannah didn't think she'd see the humorous side for quite some time.

"I had no clue," she admitted. "Apparently, being mute gives you the right to be a lying asshole." She chanced a glance at Keenan. Until then, she hadn't been able to meet his gaze and had no clue if he'd walked toward her with a sense of regret or satisfaction. All she knew now was that her insult had inflicted injury because he was glaring at her, his nostrils flaring at her low blow. "Have a lovely day."

She sauntered between them, determined to reach the elevator with her happy-go-lucky mask still in place. Only it faltered when Keenan's grip encased her wrist. He held her, firm yet tender as he peered down at her.

His eyes spoke to her. Those gray depths portraying a myriad of emotions from remorse to annoyance. But she'd been wrong before. For all she knew, he could be lapping up her suffering, devouring it like a heartbroken woman glutted on ice cream.

"Fuck you," she whispered through a dazzling smile.

His jaw tensed and the calculation in his features turned feral.

She yanked her arm away and moved gracefully to the elevator door, pressing the button with composure and poise. They were all watching her, she could feel it—Keenan, Penny, the receptionist, too.

Lunch, dinner, and Christmas seemed to pass before the doors opened and she moved into the sanctuary of the small space. Keenan approached and she shook her head in a non-verbal fuck off. He didn't listen.

He stepped into the elevator and his arrogance stole all her oxygen.

"I'm going to give you to the count of three before I cause a scene that neither of us wants."

His chin lifted as he remained still. Stubborn. She didn't want to lose her shit. She wasn't even sure what it would involve, but she continued the threat nonetheless.

"One." She swallowed over the anguish rising in her throat. "Two." Her chest restricted, tight and unyielding. "Th—"

He huffed out a breath and stepped back into the reception area. The doors began to close as she stared down the conviction in his eyes, spitting in the face of it with a glare more potent than arsenic.

The descent to the ground floor was a blur marked by buzz after buzz of her cell. She wanted to ignore it. Her brain demanded it. Yet everything inside her forced her to retrieve the device and read his excuses as she entered the lobby.

Keenan: Give me more time to handle it.

Then— *Savannah, I'll speak to Penelope again. Please, let me take care of it.*

Followed by— *Where are you?* And. *I need to see you.*

The last two were the real kickers— *This isn't what you think it is.* And *Give me a chance to explain.*

No, thank you. She was going to lock in option B and slink away with her tail between her previously spread legs.

She needed to decompress and clear her head. This wasn't merely a case of being duped. Her job was on the line. Her reputation and dignity, too. Grant, Kelly, and Amanda would expect her to come back with answers, not a declaration that she'd been sleeping with the enemy.

The ultimate enemy.

"Shit." Did they already know?

Keenan had spent the night in her room. He'd been given a keycard by one of the receptionists. Was that why the condoms in her trash had been such a big deal? Did everyone think she was working both sides?

"Fuck. Fuck. Fuck." She ran on the toes of her pumps through the front doors of the building and closed her eyes to the piercing chill in the air.

The situation was snowballing. One mighty avalanche that was burying her. Her world was disintegrating, her professional and personal life crashing right before her eyes. And it was all because of one man.

Keenan Black.

The devil in wolf's clothing.

Email Correspondence

Date: 25th December

Subject: My father

Dear Savannah,

It's Christmas and I'm without you. I thought this year would be different. I hoped I'd spend the day with someone I loved. But you're not here.

I never spend the holidays with my parents. I grew up in a household that demanded perfection. Clearly, I didn't fit in.

I was forced out of my comfort zone so many times that, as an adult, I now cling to the infrequent moments that I feel at home.

And somehow I was always there with you.

I guess I didn't want to burst that bubble.

Women have never been a challenge for me. They see the aesthetics and latch on like they would with any other man with wealth and a favorable smile. So I stopped smiling. I stopped showing my wealth, too. And I found you… not that I was looking.

Do you know that you never once questioned my integrity? Not aloud. And every time we were together I wished you would.

You trusted me, when you should've trusted Dominic.

But you weren't meaningless, Savannah.

You were everything. You still are.

Let me prove that to you. Just write back.

Keenan

Twenty

Savannah had walked the Seattle streets for hours, without a coat, or common sense to notice she was numb to the freezing temperature. She was destined for hypothermia and, lucky her, that outcome had a silver lining because it was the ideal excuse to go home without admitting to the disaster she'd created.

She was a failure. A spectacular, highly accomplished failure who didn't want to admit her heart hurt more than her pride. But it did. The pound in her chest was rampant, the heat in her cheeks announcing her humiliation to the world.

Her feet pounded the pavement until midday crept into late afternoon. Solace was nowhere to be found. Neither was understanding. She didn't know why her emotions were a wrangled mess over something far more trivial than her broken relationship with Spencer. It had to be Penny—her conniving smile, her victorious taunts.

When she returned, Kelly and Grant were in the lobby, asking questions as she passed. No matter how scripted her reply should've been from the hours spent reflecting, she mumbled incoherently and continued walking into the seclusion of the elevator.

There was no peace to be found in her room. She'd kicked off her shoes, ignored the landline phone as it wailed its incessant call, and packed her belongings. One by one she placed everything into her suitcase—her beauty products, her clothes, her laptop.

The few remaining items she left accessible were her toothbrush, pajamas, and the box of lingerie—that stupid gift. She couldn't bring herself to look toward the silver package. It was proof of how blind she'd been.

The suite phone rang again, and she closed her eyes in a losing battle to remain strong. She'd already broken her promise to answer all staff calls, no matter what time of day or night. But her cell held unread messages from Keenan. She sensed it. Which meant her only option had been to turn it off.

The trill ended, leaving her in thankful ear-ringing silence.

She did want to speak to someone. Her insides were waging war, the need for verbal therapy fighting against shame that demanded silence. The perfect candidate to receive her info dump didn't exist anyway. There was nobody in Seattle she could chat to face-to-face. And friends and family back home seemed a world away.

The phone trilled again, this time poking at her frustration. She trudged for the bedside table, yanked the receiver and snapped, "What?"

"Ahh..." It was Kelly. Sweet, innocent Kelly. "Are you okay?"

"I'll be fine." Eventually.

"Want to talk about it?"

"No. I'm good."

There was a beat of silence, a slight pause that made Savannah nervous over where the conversation would lead.

"Well, I'm knocking off for the night and you sound like you need a drink. The location is your choice. I can either create my own room card and bring up a bottle of wine, or you can meet me in the bar. Which is it?"

"No, honestly, I'm good."

"Savannah," Kelly lowered her voice, "I've spent a lot of spare time in the hospital watching people die beside my mother. Almost every day I hear people reject the offer of help. I know the difference between someone who truly doesn't need support, from those who are too scared or full of pride to accept it. So, I'll ask again—your room or the bar?"

Savannah turned to face the small space that had become her temporary home. Daylight was fading, casting the furniture in varying shadows. There was no life in here. No warmth. The room was devoid of possessions. Everything was packed. Her suitcase was on the bed. All signs pointed toward her departure and she wasn't ready for the staff to know.

"I'll meet you downstairs."

She hung up and didn't bother to look in the mirror as she walked from the room. There was no way her appearance was stellar, and no possibility that she could reach that point no matter how much prep time.

Kelly was already waiting for her at the bar, two glasses of wine seated in front of her. The area was almost empty with the faint mumble of guests floating in the air as they ate their dinner in the adjoining restaurant.

The receptionist swiveled on her stool and gave a sad smile in greeting. "I guess the meeting didn't go well."

Savannah used the bar to pull herself onto the cushioned seat as a glass of wine slid toward her.

"Thank you." She sipped the liquid, letting the sweet reassurance of alcohol tingle on her tongue. "Actually, the meeting went well for Rydel staff." Her voice lacked enthusiasm. "The CEO has been busy with other projects and was surprised by my concerns. He assures me he'll get to the bottom of the emails and that you'll have no trouble in the future."

"You say that like you're not going to be here."

Savannah stared at the golden liquid in her glass, the throb, throb, throb under her sternum demanding she release some of the built-up pressure. "I'll be leaving tomorrow." Once morning came, she'd look for an available flight. A phone call was too impersonal to announce her downfall. It was best to speak to Spencer in person. Mathew, too. She deserved the 3D version of their ire, after all.

She took another sip of her wine. Followed by another and another. Night was already falling and the time since her last meal allowed for the wonders of alcohol to work their magic quicker than usual.

"I'm actually related to 'The Bitch' of Grandiosity," she murmured. It wasn't as if anyone apart from Kelly could hear her. The bartender was wiping down tables on the other side of the room. He hadn't paid her attention since she arrived. "Mr. Rydel thought my presence would have helped the teething problems. Instead, it became clear that this is a personal vendetta against me."

"*Hey, Trent,*" a female voice shouted from the restaurant. "*Can you give us a hand?*"

Savannah swiveled to meet the wince of one of the wait staff hovering in the doorway.

"Sorry, Ms. Hamilton, but we're swamped in here. People are actually dining in tonight and it had to happen when two of the waitresses called in sick."

"They're not sick," Kelly muttered. "I think they'll be the next to hand in their resignations. A new restaurant opened on the other side of the city, and rumor has it that Layla and Tammy both had a trial run tonight."

Savannah sighed. That meant two more wait staff that wouldn't be available for the wedding. "Let me know if you need more help," she called. "I'll look after the bar."

"It's no problem. I can work both." Trent threw his cloth over the counter. "I'll keep walking back and forth."

Thank goodness for small blessings. She didn't think she should be in charge of serving alcohol at a time like this. As it was, she was practically alone in a fully stocked bar, heaven at her feet, and still she couldn't let go of the nauseating pound in her chest to be able to enjoy it.

"You were saying that all of this was a personal vendetta." Kelly glanced at her from the corner of her eye.

"Not all of it." Savannah sighed. "I don't think it started that way. But me being here isn't helping the situation."

"You just said everything went well with the CEO."

"It did." She was confident of that much.

Kelly frowned at her, the lines of confusion marring her forehead getting deeper and deeper.

"What's with the look?" Savannah downed the last of her wine and pushed from her stool. The best part of being a temporary bartender was going to be her refusal to meet the standard height for a perfectly poured glass. Guidelines be damned.

"I'm surprised, that's all. You say the meeting went well, yet when you walked back into the lobby this afternoon you looked devastated. Did I miss something?"

"That was different." She grabbed an already opened bottle of wine from the mini fridge beneath the counter and filled their glasses. "It was a personal matter."

"Right…" Kelly didn't say another word as Savannah returned the bottle and stalked around the bar to take her seat. "Does it have anything to do with the guy staring at you from outside?"

She followed Kelly's focus, her heart in her throat as she laid her gaze on the formidable figure standing near the public entrance to the bar. He stood in the shadows, his harsh features darkened from the glow of the dim bar lighting.

She didn't say a word. She was too busy trying to suppress the urge to flee or to scream or maybe shoot him a hearty middle-finger salute.

"He looks familiar."

Savannah scoffed. "He's your future boss."

The receptionist glanced back and forth, from Keenan to Savannah, over and over as if witnessing a tennis match. "The lingerie…"

Shit. Kelly worked that out way too easily.

"You've been seeing him, right?"

There was no point denying the truth, or the staff she'd put at risk because of her stupidity. But the words wouldn't form. They were caught in her throat, cutting off her air.

"What happened?"

Savannah reached for her glass, pretending to be unperturbed, just like Keenan had pretended to be interested in her. "I didn't realize who he was."

"Until when?"

Not until after the sex and seduction, the laughter and the fun. "This morning."

"Ohh."

"Yeah." Savannah nodded, determined to keep her focus on the still liquid of the wine. "Ohh, is right. I feel ridiculously stupid."

"If it helps any, it looks like he's here to apologize."

Doubtful. Oh, so doubtful. "I don't care. It didn't mean anything anyway. Just a little fun that was meant to be harmless during the nights alone."

Kelly tipped her glass, taking an extra-long gulp before sliding from her stool. "Well, I'll leave you two to figure it out."

"What?" Savannah straightened. "No. You're not going anywhere."

"Just look at him." Kelly implored her with Bambi eyes. "He's remorseful. Even I can see that under that intimidating glare of his."

Savannah weakened, glancing toward the glass door. Keenan had regressed. He was back to scowling at her. The exact same expression as the night they met.

"What's the harm?" Kelly added, grabbing her handbag off the counter. "You said you were leaving tomorrow anyway."

The harm was all soul deep. Her stomach had been wrung like a dishcloth and she wasn't sure if she could hide it if they spoke again.

"Good luck." Kelly placed a hand on Savannah's shoulder. "No matter what you decide, I hope it involves you sticking around in Seattle a little longer. The majority of us thought you were doing a really good job, and I don't think who you were screwing changes that." She lowered her voice. "And just to let you know, he's already got one hand on the door."

Savannah swallowed, hard, and wished every one of Kelly's retreating steps toward the lobby didn't feel like she was being shoved to the wolves. The swish of the door followed soon after, giving her an excuse to down the full glass of wine in three painful gulps.

She didn't need to be informed of his presence. She could already feel him beside her, probably preparing to sink another knife in beside the one still embedded between her ribs. His solid frame slid onto the barstool Kelly had been seated on, and the unmistakable scent of his aftershave sank heavy into her lungs. He was there, right there. All sexiness and superiority wrapped up in a casual package of jeans and leather jacket.

"Leave." She raised her glass then glared at the non-existent contents.

"Can I get you another one?" Grant strode around the bar, shocking her with his presence.

"Yes," she gasped like an addict being offered a fix. "Please."

The bartender inclined his head and reached down to the small wine fridge, his gaze scrutinizing her unwelcomed companion. "And you, sir? Can I get you anything?"

"No," Savannah grated. "He's leaving."

Grant nodded and poured her wine. "Do you need anything else before I head back into the restaurant?"

"No." She would leave mere minutes after him. Once the cool liquid in her glass had finished sliding down her throat, she would be out of here. Away from Keenan, to spend her last night in Seattle alone.

"Okay. I'll keep coming in to check on you." Grant walked to the end of the bar and out of view.

The hair on the back of her neck rose, the silence thick and nasty in the air. The alcohol in her stomach solidified, making her nauseated. Keenan was staring at her, she could sense it, feel it.

"I'll have to inform our legal team, yet again, that Grandiosity staff are on the premises and causing trouble." She kept staring straight ahead. "Our case for bullying and manipulation continues to grow stronger by the minute."

He turned his body toward her, his knees bumping her stool. He could kick her chair for all she cared, she still wasn't going to look at him.

"Just leave," she murmured. "Run back to Penny."

Announcing her jealousy wasn't the best strategy, but intoxication didn't play by the rules. Her veins were filling with fire, the temperature growing by the second. Soon her face would be flushed and her palms sweaty.

A bang exploded beside her, tearing a gasp from her throat. She glanced at the perpetrator—Keenan's heavy hand now palm down against the counter. He'd slapped something against the wood. A piece of paper beneath his fingers.

A note.

Her head told her to walk away. To run.

It was the rapid beat of her heart that demanded she read the words that became exposed as his arm slid away from the bar and back to his side. He revealed a bright yellow Post-It scribbled with the words—*Let me explain.*

She fought the fragility taking over her and laughed. "Please leave, Mr. Black."

There was another slap on the bar, another bang of sound that made her gasp. And yet again, she had no will to stop herself from looking at the new message.

Would you have spared me the time of day if you knew I was the CEO's son?

She stared at the question, reliving their past with his new position in mind. The answer was easy. Obvious. That was the problem. This thing between them should never have happened, yet he manipulated the silence to make sure it did.

His hand fell heavy again and this time she didn't startle at the sound of palm against wood.

Would you have given me a chance if you knew who I was?

One by one he slammed down questions, then aggressively scribbled another.

Do you think that night in the penthouse would've happened?

How far would this thing between us have gone if you knew I was your rival?

He paused long enough to poke her curiosity. She looked up at him and met the angered raise of his brow. *Asshole.* He stoked her blood to the boiling point in that mere crinkle of his forehead. He had no right to be angry. No right at all.

Another note landed before her. *The last few weeks wouldn't have existed.*

"For good reason," she hissed under her breath. "You've jeopardized my job. And for what? To get laid?" She tore her gaze from his. "Or maybe it wasn't about sex. Maybe it was to help your girlfriend get back at me for a stupid mistake in high school. Or did you do it for inside information? To make Daddy proud if Rydel occupancy levels fell below the required levels?"

Another slam landed on the bar.

She clenched her jaw, fighting against the pull to lower her eyes. She didn't want this to continue. She didn't want to read another message.

Her traitorous vision lowered anyway.

That's bullshit and you know it.

"Do I?" It was her turn to raise a defiant brow. "What's the alternative, Keenan? Why keep something that important from me? There's no point denying your manipulation. You succeeded for weeks. Congratulations."

This time his writing was slower, less frantic in her periphery. He slid the message on top of the others, his fingers remaining on the paper as she read, *I should've told you.*

She glared at him. "Ya think?"

He returned the stare as he placed the next note down. *And you shouldn't have assumed I was only capable of a low-level position.*

Incorrect. She'd thought his *employer* would've made that assumption.

"Don't even try it." She sipped her wine slowly, shooting daggers at him over the rim of the glass. "The guilt ship has sailed, buddy. It boarded all passengers this morning, never to return."

His nostrils flared and he pinned her with a look so feral and furious that she almost wanted to slink away. Almost. Instead, she raised her chin. "So, please leave."

His jaw ticked as he wrote on the Post-It pad. This time he held up the message beside his angry face—*I'm falling for you.*

She fought to keep her stare impassive. Fought and lost. She swallowed hard, fighting back the lump building in her throat. "Well, don't let the ground smack you in the face when you finally stop the descent." She slid from her stool. "Good luck with the settlement. I'll make sure Spencer has all my notes before he arrives to take over."

Something flashed in his eyes—shock, fear, panic—she didn't know and wasn't going to waste time being wistful. Instead, she turned and focused on putting one foot in front of the other. Big steps, little steps.

She fumbled her way from the bar and into the hotel lobby. The lights were brighter out here, almost burning her retinas. She really needed to get more sun.

Her heels clapped faster and faster along the floor, matching her deadly heart rate. This was the end. Her final glimpse at the Seattle staff. She wasn't going to see Keenan again either.

She wasn't sure what hurt more... Well, she did. She simply refused to admit it to herself.

Footfalls echoed behind her, spurring her to move at a pace that defied inebriated logic. She was holding her own at the moment, but the alcohol was kicking in, moving from first gear and straight into third.

She rounded the corner, the hairs on the back of her neck prickling as she jabbed the elevator button. "Come on."

The heavy footsteps stopped. She wasn't alone. And it wasn't a stranger at her back. It was a familiar frame. An unforgettable scent.

The elevator doors opened and she rushed inside to press the button for level three. Her shadow followed, shrinking the already small space with his overbearing presence.

"Get out." She held the door open and waited. Waited and waited. *"Get. Out."*

Keenan leaned against the side wall of the elevator and stared at her, arms crossed over his chest, feet crossed at the ankles.

"Do you think this is a joke?" Her arm fell to her side as she took a menacing step toward him. It probably would've been funny from his perspective—tipsy woman, trying to intimidate an ogre—but she didn't care. "I don't have the security of being related to the boss to be able to risk my career like this. You're playing with my life."

He held up the Post-It note again and the same message stared back at her—*I'm falling for you.*

"Get out," she seethed.

The doors began to close and her throat restricted with his lack of movement. They stared each other down, Keenan's determination matching her frustration as they ascended in silence. She hated the emotion he laid bare for her—the fake, manipulative emotion that encouraged her into this mess in the first place.

The interest in his eyes wasn't real. The concerned furrow of his brow was fraudulent.

The elevator dinged its deafening trill of arrival and she back-tracked into the hall, her gaze never leaving his. He remained poised, so arrogant leaning against that wall.

Once safely outside, she turned. Fled. She made two steps before she shivered at the sound of his accompanying footfalls. "You're not coming into my room." He couldn't. She wouldn't allow it. Memories already daunted her. They'd shared too much in that bed.

"Don't follow me, Keenan." She marched harder down the hall, trying to gain a lead, but he was right there, his longer, stronger legs eating up any space she made.

Damn him, and damn her for being so susceptible to whatever it was that made her addicted to his existence. Dominic had warned her. Penny had threatened her. And still she'd wound up in a mess of infatuation she never should've become involved in.

She yanked her room card from her pocket and slammed it against the locking device. There was a buzz, a gratifying blink of a green light, and then she was shoving the door open, her heart thankful for the awaiting sanctuary.

"Goodbye, Keenan." She slunk inside, and quickly pushed to close the door.

Instead of shutting him out, the glossy wood opened further under the heavy press of his palm. He stood before her, an undeniable force, a mask of superiority.

"Please," she begged. "Don't."

She backtracked, unable to maintain the close proximity between them as he stalked toward her. Her limbs were trembling, especially her hand as she raised it to stab a finger toward the exit in a silent attempt to tell him to go.

He ignored her, the door drifting shut behind him, closing them in together. His approach continued, increasing the rapid pound in her chest and the tumbling roll of her belly. She couldn't breathe. Couldn't think.

"I'm not playing games. *Get out.*"

His focus drifted to the bed, to the suitcase ready and waiting. His eyebrows pulled tight, his lips, too, as he narrowed his attention back on her and shook his head. "*No.*"

He reached for her luggage and grasped the zipper.

"What the hell are you doing?" She watched in shocked fascination as he unzipped her case and pulled out a stack of her clothes. "Stop it."

Keeping her distance was imperative, for her heart and her self-preservation, but what the heck was she expected to do when he was unpacking her belongings and stalking back down the hall to place them in the tiny closet?

"Keenan." Her voice was more hesitant than she would've liked.

He didn't stop, his presence taking over the entire room as his hands manipulated her clothes. With painful fortitude, he was doing everything she refused to admit she wanted. He was fighting for her attention, demanding she listen, insisting she stay.

Just watching him was encouraging her surrender...or maybe it was the alcohol making her pliant.

Stupid wine.

Either way, every inch of her was out of control, every nerve highly attuned to his movements.

"You made a fool out of me." She was fighting against herself, broadcasting the obvious, not to remind him, but to remind her. "You humiliated me."

He paused at the foot of the bed and the harshness of his expression didn't change. Nothing wavered except his eyes. The deep, smoky depths turned somber. Almost apologetic. He changed his course and stepped toward her, those strong hands and legs and arms approaching.

"Stop." There was nowhere left to run. She was already cowering near the window. "Just stop."

He didn't.

She shoved at his chest, and the hardness of muscle beneath her palm wrought havoc on her senses. "Why are you doing this? Why can't you just leave me alone? Why did you show interest in me to begin with?"

She needed to hear his words. To have something other than sterile pieces of paper slammed down between them.

"*I don't know*," he mouthed with a slow shake of his head. He inched closer, those beautiful lips descending to cause irreparable damage.

"Don't." She looked away, denying his kiss and any chance for him to communicate. He didn't deserve anything from her, no matter how willing her body was to raise the white flag.

His fingers encased her chin, the familiar grip stealing a silent whimper from her throat. He guided her face back to meet his and she stood riveted, unable to break the connection. "*I need you.*"

She wished she could scoff, or laugh, or glare. She didn't want to understand him anymore, didn't want to acknowledge the words that had become so easy to interpret. "I'll never trust you again. Everything will be a lie."

He shook his head. "*No.*"

He reached into his back pocket and pulled out his phone. His fingers worked in proficient taps and strokes until he held up an old message for her to read— *Nobody has ever affected me the way you do. Nobody. Ever. I leave you and within seconds I have to push myself not to turn back and go in search of you again. It might be a normal feeling for others, but for me it's a first. And although I don't have the experience to back it up, I think this uncomfortable, clingy sensation might be something normal people consider a good thing.*

"*Not a lie*," he mouthed.

He tapped over and over and then showed her the screen again. This time it was a new message—*I didn't know you were with Rydel until after you left the bonfire. And by then, it was too late. I wasn't going to stand you up at the restaurant. Even if I hadn't given you that note, I was already in too deep.*

Her cheeks heated with gullibility. It had to be a lie. He was playing her. Again. But he played her so well. He played her with such sweet proficiency that she anticipated another betrayal and still wanted to go along for the ride anyway.

She lowered her gaze to the floor between them and wished she could forget the time they'd spent together. "Can you move back a little?"

She needed room. He was too close. Too tempting. Instead, he stepped closer, bringing them toe to toe. "Keenan…"

His arm wove around her waist, pulling them together. The solid wall of his chest beat against hers, his strength making her weak as he typed one-handed—*You knew I worked with Penny*.

"Yes. I just didn't know to what extent," she admitted.

But you knew Penny worked closely with the CEO.

"Yes." She became hooked on the support of his body, sated by it, until he stepped back and she mourned the loss.

He flashed her another message—*So, like I mentioned earlier, you thought I was worthless. You assumed I lacked the skills to have a position of power. Or maybe I'm wrong. Maybe you realized what was happening between us had turned into something more than gratification and you decided to ignore the risks. Which is it?*

She stared blankly at the screen, refusing to admit to either when she had to acknowledge she was guilty of both.

"I want you to leave," she murmured. He'd dissolved her anger, which was dangerous because now she only had vulnerability to keep her company.

He lowered his screen. Typed a new message—*Do you think I wanted to become infatuated with someone who thinks I'm less of a man because I don't talk?*

"It doesn't matter." She placed her hand back on his chest and lost the fight to push him backward. "It's over. I won't risk my job any more than I already have."

His mouth curved, the slightest grin dissolving the potent seriousness in the room with the kick of his lips. "*Yes, you will,*" he mouthed.

His hand came to her cheek, then wove gently through her hair. The soft clench of her heart made panic unfurl in her belly. She was falling victim all over again. Her weakness for him was pathetic, and way too powerful.

"Leave," she repeated with conviction.

His eyes narrowed and that perfect grin faltered. He was trying to read her thoughts and she couldn't allow it. She wasn't going to let him win. Not twice in one day.

He thumb-tapped into his phone and kept scrutinizing her as she read—*Promise me you won't leave Seattle.*

"I owe you nothing."

He shoved his cell closer to her, demanding she reread his screen—*Promise me you won't leave Seattle.*

"I'll have you removed from the premises if I have to." She slid out of reach. "Take the lingerie you sent me as you go. It's in the box beside the television. The tags still attached. You might be able to return them."

He stepped forward, coming to her side. She stiffened, every muscle taut trying to defend from the enticing onslaught. There was no communication, no Post-Its or messages on his screen. There were no mouthed words or gestures with his body. He merely stood there, looking down at her, owning her with his gaze.

She raised her chin, determined in her stance as he leaned in and placed an excruciating kiss on her forehead. The brush of his soft lips was brutal, destroying her defenses.

The need to pull him toward her was painful.

Punishing.

He spared her one final, torturously long look and then strode down the hall, letting the suite door click shut behind him.

She wrapped her arms around her waist and stared blankly at the open suitcase on her bed. The thought of repacking her things after he'd touched them made her whimper. She didn't want to deny him. And in the same breath she didn't want him to claim victory.

Staying meant emotional weakness. Leaving showed professional fragility.

Numb to the world around her, she pulled her cell from her pocket and turned it on. She ignored the continuous beep of updates and the fifteen unread messages noted on her screen, and navigated to her email.

At the top of her inbox sat Patrick Black's name, the subject—All

Interviews Cancelled Until Further Notice.

She clicked on the link and smiled at the email addressed to all Rydel staff. It was an apology. A formal notice from the CEO of Grandiosity over the miscommunication and unintentional stress they had caused. He noted that all interviews were cancelled until a suitable, friendlier approach to the transition could be arranged, and promised to create a positive environment for his future employees.

Savannah wanted to cry in relief.

Something good and solid had sprouted from the ashes of her lust-inspired mistake. There was hope. At least for the Rydel Seattle team members. Her position, on the other hand, was still unclear.

She didn't want to announce to Spencer that she'd made a mess of the upcoming settlement as well as the opportunity to move on from their relationship. The professional failure was a point of pride. The personal defeat would place her in a detrimental position.

Spencer claimed to want her to move on. He kept poking at her to start dating and broadcasted the lie that he would finally have closure if she found another man.

In reality, he hoped she would try, but fail in the process. He itched to be the white knight. To make up for the mistakes of his past by picking up whatever weak and vulnerable pieces he thought would be left behind if she wasn't successful in the dating pool.

He wanted her in the exact position she was in, which didn't leave her in a hurry to get back to Seattle. The only other option was to keep her mouth shut and hope Penny didn't stoop to a level that involved tittle-tattling.

Decisions, decisions.

The unread message icon glared at her. A constant taunt. There was no time like the present to get another Keenan experience over and done with.

She clicked on the button, and gave a derisive laugh as his name sat right at the top of the screen. Her finger stroked over the letters, a brief moment of whimsy in the forest of devastation, before she tapped to open his text.

She'd been wrong. He hadn't sent her messages all day. There was only one. Only a solitary brutal notification.

Keenan: *If you leave, Penelope wins.*

Twenty-One

Savannah slunk into her chair and stared at the far wall. She hadn't left Seattle, not yet, and every day she questioned her sanity over the decision. It would've been easier to repack her things and walk away without a backward glance. Only the nasty clutch of responsibility dug its nails into her neck.

If she gave up, Spencer would replace her, and that man hadn't worked a hard day in his life. He wouldn't give a shit about the wedding. He wouldn't care if staff were stressed and fearing for their future. He'd only look at the bottom line—the line that determined occupancy levels—and as long as that was in the black, everything else would go to hell.

All that shouldn't have mattered, but then she thought of Kelly, whose mother was dying in the hospital. Or Grant, who had only just started to open up to her and speak without stress etching his voice. Or Amanda, who was working her ass off to make the wedding work under the worst of circumstances.

They didn't deserve to be abandoned, even when she was currently cursing her guilty conscience for pushing her anxiety to the max.

"You need to speak to him. It'll work out. I promise."

Savannah raised her focus from the mess of scattered pages on the conference table and met Kelly's concern. "I know."

"I mean, you need to speak to him *now*. Get it off your chest."

A defeated sigh escaped her lips as she nodded. "Give me a moment, will you?"

She hadn't seen sunlight for at least six hours. Her time had been spent in this chair, at this table, speaking to different parts of the management team in an ongoing attempt to mesh uncooperative puzzle pieces together.

She patted the scattered pages in front of her and came up with her cell. There were numerous emails, texts, and calls that she'd missed while it lay silenced on the polished wood, and she swiped past them all to get to her phone directory. Her finger tapped the unfavorable number near the top and the resulting dial tone increased her lazy heartbeat.

"Savannah..."

"Hi, Spencer." His voice batted away any homesick feelings that had festered. "Is your dad free to conference call?"

There was a pregnant pause, one that spoke heavily of his concern. "Hold on a second. I'll check."

The San Francisco radio station kept her company as she waited. A week had passed since she packed her suitcase to return home. Seven long days, with each one marred with a text from Keenan to greet her in the morning.

Every correspondence was a demand, a brief few words that exposed no emotion.

Keenan: Meet me at the Sated Palate, 8pm.

Keenan: Be at the corner of Lincoln and Park at noon.

Keenan: I need to speak to you. I'll buy you a coffee at Winchesters. 10am.

The list went on, and she'd ignored them all.

She should've been happy he'd kept tabs on her, that he'd snooped to determine she stayed in Seattle. Only every time she received a message it became harder to pretend she was unaffected by his attention. She'd learned to combat the spike in her pulse by occupying herself with work. Morale had increased. Pessimism was in freefall. Penny hadn't been on the scene, not via emails or unannounced visits.

Life had settled back into place... too quickly to be comforting.

The only task she hadn't been able to kick into submission, now that Grandiosity was in her pocket, was the upcoming wedding. Amanda had shared the long list of intricacies the bride and groom expected for the big day. All Savannah could do was cement a smile on her face to hide her lack of confidence. They didn't have enough staff to accommodate table service for alcohol, let alone provide one server for each table as requested by the happy couple.

But that was a tidbit they were keeping under their belt. For now.

The radio vanished and Mathew Rydel's voice drifted over the line, "Savannah?"

"Yes, I'm here."

"I'm here, too," Spencer added. "What's the problem?"

Nausea threatened to take hold. "I need to discuss something with you."

"You haven't stormed the Grandiosity head office again, have you?" Mathew asked.

"That was ballsy." Spencer chuckled. "The pole up Grandiosity's ass isn't something to be reckoned with."

"It was far from *storming*." She hadn't planned on telling anyone about her meeting with Patrick Black, not until she realized hiding the situation would leave her open to more scrutiny. She ended up calling Spencer three days ago, smothering him with every morsel of information that didn't involve Keenan and Penny so he wouldn't be interested in asking more questions. The strategy had worked. He'd been tired of her chatter before she'd finished speaking. "It was merely a conversation—"

"Where you threatened legal action," Mathew scoffed.

Oh, yeah. She'd forgotten that part. "It was a bluff. We both knew it."

"Well, now that they're playing nice, you need to do the same." Her boss's tone turned firm. The candor was over. "I want you to leave a favorable impression at the welcome meeting."

Welcome meeting? "What welcome meeting?"

A huff of frustration coursed down the line. "I'm starting to question what you're getting up to over there. When was the last time you checked your emails?"

Her chest thumped a little louder, a little harder, and she gripped the phone tight in her now sweaty palm. "First thing this morning," she bit back. "I've spent every waking minute in this claustrophobic conference room, trying to sort out a problem that could potentially cost us a bucket-load of money. That's the reason for my call. I need to discuss the wedding we have to cater."

AKA the task that stole away all unfavorable thoughts of Keenan.

"As is," she continued, "we don't have enough staff to cover the function. We've had too many resignations—" Kelly had been right about the two waitresses. Tammy and Layla handed in their notice at the start of the week and Savannah had no confidence in them showing up for the time they had left. "—and employees are already covering the workload of other people. I've done everything within my power to resolve the issue, but there simply isn't an easy option. I need your advice."

"Go on," Spencer spoke up.

"This morning, I've held meetings with the shift manager, as well as the event and restaurant managers, and the head chef. We've gone over the staff rosters again and again. The only way I can make this wedding work, is to shut down room service and close the restaurant for lunch and dinner. In return, I thought I could have the chef create a limited list of bar meals that the kitchen should be able to handle during the function."

She had lists on everything, because lists kept her distracted and distraction was key.

"You can't call in temporary staff?" Spencer asked.

"I've called every recruitment agency, numerous times. I've begged, more than once, for the staff who previously resigned to come back, even if just for one night. I've done everything possible, and there still aren't enough people to cover the wedding. Nobody wants to do us any favors the day before Thanksgiving."

There was silence, the deafening sound filled with disappointment.

"With occupancy at a dangerous level, I can only assume the wedding is keeping our heads above water," Mathew murmured.

"Yes. That's right." The wedding would infuse the hotel with the last burst of life before the inevitable death in a few weeks. "Without the function, we'd sink below the red line."

"Then do what needs to be done."

She leaned back in her chair. "Okay. Thank you."

"And Savannah?"

"Yeah?"

"Check your emails and make sure your attendance at the welcome meeting is noted. I appreciate you going in to kick some Grandiosity ass, but now you need to resolve any bad blood. We can't afford to be a thorn in their side."

That thud in her chest increased. "I'll try my best."

"Please do. Otherwise, I'll have to send Spencer to clean up the mess."

In other words, he'd label her inadequate, just as she'd feared.

"I understand," she lied. She'd worked too hard and tangled herself in too many strangling vines to let Spencer take over.

Mathew ended the call, allowing her to navigate to her inbox. She expected another delightful message from Patrick, or maybe a restrained email from Penny. Instead, her heart sank at the sender's name in the middle of her unread messages.

Keenan Black.

Subject: Grandiosity Welcome Meeting.

Every word was professional. Poised. He offered his apologies over previous emails sent by his staff and hoped a casual conversation, while sharing a few drinks at the Grandiosity bar, would be a better way to make introductions. The passage was eloquent, his mannerisms so foreign in comparison to the texts he'd previously sent her, that she knew the message was faux.

It was a provocation.

A checkmate.

A resounding—you-wouldn't-meet-with-me-of-your-own-free-will-so-I'll-play-hardball.

Bastard.

She shoved from the conference table and clapped her three-inch heels to the lobby. There was a mob again, familiar faces standing in a circle. This time they weren't conspiring in anger. They were smiling. Happy. Their conversation littered with laughter and optimism.

"Did you get the email?" Grant called out.

She cringed through a nod. "I guess you did, too."

He made his way to her, leaving the crowd behind. "We all did. Management, I mean. We've already passed the details on to the rest of the staff. I guess your meeting with Grandiosity really worked."

"Yeah." She tried to pull off a smile but there was no way the uncomfortable lift of her cheeks was pleasant. "Just as long as everyone is aware that we'll be in major wedding preparation mode the following day."

Grant frowned. "Is everything okay?"

"Of course," she muttered. "Perfect." There was no way she could admit the meeting was scheduled to manipulate her instead of welcome new staff. "Could you do a call-around and find out attendance numbers? I'll make sure to RSVP for us all."

No matter how cloying it was to announce Keenan's deceit, she needed her team to remain positive. This was an important moment for them. They'd be able to enjoy their Thanksgiving without fearing for their future. They could relax. Unwind.

Her discomfort was a small price to pay to give Rydel employees peace of mind.

There was also the opportunity for retribution.

A genuine smile curved her lips at the thought. If Keenan wanted to keep pushing, maybe she could show him her ability to push back, equally hard, and with a favorable amount of cleavage showing.

Email Correspondence

Date: 26th December

Subject: Dirty tactics

Savannah,

I used dirty tactics while we were together. I also used them while we were apart. But I have no plan to use them now. I want you to come back to me of your own free will. I want you to forgive me and believe my promise that it will never happen again.

Please don't blame Penelope for her involvement. Or Dominic for not telling you. It's all on me. I'm to blame, not only for hurting you but for tearing apart the Augustines with the weight of my lies.

My actions in no way dictate how I feel for you. You deserved better. I only hope you give me another chance to show you how you truly deserve to be treated, instead of Spencer.

Keenan

Twenty-Two

It took days to tick every box necessary to ensure all guests were aware of the upcoming restaurant closure. Reception had notified people on check-in. Housekeeping had updated room service folders with the temporary list of bar meals. And tomorrow every room in the hotel would have a note slipped under the door as an additional reminder, along with discount vouchers for nearby restaurants.

"Are you ready?" Grant asked from behind the reception counter.

"I'm—"

"*Savannah.*"

She turned at the shout and found their head chef approaching from the restaurant archway. "What's up, Thomas?"

He stormed for her, his normally warm skin pale beneath his heavy beard. "They called in sick."

Her calm façade fractured ever so slightly. "Who?"

"Those little twerps that handed in their notice last week—Layla and Tammy. They're both scheduled to start their shift in half an hour, and now I have no waitresses."

"Where's Sally? Why isn't she dealing with this?" Thomas wasn't the restaurant manager. He didn't need to be taking calls from meddling staff. The wedding was a big enough priority to concentrate on when the success or failure of the night would be determined by what went on in his kitchen, under his command.

"I told her I could handle dinner service so she could meet with

Grandiosity." He shrugged his beefy shoulder. "I'm averaging twenty meals on Saturday nights. Less on Fridays. It wouldn't be a big deal if those ignorant bitches hadn't called in sick. I need at least one waitress here to help out."

"Call them back. Demand a doctors' certificate."

"We can do that?"

"Yes," she growled. "We can. It's in your employment contracts— one of those tiny stipulations that we only bring to light if necessary." It was necessary now. The women in question had no sense of dedication. They were young. Undependable. And in a position to cause havoc if they pulled the same shit tomorrow night.

"I've been over their files. They have a lot of annual leave banked up. If they can't commit to the two weeks' notice they've promised, let them know we won't commit to paying their entitlements."

He gave a tired nod. "Can do."

"Are you sure you don't want to come to this Grandiosity thing for a few drinks?" She grabbed her coat off the reception desk and shrugged into the heavy material. "If the restaurant is slow, you should close up early and meet us over there."

"No." He cringed, exposing heavy wrinkles across his forehead that she hadn't noticed before. He was exhausted. Overwhelmed. Just like every other employee under this roof. "Fuck them. I'm not going to clink a beer glass with the assholes who've kept me up at night. And besides, the two chefs I have left need a point by point instruction manual if left unsupervised."

"Understandable." She only needed him to hang on for one more night. Another thirty hours or so. Then they could breathe again. "Take it easy, okay? Look after yourself."

He scoffed and strode away, leaving her to turn to the reception counter and the two people with competing levels of stress sliding off them in tidal waves.

She ignored Grant's usual demeanor and focused on Amanda. "What is it?"

"The bride wants to add four more guests to the seating plan."

"Is that an issue?"

Amanda balked. "Is that an issue? The night before the wedding? Um, well, we have to add more meals for the kitchen to prepare, more drinks for non-existent bar staff to make, more plates to clear for waitresses who apparently won't turn up anyway. Then there's the tables and chairs that need to be rearranged." She ran a hand through her tousled hair and sucked in a deep breath. "I'm at the point where I'm ready to walk."

Shit. "It's just last minute teething problems. We'll sort it out." Yep. Last minute teething problems. Last minute teething problems. It would all work out. *Fuck.* "Don't stress."

Who the hell was she kidding? It was hard not to envisage the inevitable crash and burn of the wedding when the world seemed set against the nuptials. "As soon as I get back, I'll rearrange the tables. And I can do whatever else you need. Just write a list."

"I'm entirely over this job." Amanda held up her hands in surrender. "After tomorrow, I'm taking time off."

Savannah nodded. "Whatever you need. I promise." She turned her focus to Grant and snatched her clutch off the counter. "And what's wrong with you?"

"Nothing." He patted the coat swung over his arm and then his pants pocket. "I'm all set to go."

"Fantastic." She searched the lobby, looking for the night-shift receptionist.

"She's in the bathroom," Amanda offered. "I'll stay here until she gets back."

"Thank you." Savannah clapped her hands together as if in prayer. "I promise, once tomorrow is over, everything will be smooth sailing."

It had to be.

A perfectly manicured brow rose on Amanda's forehead. "I'll believe it when I see it."

Savannah winced in farewell and walked for the lobby doors, Grant at her side. They didn't speak, not while hailing a cab, not on the few blocks' drive to their destination, and not even when they strode by the immaculately shaped shrubs lining the front path.

The glitz and glamour of Grandiosity towered before her, the

193

structure oozing with snobbery. She puffed out a breath of fog, let it disappear into the darkness, and then straightened her shoulders.

"You ready?" She focused on the building, on that shiny, glistening chandelier that beamed its message of superiority.

"Ahh... yeah." Grant rubbed his hands together, warming them in the cold. "But you're making me nervous... Should I be nervous?"

"No." She shook her head, still staring, still frozen. He was already a slave to anxiety; he didn't need her apprehension rubbing off on him. "This is going to be great."

Fan-fucking-tastic.

She led the way, climbing the stairs, and came face to face with the doorman. He was familiar. The same man from the night she'd spent in the penthouse. *Shit.* Could this night be more punishing?

She snapped her gaze to the floor and feigned the tiles had a mesmerizing hold as she walked through the entrance.

"Are you from Rydel?" he asked.

She froze, fear sliding down her spine.

"Yeah," Grant answered for her.

"Then the bar's straight through to your left. Would you like me to take your coats?"

Savannah stifled a squeal as Grant lifted the heavy covering from her shoulders and handed it over. She hadn't prepared herself. Not properly. She'd planned to schmooze with Patrick, ignore Penny, and completely avoid Keenan. But she hadn't anticipated the shame she would feel when she reentered this building.

Memories overwhelmed her, flashes of vision that made her heart race.

"Are you sure there's nothing to worry about?" Grant muttered near her ear. "You're acting strange."

She shook her head to dislodge her thoughts. "It's a new dress," she lied and swung her hand out to indicate the glistening black that clung to her skin. "I'm not sure I can pull it off." The dress had hung dormant in her closet for years, the long sleeves and knee-high hem too conservative for clubbing and too sexy for a business function.

Tonight was an exception. She wanted Keenan to see the material hugging her the way he previously had. She craved his attention along the deep neckline that exposed cleavage highlighted with a simple silver drop necklace nestled between the top of her breasts. She'd kill to have him contemplate the thought of her underwear. To second-guess if she was wearing something equally appealing as the lingerie he'd bought for her. And if they did cross paths, and their eyes did meet, she would be on his level, able to glare into those deep gray depths because she was wearing her highest heels, the ones that gave a great kick to her calf muscles adorned in sheer stockings.

"You look gorgeous."

She stifled a gasp at the breathlessness in Grant's tone.

He was looking at her. *Really* looking at her. "Stop it." She patted his arm playfully and clung tighter to her clutch. "You're making me blush."

"Sorry," he muttered. "I didn't mean anything by it."

He jogged a few steps ahead to pull the door open for her. She slowed, swallowing over the tightening in her throat. Inside was shadowed, glistening lights filling the darkness. Noise bellowed forth, laughter, clinking glassware, chatter.

Goosebumps skittered along every inch of her skin, blanketing her in discomfort. Not quite unhealthy anxiety, but awfully close. The glossy wooden bar came into view. The stools. The suits. The crowd. Each step exposed more elegance and superiority that shoved her tighter into the Inferior box.

"Savannah..." Patrick Black stepped toward her in his tailor-made suit, his hand outstretched. He was dashing, entirely pleasing to the eye for a man old enough to be her father. He would've been a heartbreaker in his day, and the trait lived on in his son who came to stand tall at his side. "You look ravishing."

"Thank you." She grinned, pasting a sly and provocative smile right where it needed to be. "You're quite charming yourself."

He chuckled, giving her hand a warm shake before releasing it. "Have you met my son?"

Heartbeats increased, the sound punishing in her ears. She tilted her chin, ever so slightly, and met visual perfection. "Yes." She kept her voice strong and licked her lower lip for added measure. "We've met."

Keenan took her hand, encasing it in his solid grip. He held her tight, peering at her with a look so fierce it almost scorched her nerves. She tried to remain in control, to keep him from penetrating the rapidly beating organ in her chest, but she was too susceptible, too weak against his charm.

She cut her gaze to his father. "He's quite mysterious, isn't he?" She spoke as if Keenan wasn't even there. As if he didn't exist even though their palms were still joined. "I bet his silent demeanor works wonders on the ladies."

Patrick chuckled. "It certainly works on my assistant."

Keenan's touch vanished, leaving her arm to fall to her side. She feigned ignorance, her lips parting in shock as he fled, the back of his tailored suit fitting perfectly over every body part.

"Was it something I said?" she murmured, her stomach turning with guilt.

"Please accept my apologies on his behalf." The influential CEO of Grandiosity encroached, placing his hand at the low of her back. "He's not the most social of people."

"I understand." But she didn't. When it came to Keenan, she knew nothing.

"And who is this young man?" Patrick focused over her shoulder.

Oh, shit. "Sorry." She winced at Grant. "This is Grant Stevenson, one of the managers of Rydel, Seattle."

The men shook hands and flowed into an easy conversation about business. She excused herself, needing space. Needing alcohol. But mind-numbing bliss wasn't an option. She had to remain in peak condition for the wedding.

A waiter passed, teasing her with a tray of bubbles as she maneuvered around guests, pretending she had a destination in mind. She didn't want to speak to anyone. She didn't even want to keep this smile plastered on her face when there was a mountain of work to be done back at Rydel and too many unfamiliar eyes looking her way. Did they know she'd been banging their boss? Had they found the security tapes that placed her in the penthouse, and cavorting in their pool?

Another tray slid past her vision, and this time the champagne couldn't be denied. One wouldn't hurt. One might actually help. It would keep her free hand occupied and stop the tremble of her traitorous fingers.

She reached out, swiped one of the flutes, and smiled in thanks at the young man who continued walking. Over the rim of the glass, she scoured the room as she sipped. Familiar faces chatted with strangers. Rydel and Grandiosity mingling with ease. Penny was in the far corner, her long, perfect legs on display, her flawless, glossy hair streaming over her shoulder.

Savannah detoured in the opposite direction and made polite conversation with the competition. She ignored the itch at the back of her neck, the one that told her someone was staring at her, talking about her, and feigned interest in the people she met.

"Savannah," Patrick called from over her shoulder. "I'd like you to meet Tanner. He's like a son to me."

She turned to meet vibrant blue eyes and a playboy smile that threatened to melt her panties. But the introduction hadn't been lost on her. Patrick was far more enthusiastic about introducing this man than he had been about his biological son.

"Hi." Her grin was genuine under Tanner's hungry stare. "Nice to meet you."

"Tanner is one of my executives. He determines what brands go into every Grandiosity room. From the televisions to the tiny liquor bottles."

"Impressive."

"I think I can handle it from here on my own." Tanner's voice was deep and smooth. Almost edible.

"I know. I know." Patrick held up his hands. "I'll leave you to it."

Savannah smothered a laugh and remained quiet until they were alone. "That sounded awfully close to matchmaking."

Tanner chuckled. "Get to know him a little better and you'll realize there's no doubt."

"Really?" This time she couldn't hold in a snort. "I thought I'd be considered the competition. Maybe even the enemy."

"There is no competition between Grandiosity and Rydel. We're in two different leagues." His warm eyes didn't even flicker with the insult. "But Patrick has been very vocal about how impressed he is by you. Apparently, you acted like GI Jane and stomped into his office, demanding his attention and cooperation."

A sneer threatened to curl her lip. "I guess it would've been shocking—a mere woman from an insignificant company dictating terms to a business god," she drawled. "Crazy, right?"

"It shocked the hell out of him." He didn't even notice her sarcasm. *Pretentious asshole.*

She gave him a tight grin and sipped her champagne. Her focus strayed from Tanner's nauseating million-dollar smile to the bar, where a formidable man leaned against the wood, staring at her.

Keenan was always staring at her.

She lowered her glass, her gaze, and her self-esteem. She didn't have the energy to fight narcissism, or whatever it was that made these men think they could treat her on a sub-human level.

"Have you ever thought about working for us?" Tanner continued, oblivious to her desire to shove the remaining contents of her glass in his face.

"For Grandiosity?" she mocked. "Wow. Wouldn't that be nice?"

Her clutch vibrated and the faint trill of her ringtone sounded over the chatter. "I'm sorry. Could you please excuse me for a moment?"

He inclined his head. "We'll talk later."

Oh, goodie.

She opened her clutch and pulled out her cell. *Private Number* flashed on screen and she answered, expecting to hear Amanda's voice on the other line.

"Savannah speaking."

"Savannah..." Yep, Amanda had called in all her anxiety-riddled glory.

"What's up?"

"There's been—"

The words were smothered by laughter and the obnoxious thump of conversation surrounding her. "Hold on a minute. I can't hear you."

She turned in a circle, ignoring the continued stare from Keenan, and spied a bathroom sign in the far corner. "I'm finding somewhere quieter." She scooted on her toes through the throng of people and side-stepped a partition to enter a secluded hall to the male, female, and disabled toilets. "That's better. I should be able to hear you now."

"Savannah... I..."

Shit. There was too much panic in the event manager's tone. Too much fear. The waitresses mustn't have shown up. Or worse, they threatened not to work tomorrow.

"The ambulance had to come," Amanda continued. "They think Thomas had a heart attack."

Savannah stopped breathing. "What?" She crumpled against the wall and placed her glass on the tile floor. "I don't understand. I was with him an hour ago."

A sob filtered through the line, hitting her ears with painful clarity. "Amanda?"

"I can't do this. I think I'm going to be sick." The event manager babbled, mumbling words that ran in and out of coherence. "He could've died and all I can think about is the stupid wedding. How are we going to feed the guests without a head chef? How are we going to pull this off when everything is *fucked up*?"

Savannah's lungs restricted with the possibility of catastrophe. She was caught in the same maelstrom as Amanda—suppressing nausea over thoughts of tomorrow when she should've been focusing on Thomas' health.

"*Please*," her voice cracked. "I need you to be strong." She let out a slow breath and prayed for the bile to stop rising up her throat. "I'll figure it out. I promise." There was no other choice. She *had* to figure it out. Hundreds of thousands of dollars were on the line.

"I'll be back there soon with Grant. Go to the bar, have a relaxing drink, and wait for me. Tell any staff to continue as best they can until we arrive."

"I..."

"I promise I'll be there as soon as I can."

"Okay," Amanda's voice shook. "I'll be waiting."

Savannah was thankful for the wall that kept her upright as her arms fell to her sides. She hung her head and breathed through the negative thoughts that threatened to drown her. There was no way out. Not from the wedding nightmare, and definitely not from the memories of silence that screamed with passion.

She'd made too many mistakes in her life. First with Penny, then Spencer, now Keenan. Seattle seemed to be her punishment, with each past indiscretion compounding her inability to fix the here and now.

"Goddamn it." She spoke to her shoes. "*God. Damn. It.*"

The rhythmic thud of footsteps approached, stopping at the start of the bathroom hall. Someone was there, staring at her. She raised her head, narrowed her gaze to a feral glare, and prepared to tell them to mind their own business.

Prepared and failed.

It was Keenan, his dominance narrowing the hallway.

There was concern in his eyes, those deep depths speaking to her through the surrounds of harsh features.

"Leave me alone." She held her chin high through the force of self-loathing and placed her cell back into her clutch. Her hands shook, trembled, each of her fingers fluttering like butterflies' wings. She was losing herself. The grip of sanity loosening its ties to her.

He approached, calm, controlled, and far from civil. There was a wealth of hatred in his breathtaking features. Yet his eyes, those conquering, undeniable eyes, produced a symphony of worry.

She pushed from the wall and winced at the tumbling anxiety in her belly. Dizziness overwhelmed her, the black of breathlessness biting at her periphery. She focused on the ground that rolled under her feet and tried to tell herself to move, to flee.

Tightness encased her upper arms and she raised her gaze, falling under his spell. Words flittered in and out of her consciousness—sarcasm, spite, hatred, even admiration. The emotions he inspired could overflow a gorge. She wanted to say them all and wasn't sure what would come out when she opened her mouth.

"You can start to celebrate," she sneered. "You and Penny... You wanted to drag me down and now you have. Congratulations."

He frowned and tightened his hold, demanding answers.

"They've quit—waitresses, bar staff, anyone and everyone because of the nastiness from Grandiosity. The hotel is barely functioning. And now..." She released a maniacal laugh. "Now, we have a wedding to cater tomorrow, and my head chef just had a heart attack." A fucking heart attack. Oh, god, she was going to lose it. "I have employees almost dying because of stress. *From you,*" her voice cracked. "*You* did this."

His gaze cut to the entrance, to the woman Savannah hadn't heard approach the bathroom hall. Keenan's focus turned lethal and the woman paled in response.

"Sorry," the intruder murmured and quickly two-stepped around them to push into the female bathroom.

Savannah didn't care anymore. She didn't give a shit if people found them together. She couldn't give a flying fuck if all her secrets were exposed. She was tired of fighting. Of hiding. She'd taken on too much. Made the wrong decisions. Dug a deeper hole to bury herself in.

"You win," she whispered.

Keenan's beautiful lips parted and she ached for his words. She ached for anything that would stifle her hatred. He yanked her, pulled her so strongly away from the wall that she gasped. Her feet followed after him, the movements made on numb legs. He dragged her across the hall, into the disabled toilet and slammed the door shut behind them.

Her chest throbbed as he leaned her back against the cold tile wall, his palms still gripping her flesh. She stared at him, her throat convulsing as his focus intensified.

"Why?" The question bubbled from her without permission. "Why did you have to destroy me?"

That's what this was all about. She could've handled the professional assault. She could've recovered from Penny's nastiness and the pressure from resigning staff. But not this. Not him.

His chin lifted, taking her onslaught head on. He leaned closer, eye to eye, almost chest to chest. She could smell the tang of scotch on his breath, could practically taste his intoxication on her tongue. She shuddered, not from hate, but from longing. The sensation clogged her veins, blurred her vision, made her despise herself so fucking much that her chest threatened to crack under the pressure.

He frowned down at her, taking his time to scrutinize her features before he stabbed a finger at his sternum. "*I'll fix it,*" he mouthed.

She laughed. "You can't. I've already called every recruitment agency across the city."

"*I'll fix it,*" he repeated.

She suffocated under the sincerity in his eyes and wished she could believe him. It would be easy. All she had to do was relax. Let go. Sink further into his arms and let him spin her a tale that made the stress wash away.

He inched closer, the approach of his lips making her lick her own.

"Don't." She shook her head, but her feet wouldn't move. There was no strength. Not of will or of body.

His mouth brushed hers, a soft, gentle stroke that only endeavored to tear her apart. She mewled, and squeezed her eyes shut to fight the devastation. She didn't want this. Not soft. Not gentle.

On cue, his fingers found her shoulders, her neck, her hair. He tugged the strands, tight, painfully hard, and deepened the kiss to a level of punishment. Harsh strokes of tongue infused her, awakened her. He held her in a vise, tempting her to flee as he encased her tighter in the trap of his arms.

Darkness retreated. Clarity approached. She wanted to depend on him. For everything. For anything. Yet he was unreliable. Even for honesty.

She pushed against his chest and broke their connection, pressing cold fingers to her scorched lips. "Don't ever do that again."

He stiffened, straightened, and the harshness returned to those glorious features. He stepped back, creating a chasm between them, and pulled his cell from his pants pocket. Confident fingers typed, and she watched in a trance as he wielded his weapon, preparing to strike her down.

I promise I will fix this for you.

She took the assault, let it sink under her skin. "Stay out of my life."

INARTICULATE

Her heart thundered in her throat as she slid to the door and gripped the handle. "I don't want to see you again until settlement."

Twenty-Three

Sleep was elusive. She'd only scored a few hours nap between waking nightmares. There'd been no shower, no change of clothes. Hell, she hadn't even seen the inside of her suite, and had called the conference room her home since she returned from Grandiosity.

Determination kept her company, the last minute fight for survival keeping her adrenaline flowing and her brain cells churning on their lonely battle. Staff enthusiasm had hit rock bottom. Optimism had been slaughtered, even though the whispers she'd heard about the welcome meeting had all been positive. There was no motivation. They were all numb with concern for Thomas and angry as hell at Layla and Tammy, who hadn't been contactable since they both called in sick. It was still unclear if they would show up to lead the glorified team of housekeeping staff through the reception table service, or if they'd sink another nail into the wedding coffin.

But they were far from her biggest problem.

The disaster was the three-course wedding dinner that wouldn't cook itself. Thomas' comment about his chefs not working well unsupervised hadn't sank in until she was standing in front of them, glancing from one dumbstruck expression to the next after she'd broached the topic of them sharing the head chef role. Evidently, the kitchen fell into a heap without leadership. And there wasn't a soul on the face of the planet available to take on the responsibility the day before Thanksgiving.

Even Spencer lacked the words to comfort her when she'd called him in a blubbering mess at three in the morning. The only thing she knew with certainty was that he was on his way, soon to be here to make everything just a little bit worse.

"Savannah?" Kelly's voice was filled with concern. "Amanda just called. She's on her way in and wanted to know if you had any answers yet."

Savannah kept staring straight ahead, her elbows resting on the spectacularly adorned bridal table as she took in the reception area destined to host a myriad of unfed people. Each table was covered with a white tablecloth, the crockery and cutlery placed perfectly at each setting. Soon the florist would be here to place the centerpieces, and the band would set up in the corner.

"Not yet," she murmured.

"What can I do to help? Can I get you a coffee? Maybe a wine." Kelly shuffled into view and tilted her head to make eye contact. "Crack?"

Savannah released a breath of laughter. "I'm okay." She swallowed over the placation. "What time is it?"

"Nine."

Shit. She'd been sitting here for hours, without a resolution to show for it. "Can you do me a favor?"

"Of course. Name it."

It was a last ditch effort. "Can you call all the recruitment agencies in the directory? Beg them. Plead with them. Tell them how dire our situation is and let them know we'll double the standard rate of pay if they can find a capable head chef to lead our kitchen today."

"Sure." Kelly's smile was weak. "Have you heard any more on Thomas?"

"Grant spoke to his wife sometime during the night." The news was her only solace. "She said he's recovering well from a minor cardiac incident. Not a heart attack."

"Thank God." Kelly's relief was palpable, her smile genuine. "I'll go make some phone calls."

Savannah remained in place to battle her demons in solitude. There *were* options, but they weren't pretty. The menu could be changed to finger food. Or the three courses could remain, if easier, more production line selections were chosen.

Neither alternative would be appreciated by a bride and groom on their special day. Compensation would be inevitable. A lawsuit likely. The Rydel name would be tarnished with more potency.

"Savannah?" Kelly's head poked through the door on the far end of the room. "Spencer is here to see you."

Spencer. The name rolled around her head, tainting everything it touched. She didn't want to stand up, didn't want to approach the lobby, but she did, her feet moving of their own volition. Anticipating this moment had filled her with dread, because seeing him stand before her with his dark suit and bright smile had sparked the reaction she'd expected. A reaction she loathed.

"Hey." He strode for her, wrapping her up in his cast-iron grip.

Relief overwhelmed her. Disgusting, repulsive relief. Positive feelings toward him weren't safe. They weren't healthy at all. Yet he blanketed her in comfort and gave her anxiety a slight respite.

"I hate to say it, sweetie," he murmured in her ear, "but you look like hell."

She laughed and shoved at his chest. "Nice to see you, too."

He pulled back, his hands sliding to her hips. "What can I do to help?"

She broke away from his potent stare and focused over his shoulder. "I'm not..." Her words trailed as three guys with small duffle bags entered the lobby. They were followed closely by numerous young women and men, around eight or so, all immaculately dressed, their hair flawless. Her stomach dived at the thought of them being enforcers for a bride who'd caught wind of the impending catastrophe.

But their intentions were worse, far worse. Penny and Keenan came in behind them, drawing the group's attention with merely their presence.

"*Fuck.*" Her whisper was filled with horror.

"What's wrong?"

She glanced at Spencer and then grimaced at the instinct to seek his guidance. This was her show. Her problem. Her punishment to take. "They're from Grandiosity."

"What are they doing here?"

"I don't know." She shook her head and met Keenan's scowl across the other side of the lobby. He spared her the briefest flicker of acknowledgement before his attention turned to Spencer, his scrutiny falling to the hand possessively on her hip. She should've jerked from her ex's touch or shoved his arm away, but his palm was filled with support, the warmth and strength the only thing keeping her upright.

"I better find out." She progressed toward her doom, Spencer still at her side, his hand still marking what he thought was his territory.

"Can I help you?" The group turned toward her en masse while she drilled Keenan with her stare.

"We heard you're in a bind." Penny's tone was sickly sweet. "We're here to help."

Savannah kept her focus on Keenan, not wanting to turn to her cousin and see the look of superiority chiseled into her make-up covered face.

"Three chefs and nine wait staff. Just point them in the right direction so they can get set up before returning later this afternoon."

Silent oblivion washed over her. A wave of indecipherable nothingness filled her head. Her knees threatened to buckle. She was going to be sick. Vomit was literally going to volcano from her nose in a display of utter relief and unmanageable rage.

"What's going on?" Amanda's voice dissolved the crescendo.

Savannah straightened and dragged her attention from an unreadable Keenan, to her apprehensive event manager. "Amanda, this is—" *underhandedness at its finest*, "staff from Grandiosity. They're here to..." *fuck with my sanity and make me go post—*

"Help," Penny cut off her internal diatribe. "We're here to help." Her cousin smiled, a fake, beaming smile that deserved a snarl in return.

"Really?" the event manager gasped. "Oh, my God, that is such good news."

Yeah, roll out the celebratory banners and confetti.

"You don't seem pleased," Spencer whispered in her ear. "You should be thanking them."

She wanted to scoff, to laugh, to guzzle a bottle of something high in alcoholic content. "Thank you," her words were etched with sarcasm, but nobody seemed to notice. Not even Keenan who kept eying the hand on her hip with disdain. "Amanda, I'll let you take it from here. I've got things to sort out."

She faced her ex and tried to shrug him off. "Can you give me a minute?"

He seemed perplexed, like he'd always been when endeavoring to read her. "Sure." He pulled her closer and placed a kiss on her temple, marking his territory in the subtlest way possible. "I'll go get a room... Unless I can share yours."

She raised a fuck-you brow and laughed. "Not gonna happen."

Her strut was calculated as she walked toward the function room— equal parts determination and independence that slowly dwindled at the sound of following footsteps. She entered the silence of the large, open area and prepared for battle as she turned.

"How dare you?"

Keenan raised a superior brow along with his cell screen—*If I'd known you'd called your boyfriend in to save you, I wouldn't have bothered.*

"He's my boss." She ignored his jealousy, even though she itched to bathe in it, to lick it off her skin like honey. "Who I'm sure you already met during the negotiation of sale."

He laughed, the silent movement taunting. His hand rose between them, his middle and index fingers both intimately crossed. "*Close,*" he mouthed.

"Yeah." She nodded. "Just as close as you and Penny."

He shook his head, denying the facts that had already been proven without doubt.

"I told you to stay out of my life. It wasn't a difficult request."

His eyes narrowed, the tension in his posture coiling tighter and tighter.

"And I guess this means I need to repay you now."

His lips curved, his smile far from friendly. There was calculation in his gaze, a look that spoke of possession and passion. He raised a brow, questioning her cluelessness, telling her exactly how he wanted to be compensated, precisely how she should go about reimbursement.

"If your help comes with strings…"

What? Would she reject the offer? Would she shove it back in his face and tell the Grandiosity staff to leave? Of course not. She was indebted to him and wasn't sure if she truly loathed the possibility of repayment.

"*No strings.*" He held up his hands in mock surrender and backtracked, his seductive demeanor leaving without her permission. His sure steps put aching distance between them, his final glance calculating, before he turned and made for the lobby.

Shit. "Wait." She needed to apologize. To take back her bitterness and show her appreciation for him saving her behind. In mere hours, he'd done what she hadn't been able to pull off in days. Even weeks. It was everything else that made her psychotically bitchy—Penny's presence, lack of sleep, the buildup of stress, the pleasured memories of last night's kiss.

He didn't stop, didn't falter in his sure stride as he left her on the periphery of the excited conversations coming from the lobby to sulk in her own childishness. He only gave her a wicked view of his sexy jean-covered ass, and a heavy dose of temptation to make her all the more grumpy.

Twenty-Four

Savannah left Amanda to oversee the wedding at the back of the function room, and bumped the swinging kitchen door with her hip, exposing the stainless steel and tiled area in all its chaos. "Tell me what to do and I'll do it."

She'd flittered from one job to the next all day, determined to keep herself moving so she didn't slump into an exhausted heap. For everyone else, the night was running smoothly. Guests were seated, listening to the besotted groom wax lyrical about his glowing bride. Spencer hadn't lifted a finger since Penny and Keenan had returned earlier in the night. Her ex had discovered that chatting up her cousin made for an excuse to get out of the workload and probably thought it was the perfect strategy to make Savannah jealous.

The only thing poking at the green-eyed monster was the seductive grin Keenan currently gave to a giggling Rydel housekeeper who was posing as a waitress. Apparently, they both knew sign language, which seemed to spark a looming happily ever after for the woman who kept batting her lashes at the eligible bachelor.

"Start serving guests." A plate was pushed forward from a Grandiosity employee. "The sooner we get the meals out, the better."

"Sure." Savannah grasped the porcelain and pushed past the swinging door into the dimly lit function room. She followed the line of Grandiosity wait staff leading to the table being served. Everywhere she turned there were smiling faces—the bride, the groom, guests, even Amanda.

They'd succeeded.

They'd pulled it off. And tomorrow she would celebrate. Tomorrow, when her feet weren't throbbing and her head wasn't filled with cement, she would let her hair down and focus on a way to apologize to Keenan. After hours contemplating an amicable, professional way to approach him, she'd come up with nothing. Instead, she'd become an automaton, striding back and forth from the kitchen, serving guest after guest, while she punished herself with the image of him flirting with the hired help.

Time passed without meaning, each speech fading into the next until she glanced up from placing the final dessert bowl on the far back table and sucked in a breath at the man staring at her from his leaned position against the entrance doorway.

She lowered her focus, convinced it was a coincidence they'd both spied each other at the same time, only to be proven wrong when she lifted her gaze again. He hadn't moved, hadn't quit staring at her with his arms crossed over his chest, his shirt sleeves folded, and his attention decimating the final vestiges of her strength.

Mentally, she crumpled. She lost coherence under the spell of his eyes. Then with the next inhalation everything rushed back—her energy, her memories, even her desire. She walked toward him, eager to get her apology over and done with while he was finally alone.

"Hey." She gave him a half-hearted smile and kept her voice low. "The wedding was a success…"

He inclined his head, his expression blank as he took in the room.

"Your staff were a godsend." *He* was a godsend, although she wasn't entirely convinced he wasn't the devil.

His casual nod left her wanting more, craving a reaction, something fierce and emotional to match the growing force inside her chest. Most of all, she coveted an apology. His apology, and the belief that he regretted the deception which had cut her deep.

"You didn't have to help me."

He dragged his attention from the guests and looked at her. *No.* He looked into her, seeking secrets and making his presence known in her most intimate of thoughts. She fell under the spell of that look. She capitulated. She caved.

He jerked his head toward the lobby, then pushed from the wall and walked away. A stronger woman would've protested. A smarter woman would've hightailed it in the opposite direction. But she was none of those, not right now.

She scooted to the kitchen, retrieved her cell from the counter, and pretended she didn't understand the questioning frown Spencer aimed at her as he continued chatting with Penny.

This was a case of killing two birds with one talented stone. Communicating with Keenan was inevitable. They had a lot to work out, with payments for the Grandiosity staff sitting at the top of the list. And once they were finished, she would receive the grateful bonus of being able to sneak to her room without Spencer shadowing her.

There was nothing sordid or affectionate about the way she trailed after the man who conspired against her. Nothing emotional or calculating. Nope. It was entirely business. That's why she walked with the added confidence in her stride and the authoritative tilt of her chin.

She was owning this—the apology and thank you that would wipe their slate clean. Or she had been until she entered the lobby and found him beside the reception desk. He captured her with those eyes, his attention unwavering as he retrieved his coat from the night shift receptionist and shrugged into the material with enough suave sophistication to rewire the beat of her heart.

Her feet slowed, telling her to proceed with caution because clearly her mind wasn't up to speed. He jerked his head again, a slightly arrogant nudge toward the entrance.

No. She shook away the invitation. He was exuding trouble. Tempting, palpable mischief.

He grabbed his cell from his pants pocket, worked the screen, and made the device in her hand dance. She peered down at his message and her stomach descended for the ride.

Keenan: *I need to show you something.*

She stiffened at the direct hit to her restraint. Humoring him would only cause complications. So why did she continue to walk in his direction? Why was her blood pumping a little faster at the slightest tweak to his lips?

She met him at the lobby doors, his hand poised on the handle. "What do you need to show me?"

He mouthed something indecipherable, or maybe she didn't understand because she was too focused on his eyes, the gray now vibrant, almost blue. He pushed into the night and held the door open for her to proceed. The freezing air infiltrated her lungs and she shuddered from the vast change in temperature. Within seconds, his coat was slumped over her shoulders, his mouth-watering scent enveloping her like a drug.

"Thank you."

They walked side-by-side along the path, the silence between them far from comfortable. It was magnetic, his pull loaded with energy that obliterated her need for sleep as they approached the road. There was a clink of a keychain, a flash of lights from a nearby vehicle, and then slowly dawning realization.

"This is yours?" She remembered it from dinner at her aunt's house. The shiny silver sports car had been parked in the drive the first night they met.

He nodded as he ate up the distance to the passenger door and opened it for her. There was no cockiness in his features. No arrogant smirk. There was no expectation at all, only the lone hand that indicated for her to get inside.

Her lips parted on a silent protest. She wanted to announce her distrust, to tell him sliding into his car didn't change anything between them. But his actions today meant she owed him. Big time.

"I can't be gone long." She made her way to his side. "I need sleep."

He nodded, the solemn gesture announcing he was fully aware of her exhaustion. She was stupid to think her appearance would've escaped him. She still wore her clothes from the night before, the dress now crinkled and her stockings bearing a long runner up her right inner thigh.

She spared a final glance toward the lobby, making sure her

stupidity wasn't being witnessed by staff, especially by Spencer or Penny, before she slid into the soft leather seat. The door shut behind her, the seconds until Keenan joined her ticking by with an unfavorable growl from her intuition.

The keys were thrust into the ignition, the engine purred to life, and her sanity waved goodbye to her from the sidewalk as he pulled from the curb. He accelerated through the city streets, gliding around corners, making the road his bitch with such ease and efficiency that her womanly parts couldn't help but notice. Within minutes, they were on the freeway, then an exit ramp and farther still. The brightly lit streets became darker, the large buildings turning into residential properties.

He was taking her away from the hustle and bustle, from the lights and the visibility. The shadowed streets filled her with comfort, as if the solitude could hide the secret of falling for him again. There was no radio, no sound, apart from the smooth growl of the engine which thrummed in her chest.

She palmed her cell, unlocked the screen and re-read his message—*I need to show you something.* She skimmed her thumb over the words, stopping at one. *Need.* His request wasn't a wish or a want. It was a necessary requirement.

The same necessity echoed in her chest. She *wanted* him to turn the car around and drive her home, but what she *needed* was closure. To cut off the redundant desire for him and move on. Without an amicable conclusion, her head wouldn't cease thinking of him. Her heart wouldn't quit fluttering at the thought of his name.

She had to stop. He had to stop. Everything and anything had to come to a halt so she could regain her professionalism and do what she'd been sent to Seattle to do.

"Where are we going?" She'd only been this far from the city once, the night of the bonfire, and they were traveling in the same direction, down roads that turned desolate, with houses that increased in size and land that spread out between them.

"I think you should take me back to..." Her words drifted as the mansion from their past came into view, the impressive structure now alight from innumerable angles. She sucked in a breath, held it, and let the pressure trigger her adrenaline.

The home was bigger than she remembered, more monstrous in all its pretentious beauty. The top level mimicked the bottom with matching windows and curtains. There was a balcony above the double-door entry, a three-bay garage, and an immaculate garden to make it picture perfect.

The car slowed at the looming front gates, while her heart tried to climb into her throat. "This is yours." It wasn't a question. She was now well aware of all the blindingly obvious clues she'd missed.

He hadn't lied. His position at Grandiosity hadn't been a secret. The puzzle had been there for her to piece together. She'd just been too preoccupied to notice.

The gates parted before her, cracking her ribs apart at the same time. "You should take me home." *Christ.* Even her words betrayed her. There was no conviction, no determination or demand.

He remained unresponsive and drove the vehicle along a gravel path to park in front of the stairs leading to the entry. The engine died, the keys were removed, and he slid from the car, leaving her in thick, tangible silence. She ignored his movements in her periphery, the way he strode around the hood and came to her side.

Her door opened, the freezing chill not penetrating the heated bubble she'd placed her thoughts in. He held out a hand and those fingers taunted her. They mocked her. She could already sense the spark his touch would ignite. The pleasure would be traitorous. Her white flag would raise without her permission.

"I can get out on my own."

She waited until he stepped back, and then pushed from the car, her cell clutched in her sweaty palm. Visions from the past bombarded her. He'd commanded her silence. He'd made her fearful of being caught. He'd played her, and somehow she couldn't find the will to hate him because those moments were some of the most exhilarating in her life.

"I need to get the bank documentation on the Grandiosity staff that helped today. I want to pay them as soon as possible." She was deflecting, endeavoring to turn the seductive vibe into something more professional. "And I haven't thanked you yet, have I?" She couldn't remember, she couldn't even concentrate. "If not, thank you. And I'm sorry for my attitude this morning. You and Penny caught me off—"

He encroached, seeping into her personal space as she backed herself against the hood. Her nerves responded accordingly, tingling with a complete lack of regard to her emotional turmoil.

"Don't," she whispered into the night. She couldn't handle his proximity. His temptation. Her inhalations increased, the depth of her breaths resembling someone under interrogation and would soon parallel that of a marathon runner.

He took another step and monopolized her vision as he raised his hand toward her face. She stiffened as his fingers approached, preparing for the unauthorized pleasure his grip on her chin would inspire.

She was defenseless against that hold.

Helpless.

But he didn't touch her. His hand fell to his side and the disappointment that burst through her veins only cemented her stupidity. "Was that night a game?" The need for answers bubbled from her lips without consent. "And every night that followed?"

"*No*," he mouthed. "*No game.*"

She tore her focus away, already losing the will to remain angry. How could she when his wordless apologies addressed her libido, not her common sense?

"Is this all you needed to show me?"

There was no answer.

She looked up from under her lashes and hated how her heart squeezed as their gazes collided. His lips parted, then closed. His focus flickered between her eyes, from one to the next, back and forth, his zealous scrutiny shrinking her defenses. He shrugged, the answer filled with a yes, a no, and a maybe.

"You can take me back now." She pushed from the car, forcing her feet to move.

Then there it was. His touch. The connection that made her knees weak and her heart respond with arrhythmia. Goosebumps cascaded down her back, along her arms, and slid between her aching thighs. Every inch of her was covered in skin that literally burst forth for more of his attention.

Don't turn. Don't turn. *Please*, don't turn.

She turned and hated that his pain seemed to outweigh her own. His expression was etched with remorse from the shadowed depths of his irises and the creases marring his forehead.

"You're an asshole." The statement whispered between them. "You should've told me."

He nodded as if he understood, but he didn't. He had no clue what he meant to her, or how harsh his betrayal had hit.

"No, I mean a *really big* asshole."

He flashed his teeth in a sheepish smile that melted her like cheap candle wax. He'd won. With that smile and the sorrow in his eyes, he'd slaughtered her restraint. He tugged her into his body, then led her backward to lean against the warm car hood.

"What do I mean to you, Keenan?" She wanted the reason for being here painted in black and white. The truth set apart from the lies.

His brows furrowed, his pain evident as he palmed her cheeks and held her captive. He leaned into her, his thighs pressing against her while those beautiful lips approached.

She didn't want his kiss. She wanted answers. Yet the silken sweep of his mouth told her everything she yearned for. The brief, barely there brush of exquisite softness curled her toes and doused her in sensation. He stoked a warmth inside her, the delicate caress of his affection burning hotter than lust ever could.

She placed her cell on the car hood and gripped his wrists. He was ice, his skin chilled at an unhealthy level. "You're freezing."

He didn't respond. Didn't confirm or deny.

"You should take me back to the hotel."

"*No.*" He shook his head and parted her legs with his knee, sending the first clenching pulse of desire to her core.

"Spencer will be looking for me."

A flash of possession narrowed his eyes. She waited for his anger and received a brutal smashing of his lips instead, his mouth taking hers in a victorious assault. His palms left her face, one arm moving to encase her waist while the other hand tangled in the mess of her ponytail. He stroked her tongue in harsh lashings and brought them chest to chest, pelvis to pelvis, every inch of her being paid homage by the brush of his body.

She clung to his shoulders and whimpered, but the connection was dizzying. It made the world disappear and her troubles vanish. She wasn't thinking. Only feeling. And that was a dangerous position if their past was any indication.

"Stop." She shoved at him and fought a cry as he retreated. "I can't do this. I'm not sleeping with you."

He glared at the ground, as if it took an enormous strength of will to pull himself together. His head tilted, slowly, showing the briefest acknowledgement of her request.

"Please take me home. I need to pass out."

He retrieved his cell from his pants pocket and typed—*Then stay here.* He typed again. *Stay with me.*

"No," she chuckled and gave another shove to his chest, only to have her wrist engulfed by his grip. Her humor faded as his seriousness bore into her, pleading with her. "Don't," she warned. "Don't be nice when nothing good can come from this."

He leaned in, almost nose to nose. "*Stay.*"

"Keenan..."

"*Stay.*"

She tangled her fingers in his shirt and shivered at the chill emanating off him. He wasn't giving her an option, she knew that. He was laying down the first layer of his attack, hoping she'd take the path of least resistance so their battle of wills didn't escalate to the next level.

Her ragged breaths panted between them, her need to fight not as prominent as it should be. The truth was, she wanted him. She wanted *this*, whatever the hell it may be. She just didn't want to be blindsided again.

"Please don't make me regret this."

He brushed the stray strands of hair from her face and nodded with solemn conviction. "*I won't.*"

But it was too late. She grabbed her cell, already regretting the heavenly way he entwined their fingers and the first step they made toward his house, because with that brief movement, she said goodbye to her heart and gave him all the power in the world.

He led her inside, into the warmth that infused her with drowsiness. There was a flick of lights—outside off, inside on—then he was guiding her up a spectacular staircase that overlooked a sparkling chandelier.

"I assume you have at least one spare room." She slowed and released her hand from his hold.

He paused at the top step and turned to face her with a succinct nod.

"And I assume you plan on putting me in there..."

His lips twitched, while the rest of him remained fierce, under control. He descended the two stairs between them and made her squeal as he lifted her off the ground, one arm beneath her legs, the other cradling her back.

"Flexing your muscles won't change my mind." Well, maybe it would, but she was going to hold out a little longer.

He carried her down a hall, past numerous closed doors, and into a room owned by his scent. With a flick of the lights he exposed her to a king-sized bed that would easily be dwarfed by his brilliance. The dark wood side tables were unadorned, the chest of drawers holding a flat screen television and nothing else. On the other side of the room, an open door led to darkness. And that was it. There was nothing to give her insight into his character, not a family photo to be seen. His private room was as revealing as his silence.

"Please put me down."

He complied and moved ahead to pull back the ruby bed coverings and pat the mattress like a father to a child.

"Where are you going to sleep?"

He frowned, giving her a let's-be-reasonable look. But there was no reason, no sense, and no self-preservation. He crooked a finger, enticed her to his side and placed his hands on her shoulders to gently guide her to sit on the bed. With gentlemanly finesse, he removed her jacket, placed her cell on the bedside table, then lowered to his knees to tug off her shoes, like a pauper to a princess. All she could do was watch while he became her knight in tarnished armor. A waking dream she didn't want to fade.

"I should probably have a shower..." She felt dirty, her skin tinged with sweat and grit that didn't call to her quite as much as the need to close her eyes...or kiss his lips.

"*Sleep*," he mouthed and slid his hands up the outside of her thighs, his steely gaze peering up at her.

Yeah, because slumber was possible when his touch crept toward the most sensitive part of her body.

He gripped the tops of her thigh-high stockings and tugged, lowering them inch by agonizing inch. The further he strayed from her pussy, the more her throat tightened in protest. Soon she'd be starved of oxygen, the fight between exhaustion and lust pushing her toward unconsciousness.

He dropped the flimsy material to the floor and lifted her ankles, encouraging her to lie on the bed. "*Sleep*." He stood, unbuttoning the top of his shirt, and then walked to the door to flick off the light.

He was joking, right? He'd run his hands under her dress, removed her stockings, teased her with the glimpse of his chest, and now expected her to drift off? That was going to be a challenge worthy of its own reality TV show.

She imagined him undressing, could practically see it in Technicolor when she heard the hollow thunk of his shoes, the clink of his belt, and the delicate whoosh of clothes hitting the carpet. The bed covers rustled, and she measured her need for breath as he slid in beside her.

Everything around her stilled—the air, the bed, Keenan—yet she was buzzing, her thoughts bouncing from one thing to the next. She needed his seduction, his lust, his greedy passion, because this caring side of him left her uneasy. It implied emotions she didn't want to acknowledge, in him or herself.

"You scare me, Keenan," she murmured. "Being like this with you scares me."

He slid closer, wove an arm around her waist, and nodded against her shoulder.

"I don't want to like you." She rolled away from him, his agreement drying her throat. "But I do." Too damn much to be healthy.

He spooned in behind her and pressed a brief kiss to the back of her neck. She didn't know what she'd expected from her admission, maybe cockiness, or the grind of his erection against her ass. Instead, his sweet affection infused her with something that seemed a lot like heartache.

She was lost to him, carelessly and undeniably. And it wasn't the usual instigators that made the pain tighten her chest. She wasn't thinking about their positions in rival companies, or Penny, who would enjoy tearing them apart.

All she could think about was settlement day, and how she'd have to leave him to return to San Francisco, no matter how close they became.

Twenty-Five

For the first time, Savannah awoke with Keenan still peacefully lying beside her. He was breathing deeply, his hand possessively on her back, his presence making her core tingle in the most torturous way.

Sleep had softened his features. There was no scowl or tight jaw. He was flawless in his slumber. Less imperious and entirely endearing. She wanted to remain like this forever, because waking him meant facing reality.

He'd admitted he was falling for her, and she experienced the same descent. Only she wasn't eager to embrace it. She would prefer to forget the complication and count down the days until settlement on her own. Safe in solitude. But the sight of him, the excitement and invigoration while being around him, made reality less worthy of her time. The thrill of him was far more important. The desire to be with him like a drug.

His eyes opened under her gaze and a gentle kick curved her lips. She clung to her pillow—his pillow—and sank under the spell of him blinking back at her.

"*Morning*," she mouthed the word, maintaining the quiet.

"*Morning*."

She wondered how many women embraced his silence and how many demanded to fill the void with unnecessary chatter. She wondered about everything and anything that pertained to this man. She itched to know it all—the secrets, the degradations, the achievements.

His hand began to rub in slow circles, the warmth of his palm infusing the low of her back to spark a fire in her core. Around and around, he swept away the sleepiness and increased the dosage of his appeal. He inched toward her, his smoky irises so close, so intimidating, as his touch rose. He teased her waist, her ribs, the sensitive part of her shoulder and up to her neck, his fingertips barely brushing her tingling skin.

Casually, he marked her, drawing his affection over her chin, along her cheeks, and against her bottom lip. She couldn't hold in the whimper when he stopped.

His eyes blinked in lazy strokes while he raised his hand between them. His fingers outstretched, as he indicated his face in a swirl of movement, then closed them tight before reopening them all at once.

She frowned, unsure of the gesture.

He mouthed a word, an indecipherable movement of lips, that increased her confusion.

She prepared to question him, had the syllables on the tip of her tongue, and paused. She didn't want to tamper with their moment. She didn't want to spoil the silence and become like every other woman he'd been with.

A devilish grin of understanding was her reward. He did the action again, slower, indicating his face in an intricate pattern.

This time she understood when his lips parted. This time she knew what he was telling her, not from the word he mouthed for a second time, or the sign language, but from the look in his eyes. The gaze that told her exactly what his fingers had tried to announce.

Beautiful. He thought she was beautiful.

She sank her head into the pillow, trying to hide the way her cheeks flamed in a celebration of vanity. His touch tickled her neck, below her ear, then his grip was on her chin, gently guiding her vision back to his.

This time he raised both hands, fingers clenched, thumbs up and wove them in a mimicked movement like an hourglass. That sign was universal, probably used since the dawn of time.

Sexy. He thought she was sexy.

She chuckled and shook her head in admonishment. The least he could do was teach her something that might further their communication. Maybe how-are-you, or yes-your-butt-does-look-good-in-those-pants.

His lips quirked and his right hand flickered in a mass of movement. Not just one sign, but a mass of different gestures one after the other.

Her frown must've said it all. She was clueless.

He slid down the bed, his descent lithe yet controlled as he rolled on top of her, his weight sinking into the needy parts of her body. She feigned ignorance even though she had a crystal clear idea of what he was implying from the erection he ground against her pubic bone.

He leaned to one side, resting his elbow beside her upper arm and signed again.

She shrugged, hoping her feigned lack of intellect would lead to more of his heavenly teaching.

He smirked at her, formed a circle with his thumb and index finger and then used the index finger of his other hand to penetrate the circle in a lascivious simulation of sex.

Her bark of laughter enveloped the room, accompanied by his soundless chuckle that vibrated against her chest. They stared at each other, reading thoughts and finding secrets for breathless moments.

"Have you always been silent?"

Bliss left the room in a vacuum. He broke eye contact, his emotions masked by a lack of expression as he made to roll off her.

"Don't." She grabbed his arms and kept him close. "I'm sorry. I shouldn't have asked." Not yet. Not in this moment.

"What time is it?" She was seconds from caving, mere beats of her pulse away from letting him know he'd won her heart as well as her body. Her tongue worked around the declaration, her lips were starved of the words to assure him his silence was inconsequential, only she wasn't ready to concede defeat just yet.

He leaned to the side, grasped his cell from the bedside table and flashed the screen her way. The move was probably made to show her the time, yet all she could see were three missed calls from Penelope Augustine.

"I think someone's trying to get a hold of you."

His morning lethargy morphed into an annoyed glare as he cleared the notifications.

"Why would she be calling?" The need for answers wasn't inspired by jealousy. Not entirely. It was based more on confusion over why her cousin was trying to hold a one-sided conversation instead of communication via text or email.

He typed and flashed her the screen again. *Thanksgiving lunch.*

"Oh, shit. I completely forgot." She tried to move, to sit up, but he wouldn't budge from his position between her legs. "How long until you have to leave?"

He grinned and tapped at the time stamp on his cell—*1:38pm*

"You missed lunch?" She shoved harder this time, working her arms and knees to make him roll back to his side of the bed. "How the hell did I sleep that long?" She sat up and flung back the covers. "I have to get back to the hotel."

She needed to call her mother. Spencer, too. Her ex would demand answers to her whereabouts. Answers she wasn't willing to give, but would need to respond to.

Keenan relaxed onto his side and levered his free hand under his head. "*Why?*" His eyes narrowed, announcing he knew exactly why she was worried.

"I should make sure the wedding finished without a hitch."

His brow rose, creeping higher like a bullshit meter. She prepared to fight the muted accusation only to be saved by his cell, the screen alighting with a new call from Penny.

"Did you tell her you weren't going to lunch?"

He gave the tiniest incline of his head.

"So, you've been in contact with her this morning?"

His chin raised, as if in defiance, as if he were warding off a jealous accusation. But it wasn't jealousy. It was something far more important.

"Does she know I'm here?" She crossed every metaphorical body part as the question whispered from her lips.

The slightest wince was her answer.

"Jesus Christ, Keenan."

She slid from the mattress and snatched her cell from the bedside table, unable to remain stationary. He followed, his footsteps louder as he inserted his authority into her personal space.

"My staff are finally becoming comfortable with the changeover," she grated. "I can't lose the civil communication between Grandiosity and Rydel now. If she starts creating drama, I'll..." She threw her hands in the air and huffed. "I'll... I'll claw those baby blues out that you seem to love so much."

He stepped into her, his solid build demanding calm she couldn't muster.

"She's in love with you."

He didn't offer a response.

"Tell me I'm wrong." She needed to hear it was professional loyalty making her cousin protective. Not affection. Not lingering feelings from the past.

He stepped back, signaling a surrender that didn't match the frustrated scowl etched across his forehead. "*Don't*," he mouthed.

"Don't what? Don't freak out because being here with you is a repeat of the stupidest and most unprofessional thing I've ever done? Or don't worry that you've told Penny I'm the reason you can't be with her for Thanksgiving?"

His eyes narrowed, his rage piqued. He strode for her, making her backtrack into his bedroom wall from the sudden spike in her arousal. She stood frozen, her chest rising and falling with apprehensive breaths, her mind churning over how she would handle another dose of callous emails from her cousin.

The stress of the wedding was over, the welcome meeting with Grandiosity had cemented a positive attitude in her staff, and she'd anticipated a lack of drama moving forward. Was being here worth losing the price of stability, not only for her, but for the whole Rydel team?

"I need to get back to the hotel."

He stepped closer, his feet inching between hers. He jabbed a finger at his chest, thumped a fist over his heart, and then pointed at her.

She balked at the gesture as her mind replayed the movements in a continuous loop. *Jab, thump, point. Jab, thump, point. Jab, thump, point.*

He loved her?

No. He'd mentioned he was falling for her. Not love. There were miles between those two steps. A universe of space marking the seriousness of each level of affection.

"I-I..." She backtracked. "I need a minute." She clung to the cell in her hand and fled from the room, increasing her pace down the hall and descending the wide stairs two at a time.

Her cell vibrated as she reached the lower level.

> **Keenan:** *I think I'm in love with you.*

"Christ." She kept walking, through a television room with wide, cushioned recliners, into the modern, spotless kitchen, then down another desolate hall that wasn't unfamiliar. She never would've guessed Keenan was capable of professing love, let alone feeling it. Especially for her.

He was too cold. Too protected by his silence.

Her cell beeped again.

> **Keenan:** *Hiding?*

Hell, yes. That's exactly what she was doing. She approached the archway leading to the bathroom she'd been introduced to the night of the bonfire and didn't deny the energized goosebumps from covering every inch of her flesh.

Ahead was the entrance to the toilet, but her interest rested on the door opposite the mirror. She lunged for the handle, escaped into a new hiding place, and closed herself inside. The sight of the deep bath and spotless shower made her moan. The desire to wash away the dirt and grime and fear becoming a living, breathing thing.

She placed her cell on the rim of the bath, unzipped the back of her dress, and shimmied until the material pooled at her feet. She couldn't think past the need to be clean, to be able to start fresh. Her lingerie was next, her bra and panties adding to the pile of stale clothes before she leaned into the shower and turned on the taps.

She paced, back and forth, back and forth until steam billowed at her feet. On the tips of her toes, she stepped into the open-ended shower and groaned as the water enveloped her entire body.

This was meant to be an easy task—go to Seattle, calm staff frustrations, establish a professional relationship with Grandiosity. Only she'd fumbled at every turn. She alienated Penny, again. She became entangled with a man who should've been off limits, again. And the repeated failures didn't stop her from wanting him. The desire was still there, clawing at her chest, squeezing at her lungs.

When had stupidity become her A-game?

She grabbed at the soap in the holder and scrubbed away the lasciviousness. Every inch of skin was scoured, cleansed, and yet the dirt remained, hiding in her pores, clinging to her hair. She couldn't get it off.

She didn't *want* to get it off.

The sensations that enveloped her when she was with Keenan were addictive. He touched places and inspired emotions she hadn't found enticing before. He rewired her morals and rewrote her goals.

He changed her.

But what was more important, a man or her job? Who meant more to her, her cousins or the guy who made her body sing?

A foreign click brushed her ears, followed by the slow sweep of the door. She sighed as the water sprayed her face and Keenan's presence reignited goosebumps.

"I should've turned the lock," she murmured and opened her eyes to the answer she had to quit denying. What she needed was sitting on the edge of the bath now dressed in cargo pants and a long-sleeve shirt, staring at her with unease.

She washed the soap from her body, wiping her hands over her thighs, her stomach, her breasts. He followed the progression and gripped the rim of the bath in clawed fingers. His admiration made every nerve stand to attention and beg for more. She could deny the world existed when she was trapped under that heated scrutiny.

He grabbed at the hem of his shirt and lifted, tugging it above his smooth stomach, his muscled pecs, and over his head. Then those talented fingers lowered to the buckle of his belt.

Oh, heavenly temptation. She salivated for a glimpse of what was tenting his pants. Her mouth insisted on a taste of what was beneath that zipper.

"No." She shut off the water and surveyed the four walls in search of a towel.

He raised his chin to her rejection, stood, and strode from the bathroom, leaving the sound of slammed cupboards in his wake. When he walked back into view, he held a towel outstretched in his arms, the fluffy white material coming with the unspoken message that he needed to be the one to drape it over her shoulders.

"Thank you." She turned and backed into him, letting him cover her. The closer she came, the stronger his scent grew. He'd put on aftershave—intoxicating, dreamy aftershave.

"Can you do me a favor?" She pivoted back in his direction and lazily ruffled her hair with the corner of the towel, letting him look his fill.

He met her eyes and raised a brow. A superior, playboy brow.

She shouldn't be doing this. Shouldn't be thinking what was running through her head, yet the thoughts wouldn't fade. "Are you able to finish what you started?"

"*What?*" He frowned.

She wrapped the damp material around her, securing it above her breasts, and walked from the room. She led him into the adjoining area and assumed a position from the past—her hands against the counter, her gaze focused on his reflection in the mirror. "Finish what you started the night of the bonfire."

He grinned, slow, lethargic, and so fucking sexy her pussy clenched with his approach. His body nestled behind her, his chest to her back, his crotch to her ass. His lips lowered, his mouth finding the decadent place where her shoulder met neck, striking the match of lust-filled insanity.

She moaned, unable to strengthen herself against the one kiss that raised every hair on her body. He awakened her with skill that defied logic. He was a prize, not a misgiving. A treat, not a punishment.

Sparks ignited at her thighs, his fingers creeping under the towel, inching higher. She rubbed against his erection, the rhythmic circle of her hips tormenting her clit and making it throb. "I'm falling for you, too." She craned her neck, giving him better access for his talented mouth. "I adore you."

His gaze cut to hers, his kiss-darkened lips glistening. His desire was tangible, and so was his affection—his unspoken promise.

"But I need to keep this a secret. I need you to tell Penny that we didn't work out. That I left with no plans to return."

His chin raised, his jaw clenched.

"Promise me."

He gave a gruff nod, his fingers digging into the bottom of the towel.

"Good." She grinned at him. "Now finish this."

A growl vibrated into her back as he smoothed his hands over the material at her thighs, her waist, up to her chest. With provoking restraint, he released the hold of the towel and let it fall to the floor in a flourish.

He appraised her, placing a high value on her body if the intensity of his gaze was anything to go by. There was a clink of his belt, a grate of a zipper, then the warmth of skin to skin at her thighs, his erection nestling into her ass.

She wiggled, adoring the friction, and received a hiss of appreciation in return.

He gripped the wet strands of her hair, pulling them into a makeshift pony to release droplets of water down her back. The invigorating wave washed along her spine, to the crack of her ass, and then the heat of her pussy. She gasped at the barely there brush of sensation, the fluid mingling with her own and cascading down her thighs.

"Do it again." She wanted more. Needed more.

He wove her hair around his fist, pulling to the point of pain, causing a rush of chilled water down her back. *Oh, God.* It was akin to being teased with a feather, the slightest movement igniting an explosion of tingles.

She closed her eyes, sucked in a breath, and became malleable as he leaned into her, bending her over. The brush of his palm wove around her hip, to her abdomen, then lower, to her clit. She jerked with the first touch, the initial rush of perfection. Her core fluttered, his fingers and the head of his cock sliding through her slickness at the same time.

"Keenan..."

He leaned to the left, reached for a drawer below the counter, rifled through the contents. She jolted when he slammed it shut with a huff and then leaned to the right to do the same. This time he came up with a shiny silver packet, his shoulders loosening in relief.

"Crisis averted?" she drawled.

He gave her a playful glare. "*Yes.*"

She grinned as he tore open a packet and sheathed himself, his muscled arms tensing with the chore. Then he was positioning himself between her thighs, the smooth latex parting her folds and gliding through her wet flesh. She bit her lip, waiting, and inhaled tiny little gasps. The buildup was enough to inspire an orgasm, the inner walls of her sex already pulsing, silently begging.

She bucked, instigating the first plunge of his cock into her sex. It was a culmination—their seduction coming full circle to finally start afresh. And God, it felt like heaven and hell. Right and wrong. Skirting responsibilities had never felt so good. The virginal buzz of professional defiance made him all the more alluring.

His focus met hers in the mirror while his fingers worked lazily back and forth on her clit. There was no rush for him, no starvation. He held her captive in his arms, in his gaze, and then slammed home, his cock driving a moan from her throat.

She wanted to deny the power he had over her, wanted to suppress it and hide it away for nobody else to see. Yet there it was, a vivid picture in the mirror, the truth her only vision.

"Make me come."

He grabbed her hair again, sending more water cascading down her back to the place where they joined. He pulled tight, controlling her, not only with his grip, but the overwhelming focus in those eyes. His stare touched her with the same ferocity as his hands. She could feel it sweeping over her neck, her breasts and lower, delving to the place where his fingers stroked her clit.

He moved inside her with mastery and control. Every plunge long and slow and deep, every withdrawal gradual and teasing and flawless. She moaned for more, sinking into his adoration and lapping it up with each gyration of her hips.

He didn't loosen his grip on her hair, he kept her like a slave. But the invisible bonds of attraction were tighter. They squeezed her lungs and tensed her womb. Everything about him was undeniable—the rough scratch of his stubble, the control in his arms, the passion in his lips.

The press on her clit became harder, and she moaned at the unconscious buck of her hips. The only sign of his waning restraint was the almost imperceptible flare of his nostrils. The tiniest flicker of irregular breathing that made her moan again, over and over, inspiring his thrusts to a faster rhythm.

She bit her lip to fight the need to kiss him, and gripped the wrist between her legs. All she needed was a little more. A tiny bit faster, the slightest bit harder. She clutched tight, silently begging with the clench of her hand, her molars, and her pussy.

"You make me wild."

He drove his teeth into her neck, announcing he felt the same. Obliterating her with a connection that was entirely wrong, yet undeniably right.

Her core fluttered, once, twice. The orgasm was there, within her grasp, and she closed her eyes to let pleasure take hold. But Keenan didn't allow it. His withdrawal from her body was severe, along with the aching release of her hair. He gripped her chin instead, demanding she watch before he nudged his cock back against her entrance and sank home in a harsh thrust.

He drove into her over and over, his features tightening, his restraint buckling. There was no way she could hold out. He was too thick inside her, the delicious fullness and the press against her clit absolute perfection.

She kept her eyes open this time and cried out with the first chaotic pulse of her pussy. Her nails dug into his wrist, her other hand reached for his hair, pulling his mouth to her neck. His suction and teeth ensured he'd retreat after leaving a mark.

His deep growl inched under her skin, his rhythm lost to mindless bucking as he entwined their euphoria. It didn't stop. Her core continued to succumb to his orgasm, clutching tighter and tighter until finally satiation and exhaustion slowed their movements.

Bliss faded, but Keenan didn't. There was no retreat. He held her, his hand leaving her pussy to weave around her waist, the other resting gently at the base of her neck. His lips fell to her shoulder, again and again. The peppering of butterfly kisses almost brought her to her knees.

This wasn't mere carnality. It never had been. Since they first met, something more had bubbled beneath the surface, demanding to be heard through the silence.

She'd been attracted to Keenan at first sight. She'd been intrigued by him before leaving her aunt's house the night she arrived in Seattle. Her lust had hit a benchmark at the bonfire, but through each day spent together, the most influential sensation was the aching beat in her chest. Her heart was driving this. Her affection was the dictator.

"I came so close to going home." She met his focus in the mirror. "I planned to leave the day I walked into your father's office."

"*I know.*"

She hoped so, because one wrong move by either of them could put her back in the same position. "Just remember your promise." She reached over her shoulder and ran a hand through his hair. "If Penny causes trouble again..."

He shook his head, his focus turning determined, demanding she quit her train of thought.

He didn't understand. He had no clue what it was like to ponder a future with him. To paint the happiness in vivid clarity within a woman's imagination. She was sure Penny would've felt the same.

There was little doubt her cousin still did.

"If I were her—" She'd what? Spencer had never inspired feelings that wrought havoc on her system. She'd never been in a relationship where her next breath seemed dependent on someone else, like they were pulling it from her lungs.

Keenan raised a brow, asking the same question.

"I'd fight for you," she admitted. And there wasn't the slightest stretch of truth in her admission.

Email Correspondence

Date: 27th December

Subject: Why didn't you fight?

Savannah,

You said you'd fight. Do you remember?

On Thanksgiving, you said if I were yours, you'd fight. I remember because I held tight to those words, hoping they might save us in the end.

But you didn't fight. You gave up. You walked away, fled Seattle, and proceeded to ignore every email and text I sent your way. You didn't even let me explain.

When will you make good on your promise?

Keenan

Twenty-Six

One night in his bed turned into two. At first, she'd packed a change of clothes and her toothbrush. Then it was her overnight bag. And more recently, her entire suitcase. They'd morphed from lovers, into a couple, reaching relationship goals she'd never aspired to achieve.

The only nights they spent apart were the ones she refused to share in his presence. Every Monday and Thursday when he held after-hours meetings with Penny. At his house. Alone. It was a routine he assured her they'd been doing for years to combat his restricted communication in the office, and no matter how much she loathed their connection, she had to trust him.

If he wanted Penny, he could have her with the lowering of a pants zipper. Yet he spent every free moment by Savannah's side. For weeks, they isolated themselves in his mansion. He taught her the basics of sign language, she introduced him to a text-to-voice app that allowed them to communicate when she wasn't in a position to read his lips or his cell screen. She learned the intricacies of Keenan Black—the ones he allowed her to see—and it seemed she hadn't scratched the surface of the stories he held inside.

He never mentioned his family. He wouldn't explain why he hadn't seen them at Thanksgiving or if he had plans to share Christmas with them. Father and son had a working relationship. Period. She assumed it had something to do with his silence, but she couldn't gain clarity because he refused to acknowledge the topic. His lack of speech was off limits. And she didn't have the callousness to push him. Not fully. She always asked questions, and every so often he'd suck in a breath and part those gorgeous lips in what she thought would be a moment of trust. Then he'd shut himself off, escaping in a look of sorrow that made her vow not to ask again.

Once the seclusion of home life became too much, they ventured out. She drove to Snoqualmie Falls while he successfully seduced her with the sterile, robotic sound of text-to-voice. Another day was spent at Point Defiance Zoo, and he'd recently surprised her with a scenic flight over Seattle.

This morning marked the final hours of their first weekend escape. He'd rented an immaculate cabin in Leavenworth. A one bedroom, one bathroom paradise with the prettiest view she'd ever seen through the wide open windows looking out over the snow and the Wenatchee River.

"I guess you didn't want to join me?" She poked her head outside the bathroom door and finished drying herself with a towel. He was a slave to work, but every time she showered, he wound up naked beside her. Whenever she began preparing meals, he discarded all his communication devices and pitched in. And whenever she was in a wicked mood, unable to tear her suggestive stare away from him, he'd pour her a glass of wine and taunt her with his smirk until they became a mass of tangled arms and legs and lips.

He was carnal, successful, and cavalier.

He was perfect.

Only this time he didn't respond.

She yanked on her pants and blouse, then inched her head out of the bathroom. Her pulse spiked for a moment, waiting for him to jump out at her, to shove her against the closest wall and steal her breath with his kiss. But he didn't. There was no sound of footfalls, no television, only the crackle of the fire from the main room.

"Keenan?" She padded through the bedroom to find him motionless on the couch.

He was sitting upright, his head resting against the back of the sofa like he'd sat down and instantly became overwhelmed with exhaustion.

"I didn't realize you were so tired," she whispered, creeping closer. "Did I steal your stamina, grandpa?"

His lips kicked, the tiniest grin announcing his consciousness. She'd learned to recognize his fake smiles, the ones he gave to placate strangers. But this was one of hers. He gave her patented grins and smirks. Ones exclusively made for her.

"Is it time for your nap?" She stopped in front of him and squealed when he leapt at her, pulling her down to be mercilessly tickled.

"Don't!" She screamed and wiggled for her life. "Please!"

He ended the torture with a kiss, tangling their tongues, combing his hands through her hair. When he backed away, she whimpered, still unable to come to terms with never being sated. No matter how much he gave, she wanted more. More kisses, more affection, more attention. She didn't think she would ever get enough. At least not in the weeks she had left.

"Is that all I get?" She pouted.

He guided her to straddle his thighs, his heavy-lidded eyes staring back at her. There was no lust, no carnality. He was devoid of energy.

"You *are* exhausted." She cupped his cheeks, taking in his heavy breathing and pale skin. "Are you getting sick?"

He shook his head, the movement slow and unconvincing.

"Then what's wrong?"

He reached for his cell on the armrest and typed with a smirk— *You're killing me. I can't keep up with you.*

"Really?" She rocked slowly against his crotch, proving otherwise. "I don't think all of you agrees."

He gave a breath of a chuckle and closed his eyes, letting his head fall back against the sofa.

"Keenan?"

Something was wrong. A slowly building throb of guilt started to take over her chest. She should've been paying more attention. She should've noticed sooner. He'd been less energetic for days. Their nights had begun ending earlier, the mornings starting later. She'd vaguely laughed at the idea that his fatigue may be a case of too much horizontal exercise and not enough sleep. But this was more than that.

He wrapped his arms around her and continued to rest.

"Would you tell me if something was wrong?"

His eyes opened and a lack of reassurance stared back at her, the same wariness she'd come to expect when she pried.

He shook his head. *"Nothing is wrong."* He brushed the stray hair behind her ear and smiled. *"Tired."*

He was lying. Placating her.

She knew better than to fight for answers. He never caved to her determination. He only ever told her what he wanted her to know. Even though these moments had begun to fade, it was that stubborn secrecy that had made her cling tight to the words her heart wanted to give to him. Three little words she'd never spoken because she wouldn't release her last shield against vulnerability if he wouldn't either.

But she could give him something. A tiny piece of her that nobody else had. "You know, I never thought I'd care about a man, the way I do for you."

His eyes softened, the tiniest spark of understanding gleaming back at her.

"My father left when I was a teenager. For me, it was out of the blue. I didn't see it coming. I didn't even know there was a problem in my parents' marriage. He just left. One day he was my father, the next he wasn't. He never called. Didn't write..." A gentle hand swept her hair behind her ear, comforting the memories she usually chose to ignore. "I didn't think it affected me much. I was leaving school at the time and starting my career. I kept myself busy and pretended it was a part of growing up."

But it wasn't normal, and it had affected her. How else could she explain the lack of love in her life? She'd broken contact with Dominic, wasted time on relationships she knew had no future, and cocooned herself in a safe existence.

"I've never had this." She waved a lazy hand between them. "I've never felt like this."

"Me, too," he mouthed.

Her heart squeezed at the sincerity focused back on her. It was true. He did feel the same way, just maybe not enough to divulge whatever was hiding in his eyes. She sat there, taking in his motionless affection, his silent appreciation. Waiting. Hoping.

There was another wistful swipe of his finger through her hair. A brush of his thumb along her cheek. He bathed her in adoration and continued to leave her starved for his secrets.

"Let's go home." She placed a gentle kiss on his lips and scooted backward to stand on the floor. He wasn't ready yet, and that was okay. She could deal. At this point, she had no choice because leaving him wasn't an option. "You can sleep while I drive."

He did. Keenan dozed the entire way home while she watched the snow slowly dwindle the further she drove toward Seattle. She wanted to mother him, to escort him to bed, wrap him in blankets and figure out how the hell to make chicken noodle soup.

Only smothering him would give him more control. She needed to do the opposite to remind him of her impending farewell.

"We're here." Her words were soft, slowly lulling him into the land of the living.

She opened the gates with the spare remote he'd given her, and drove to the front of his house. Her sternum ached as she cut the engine and met him at the back of the car.

He reached for her luggage, and she placed a hand on top of the suitcase to stay him. "Leave mine there."

He raised a brow, not releasing the handle.

"I've been monopolizing your time for weeks. You need a break to recharge."

He shook his head and began lifting the case.

"Yes." This time she pressed down harder, and one by one lifted his fingers from the handle. "You're unwell."

"*No.*"

"No?" She closed the trunk, well aware she'd almost taken off his hand in the process. "Then what is it?"

His narrowed gaze returned, the fast snap of something defensive falling between them. Everything had been smooth since Thanksgiving. Too smooth. Too choreographed to perfection. Keenan had helped her to find staff to fill the vacant positions. Penny had become a fading memory within the Rydel building. She'd even told Spencer she'd met someone, and he hadn't lost his mind, only his control over profanity for a few minutes.

A future with Keenan was within her grasp. They were a breath away from together forever. The only thing stopping her from searching local employment opportunities and instigating a permanent relocation plan was that look. That painful knowledge that he hadn't given his all to her yet.

"Forget it." She didn't want to cause a fight. "I know you have things you don't want to tell…" It was a push, a provocation.

He pulled out his cell, typed—*You mean everything to me, Savannah*

Her heart clenched, practically initiating a cardiac event.

"Then trust me."

He grabbed her wrist, his expression screaming for understanding. "*I will.*"

"Just not today, right?"

He winced.

"It's okay." She soothed the discomfort between them with a soft smile. "I know you're not ready to share everything with me. I can wait." At least a few more weeks, anyway. The days left to discuss the future were dwindling. She didn't want to force his secrets from him with an ultimatum, but she also wouldn't start uprooting her San Francisco life if she didn't have all of him.

"Text or video call me before you go to bed." She kissed his cheek and backtracked. "Make sure you rest."

He stepped away from the car, his arms crossed over his chest and a petulant frown marring his brow. A little extra distance would be good for them. It would also be her first opportunity to start Christmas shopping.

"Don't be grumpy." She opened her driver's door and gave a sneaky smile even though she didn't want to leave. "As soon as you're full of energy, I plan on stealing it away again."

Twenty-Seven

The drive from his house was more desolate, the solitary trees waving in the breeze, telling her to go back. She had to do something to drag away his defenses. At least push them to the side a little.

But how?

Time didn't helped. Passion hadn't either. She had to give him more.

"What if I tell you all my secrets?" she whispered to herself. "And said that I was so close to being in love with you, so close to being entirely vulnerable and all I needed was your trust? What if I told you that it hurts to breathe when I think about boarding that plane to San Francisco? If I gave you those secrets, would you give me yours?"

She imagined his response, the subtle lift of his chin, the shock in his eyes.

And still it wouldn't be enough.

He'd already described his emotions in vivid detail. He'd painted a picture of affection and lust. Love had been on his lips, too.

She needed to do something bigger. To forget about her previous stipulations and the restraints on the relationship that revolved around secrecy. For weeks she kept their time together to herself.

A few people in Seattle were aware she had a lover. Kelly had specifics, Grant only had an active imagination. Neither questioned her. It was an unspoken rule, and the only thing to show for her time away from her hotel room were the surveillance cameras in the parking lot.

She'd hidden Keenan. Not merely for her career, or to ward off Penny. It was also to gain a foothold on whatever was building between them. She enjoyed the hell out of his company and didn't want anyone encroaching on their space. But maybe it was time to let it all go.

The answer to gaining Keenan's trust could be as easy as telling the world they were together.

She pulled to the side of the road, a smile tugging her lips as she clicked her cell into the hands-free unit. Her heart and her hands trembled in excitement with the press of the call button. The ring tone had her holding her breath.

"Yeah."

The unenthusiastic welcome muted her buzz. "Hey, Dominic." She wanted him to hear the news from her first. Not second-hand when her mom went on a gossip spree. He deserved to know she was in love, even though he hadn't thought it possible with Keenan.

"Hey, yourself." There was no charm, none of the usual playfulness.

"It's been a while. I was hoping to catch up and see how you're doin'. How was your Thanksgiving?"

"Evidently, not as busy as yours, because I had the decency of picking up the phone."

Damn, that swipe cut deep. The guilt over dismissing his Thanksgiving call had weighed on her for days. She hadn't been willing to lie to him about her whereabouts. The only option had been to keep her distance. She'd messaged him back, claiming to be on the verge of losing phone battery and hadn't found the guts to call him since. But they'd texted over the weeks. Only now it was becoming evident that his short replies weren't due to being busy.

"I'd worked late with a wedding the night before." She still wouldn't lie to him. "Comprehension wasn't my strong point for days after."

He scoffed, the sound tinged with loathing. "No kidding."

She gripped the steering wheel and tried to imagine the look on his face as he spoke. Tried and failed. Dominic wasn't prone to anger around her. They were buddies. Friends. Or they had been until the bug crawled up his ass. "What's that supposed to mean?"

"That's supposed to mean that I'm sick of this bullshit. And I'm fucking annoyed that you ruined our Thanksgiving."

Something blossomed in her chest. Something dark and grave and unwelcomed. "Ruined..."

"Mom was upset that Keenan cancelled lunch without notice. Penny was an A-grade bitch because he was with you. And frankly, I was fucking disappointed that, yet again, you didn't take my advice and stay away."

Her mouth gaped. Her throat tightened. The visual of Penny as an A-grade bitch was crystal clear, thankfully keeping her mind away from the image of Aunt Michelle's reaction to Thanksgiving.

"Why are you telling me this now?" Her voice was low, barely audible through the white noise. "Why didn't you yell at me back then?"

"I was angry. Still am. But I'd warned you—"

"I like him, Dominic. I *really* like him." There, she'd said it.

Her chest expanded a little. Relief sped through her veins. The truth wouldn't set her free from this conversation, but it gave her hope for when she was with Keenan next. "I'm contemplating moving to Seattle."

"Savvy, you're only history repeating itself. Trust me," he offered softly, as if she were a child who didn't understand. "Contemplating anything with him is a mistake."

"Why, because he can't speak? You think I don't know him because he hasn't given me words?" She shook her head. "Well, you're wrong. I've been with him since Thanksgiving. I've practically lived with the man for weeks." All his secrets may not be at her disposal, but she understood all the important parts. She knew he loved her. She knew he was determined and focused and smart. She knew they fit together—heart, mind, and soul. And she also knew her life was far more vibrant with him in it. Words or not.

"No, you know what he wants you to know and nothing more."

"Well, that's enough for me."

"Good for you. Just don't expect me to pick you up when he knocks you down."

She scoffed. "He won't." She couldn't fault Keenan's commitment to her. She was almost ready to jump on a sword for him, at the very least stick up for him against Dominic's assault. "If you were a true friend, you'd let him be happy."

"He's not happy, Savannah. That's what I'm trying to tell you. If he was happy, you'd know the truth."

"I guess we need to agree to disagree."

"To be honest, I don't need to do shit. He's asked more than enough of my family because of you. I'm not giving any more. While you're with him, don't bother calling me again."

Air escaped her lungs in a painful exhale. He was no longer giving her advice. He was laying down the law. Making her choose—him or Keenan.

A childhood of memories flashed through her mind. His smiles, his laughter. The times they'd caused trouble and mischief, along with the unending conversations about all those life or death challenges of school. All of it was there. Just there. Then suddenly it was gone.

"Don't worry," she whispered. "I can commit to that."

Twenty-Eight

She turned the car around, ignoring the desolate road and taunting trees. Sick or not, she needed to see him for a few seconds more. To hold him. To reassure herself that this slight case of apprehension was unwarranted before she spent the night alone.

If it was Penny's history Dominic was referring to, then it wasn't a repeat at all. Keenan had told her that much. They'd had a fling. An affair based on sex and nothing else. Just like Savannah's mistake with Spencer.

What she had with Keenan was deeper.

Steady and sturdy. Yep, they were solid...

"Shit." She slammed her hands against the steering wheel and cursed her cousin's name. She had to forget it. Ignore it. Put it to the furthest spot in the back of her mind and throw stones at it.

Whatever jealous, childish obsession the Augustines had over Keenan wasn't worth fretting over. She was going to make this right. Tomorrow morning she'd call Mathew Rydel and give him the news. She'd admit to falling in love with the competition and assure him, contrary to the truth, that it hadn't affected her role in Seattle.

Then she'd call Spencer. And her mother. She was going to let the whole world know she was owning her relationship with Keenan. That she knew him better than anyone else and was laying her heart on the line to prove it.

She knew Keenan. She knew what made him laugh and what made him angry. She could read his thoughts and sense his unease. She doubted anyone else in the world could read him better.

His house loomed ahead, the building filled with memories that made her heart grow reassured. She opened his front gates with a press of the remote button, and raised his garage door with another. She wasn't going to ask for answers. Nope. She was going to stifle that crap. What she was going to do was walk in there, kiss the apprehension from her lungs, and stick by him while he overcame the flu or cold or whatever illness was dragging him down.

She was going to love him just to spite all the people trying to pull her away. She was going to devour every inch of his skin. Mark him with her teeth and savor him with her tongue.

Her grin spread ear to ear as she parked in his garage and cut the engine. This was what was going to get him to open up. She could feel it.

The faint whoosh of running water welcomed her into the house. The soft tumble of her belly accompanied her enthusiastic footfalls down the hall. From the staircase at the front door, she could hear the shower and a soft hum of music from his room. He would be naked. Wet. Entirely lickable.

The higher she climbed, the louder her heart pounded in her ears. The rush of water became clear, and the lyrics floating through the air were almost decipherable. But it was her chest that begged to be heard. This time she wasn't going to hold back. She was going to say those words. Those three, vulnerable words. Each one slowly. Succinctly.

I love you.

She reached his door and poked her head inside, finding his suitcase still packed near his bedside table. She could see him through the open bathroom door, too, the water cascading down his back, over his ass, along his muscled thighs. He was divine. Truly a magnificent specimen.

Only, the image before her didn't sit right. Her intuition was sounding an alarm.

He turned toward her, his eyes closed as he scrubbed white foam from his hair. She'd never forget that sight—his gorgeousness, his appeal that was wrapped up in a bundle of pure agonizing torture.

She struggled not to retch as pain exploded in her chest.

There was no radio, no tunes flowing from his cell that sat dormant on his bed. His lips were moving, not in mime or in breath. His mouth was dancing in song, the melodic sound of his voice filling the air.

The verbal betrayal didn't cease as he turned off the water and opened the shower door to reach for a towel. Lyrics continued to haunt her, sinking into her brain, never to be forgotten. Bile began mass production, the churning of her belly making her cling to the doorframe for support. As he began drying himself, she inched out of view, numb to the sound of his ringing cell on the bed between them.

There was no will to move. No voice to scream.

He padded to the foot of the bed, the towel secured at his hips as he swept up his cell and answered the call.

"Dominic." His smooth, effortless address to her cousin sliced through her skin like a razor. He had a voice. He had a smooth, deep, masculine voice that Dominic had known about.

They had all known, hadn't they?

"W-what did you s-say to her?" The accusation in his tone pulled a gasp from her throat. They were talking about her. Discussing what had happened to bring her here.

Stormy eyes snapped to hers and undiluted panic came face to face with her pure heartbreak. He dropped his cell to the bed as her lips parted and panted breaths escaped without permission. She raised her chin to combat the emotional assault. "Don't stop on my account." Her throat constricted. "I'll go so you can continue your conversation."

Hysteria set in, thick and cloying. She lunged for the door, slammed it shut in a vain attempt to stop him chasing her, and then ran.

Her progression was mindless. Senseless. She couldn't think past the remembrance of his tone, couldn't breathe through the humiliation. With every pathetic, mimed word and every text-to-voice, he'd degraded her, making her worthless. Making what they shared meaningless.

Why? She wanted to scream the word and have it vibrate off the walls.

Her feet slowed, the questions compiling. Then she heard the sweep of his door, the loud thwack as it ricocheted off the wall, and then his predatory footfalls.

She took the stairs two at a time. There wasn't an excuse that could ease her, not one explanation that could settle the nausea. She'd fallen for someone who didn't exist. A future had been planned with a man she didn't know.

"*S-s-stop!*"

The violent stutter echoed into the lobby and pulled her up short. Ice shivered down her spine and rooted her feet in place. There was nothing polished or fluid about his speech. It was fractured, split in torturous pieces. Turning wasn't an option. She couldn't face him, but yearning took over and her feet swiveled without thought.

He stood at the top of the stairs, his destructive glare shrinking her. His hands fisted at his sides as water trickled from his hair, down his cheeks. His chest was thrumming, large breaths shaking his shoulders. He opened his mouth and she stiffened, preparing for another knife to embed her chest.

"Y-y-you w-w-w..." His lips snapped shut. Horror contorted his features, then it morphed, growing into something more volatile, changing into an emotion she couldn't fathom—anger.

She stared in fascination, unable to comprehend how he could be the guilty party, yet the one with all the rage.

"F-fuck y-your p-p-pity."

Each word was maimed more than the last, casting aspersions over every day they'd shared.

"Pity?" She shook her head. "Oh, no. I don't pity you. I *despise* you," she spat. "I *detest* you." Her lips trembled, her eyes burned. Her world was crumpling at her feet and it was all because of him. He'd created a life that didn't exist. He'd bathed her in lies and made her fall in love with them. "I've been hurt by words before, Keenan. But never have they inflicted as much pain as your silence."

They stared each other down, his nostrils flaring, her shoulders holding strong.

She grieved for the future they'd lost. She mourned the memories that were now unthinkable. Most of all, she agonized over the pounding heartache making it hard to stand tall. She had loved him. True love. Real love. The feelings that would never have allowed for betrayal and callous deception.

"Just in case there was anything lost in translation..." She glared, taking his animosity head on. "We're done."

His chest convulsed harder, up down, up down. In a flash of movement he sank his fist into the drywall, leaving a gaping hole as he withdrew. Then he admitted defeat. She could see it. His shoulders slumped, his eyes lost their ferocity, and he simply walked away, disappearing down the upper-level hall.

She stood immobile. Her feet mere inches from the stairs, her heart mere pulses from its last beat.

Dominic was right. She didn't know the first thing about Keenan. He was a stranger, a manipulator, and a thief. He'd stolen everything she had to offer—the security of her job, her family, and her heart. He'd taken everything. And she'd let him. She'd given it freely, even after repeated warnings.

"We're done," she whispered to herself and walked to the garage. Tears blurred her vision as she opened her car door, sank into the driver's seat, and focused on her cell in the hands-free station.

It sang to her, offering an escape plan at the press of a button. One she couldn't pass up. A few taps on the screen later and the monotonous ring carried through her car.

"Savannah?"

She sucked in a sob and squeezed tight to keep it down. "Spencer, I've burned out. I can't do this anymore. I need to come home."

Twenty-Nine

Date: 28th December

Subject: Goodbye

Dear Savannah,

'I'm sorry' seems like a poor excuse for an apology. It's ridiculous how many times I've written those words only to delete them because they don't hold enough conviction.

But I am.

I'm completely and utterly ruined by how sorry I am.

There's no explanation to appease the guilt. I knew I was hurting you without your knowledge. It was deliberate. I kept telling myself that this thing between us was only temporary. You were always meant to leave. And with your departure, the deceit would've died with it. Yet you tattooed yourself under my skin, and even now that you're gone, I can't let you go.

I don't expect you to want to understand what it's like to be a capable man stuck in an incapable body. But the hard lessons in life have taught me that a lack of speech is intriguing and challenging, yet an uncompromising adult stutter is a nuisance and the easiest way to be degraded by everyone—professionals, friends, and strangers alike.

I rarely share my ability to talk or the inadequacy that comes with it.

Apart from my father, who despises my lack of fluent speech, Dominic, Penelope, and your aunt, nobody else knows of my secret. The staff at Grandiosity aren't aware. I'm not in contact with anyone from my school years, and I've distanced myself from extended family, too.

So although your humiliation is justified, please be aware there was no malice behind it. It was merely my way of trying to stand tall beside the perfection of you.

And you are perfect, Savannah.

You're everything.

My everything.

But now it's time to stop torturing you with my contact, and say goodbye. I won't email you again. You now have all the things I couldn't say while we were together, and the only thing left is what you need to know moving forward.

I adore you.

I've adored you since you first teased me with your smile on the Augustines' porch. There will never be another woman to fill the hole you've left. And I hope, one day, you will forgive me for breaking both our hearts.

Keenan

He sat back in his chair, reread his email and tried to ignore the overabundance of estrogen woven between the letters. He wished he could tell her more. Not only his nonsensical feelings, he wanted her to be aware of the history behind his decisions.

But it was time to quit communication.

Weeks had passed without a word from her. He couldn't gain her attention. Not from the texts, or the attempt to video call. Not even the flowers and expensive gifts. Nothing inspired a response.

Not a damn thing.

Her rejection was far more aggressive than the years of pity he'd endured. Every refresh of his inbox stole a piece of his pride, and he'd do it again and again and again if he didn't think he was hurting her with each slide of his name amongst her emails.

She didn't want to hear from him. Not now. Not ever. And it was understandable. There wasn't anything more vile than a man who shielded himself from pain by exposing a woman to it.

"Are you coming to family dinner?" Penelope asked from his office doorway. "We're expecting you."

He shook his head and clicked on the button to send his email into cyberspace. He didn't have the strength to face the Augustines yet. Solitude was preferred, especially when Dominic had made it clear he wasn't welcome.

"Your silent treatment is starting to piss me off." She stepped into his office and clicked the door shut behind her. "Why am I being punished?"

She knew why. It didn't stop her from asking, though. Penelope had taunted him non-stop since he vowed he wouldn't talk unless it was to Savannah. If he couldn't speak to the woman he loved, he'd speak to no one.

Chivalrous? No. It was an excuse to slink further into his own little world and ignore everyone else's existence.

He shooed her with a flick of his wrist and an annoyed glare. Hurting Penelope wasn't something he enjoyed either, but this situation brought back memories of when he'd deceived her in the same way. The only difference was her willingness to forgive and the constant reminder that she still wanted to be with him.

If only he loved her in return, this never would've happened. But his feelings didn't mimic hers. She'd grown to be like the sister he'd never had among the family who had taken him in as one of their own. The Augustines were the only people he'd trusted with his stutter, and it hadn't come easily. One word turned into two, a greeting into a farewell, and soon he felt comfortable slipping his voice into their conversation.

He did it on his own terms, in his own time, which meant he didn't butcher his communication like he did everywhere else. Savannah wouldn't understand that, though. She wouldn't realize it took months and months of constant nagging from Dominic to get him to attend 'family dinner' after he'd broken Penelope's heart. She wouldn't know it took over a year to answer the simplest questions from Mrs. Augustine over what portions he wanted at dinner.

Nobody knew that but them. And he'd thought that would always be the case.

"I wouldn't recommend letting down my mother again," Penelope continued. "Ignore her enough and she'll drive into the city and drag you back to her dinner table."

He conceded a half-hearted smile. Mrs. Augustine wouldn't dare. She was too sweet. So sweet, in fact, that her kindness had meant he'd been able to manipulate her into keeping secrets from her only niece.

"Come on." She approached his desk and cocked her hip against the wood. "You're spending New Year's with us. I won't take no for an answer. So you should come tonight to get the awkwardness over and done with."

"*No*," he mouthed and stood to retrieve his coat from the back of his seat. His current attitude wasn't conducive for celebration. He'd spent Christmas alone. He'd do the same with the bringing of the New Year.

He slid his arms into the thick material and made to step around his desk, only to be blocked by her slender body.

"Keenan..." She placed a hand on his chest and looked up at him with those beautiful blue eyes that Savannah had threatened to claw. "When are you going to let me in?"

He ignored the question, her touch, and the reminder from the past, and repositioned his collar.

"Refusing to speak won't make anything better."

He stepped away, but she countered, sliding back into his path. Her hand lowered to his waist, underneath the jacket, to the thin business shirt beneath. "She's not coming back." Her pretty face turned somber. "You need to let it go."

She was right.

Settlement was tomorrow, and if Savannah was attending the scheduled meeting in the morning he would've heard of her arrival by now.

"Don't do this to your—"

His computer dinged with an incoming email, the innocent, most mundane sound resulting in the stiffening of his entire body.

"She's not going to get in contact with you." Her eyes implored him. "Why are you doing this to yourself?"

She wasn't wrong. She hadn't been in any assessment or statement since Savannah left. But not confirming on his office computer would only mean he'd pull out his cell to make sure. His imagination was more of an optimist than he liked to admit.

He backtracked and leaned over his office chair to stand immobile, his gaze caught on the unread email sitting at the top of his inbox.

"What is it?"

His throat tightened and the slightest flicker of hope ignited in a chest devoid of warmth. Her name was there, at the top of his screen, the accompanying subject read—

AUTOMATED RESPONSE: Out of Office.

Penelope came to his side. "Open it."

He already was, his fingers doing a double-click on the mouse.

Please be advised that as of 27th of December I will be in Seattle overseeing the changeover of the Rydel property. Once settlement is complete, I will be taking an extended vacation and any queries should be forwarded to my assistant, Rebecca, who will endeavor to find the right person to answer your questions.

Kind regards
Savannah Hamilton - Rydel Hotels

His stomach bottomed out.

"She's here," Penelope whispered.

In Seattle. At Rydel. Mere blocks away.

He turned to the woman who was supposed to have ensured he was immediately informed of Savannah's arrival and signed—*Did you ask our staff to keep an eye out for her*?

Her lips worked in a blatant admission of neglect. "It was an unprofessional request. I knew we'd find out soon enough if she returned."

He exhaled a breath at the invisible blow she'd landed to his gut and strode for the door.

"Keenan, please." Her footsteps followed behind him. "Let me help."

He swung around and glared. *Help*, he signed and backed it up with a violent mime of his lips. *Why*?

"I want you to be happy." She swallowed, hard, her delicate throat convulsing in a torturous movement. "I know there's never going to be an 'us' again. I know you don't love me the same way I love you. I struggled to come to terms with that... And then you being with her, even when it was only casual... I struggled so hard, Keenan. But now, all I want is for you to be happy."

He hated her pain. He hated it almost as much as he hated the memory of Savannah's unshed tears.

"Let me help," she pleaded. "Let me come with you."

Her hand raised between them, trying to forge a connection, and all he could do was stare. He'd hurt Savannah. He'd hurt Penny and Dominic and Mrs. Augustine. Wherever he went, he left a trail of destruction and a path of tears he never wanted to be associated with.

He just wanted to be normal. For every moment of his life to be devoid of degradation, or the fight to show his worth. To live without scrutiny like he had when he'd been with Savannah—the two of them in seclusion, away from judgment and negativity.

"*No.*" He grabbed her hand to place a placating kiss on her knuckles. Having her at his side would be a blessing. He needed to establish Savannah's room number, gain access to her floor, and communicate with anyone who got in his way. But Penelope wasn't the person to drag along for the ride.

"You need me." She squared her shoulders and reminded him of how many times he'd cursed his father for employing such a stubborn woman. "Believe me. I know how to make her angry, but I also know how to make her listen. I'll be able to help."

Fuck. He didn't have the luxury of arguing about this with her. Even if he won, she'd follow.

"*Okay.*" He nodded and moved to open the office door.

"Thank you."

He shook his head, disregarding her words because clearly they weren't necessary. *If* they did find Savannah and *if* she did spare him a moment of her time, he was almost positive they would all be left broken and bloodied in the aftermath.

Actually, with Penelope at his side he was sure it was a foregone conclusion.

Thirty

"**I**'ll do you a deal." Penelope placed a hand on the Rydel reception counter and batted her lashes at the woman staring back at her. "You cut the bullshit and tell me which room is reserved under Savannah Hamilton, and you get to keep your job once we take over at midnight."

"Ma'am," the woman smiled, smug as hell, "as I've told you before, Savannah's name isn't registered as a guest. I'm happy to show you the search screen if you don't believe me."

They'd been drilling her with questions for ten minutes. From what he could tell, she hadn't given them false information. Yes, Savannah was in Seattle. Yes, she'd been in the hotel today. No, she wasn't scheduled to attend the final hand-over meeting in the morning.

If she wasn't lying, that left him with fewer opportunities to win her back.

"So, she's staying here, but not under her own details?" Penelope grated. "Is it a false name, maybe?" She turned to him and gave a this-woman-is-going-to-die look. "Do you know her favorite Disney character? 'Cause we could be guessing fake names all damn night."

No. It wasn't a Disney character. He feared it was far worse as he signed seven excruciatingly painful letters.

Penelope responded with a wince and turned back to the receptionist. "How about Spencer Rydel? Is she staying with him?"

A bright smile beamed back at them. "From my knowledge, yes, she is staying in a room booked under his name."

"Fuck." Penelope swung around again. "Do you still want to do this?"

He inclined his head, prepared for whatever punishment he had to take. It hadn't escaped his mind that she might have gone home to her ex. The guy had been all over her during the wedding, only pausing his affection to try his luck with Penelope.

"Give me a room number."

"806," the receptionist rattled off without looking at her screen.

"That's Savannah's room?"

"Oh, no." The woman snickered and tippy tapped on her keyboard. "You didn't specify. And besides, I can't give you that information. It's not only a breach—"

"Yes, yes, a breach of company policy."

"—it's also a safety issue..." She lowered her voice. "However, if I go to the bathroom and someone looks at the search I've pulled up on my screen, it's beyond my control." The woman stepped back from her computer and unclipped a security pass from her pants pocket. "I'm just going to leave this here." She slid the plastic card next to her keyboard as she eyed the other receptionist on the far end of the desk.

Penelope didn't spare a second waiting for the woman to leave. She snatched the security card, handed it over her shoulder to him, then turned the computer monitor around.

"There's two rooms under his name." She spared him a quick glance. "509 and the penthouse."

He held up a hand. *"Five."* He was pinning his hopes on Spencer booking the penthouse for himself and a standard room for Savannah.

Pinning and praying.

"Lead the way."

He strode through the chaos of the lobby, maneuvering around employees taking furniture into the building and others who were taking it out. The elevator ride was hell. Thirty seconds of contemplative agony, where he questioned his motives.

Then his knuckles were on door 509 and he began to knock with hard strokes.

"Do you want me to say anything specific?" Penelope asked.

He shook his head and stared at the door, wordlessly begging it to open. A ragged breath tore from his lungs, then another, and another until the lock released and he was staring at the woman who owned him.

She stood in the doorway, dressed in a long navy skirt and buttoned up cream blouse that clung tight to her breasts. She was the epitome of his future, his happiness rolled up into one sensational package of sexy legs, gorgeous hazel eyes, and the unmistakable jut of her dignified chin.

The mere sight of her made him feel worthless and determined to succeed at the same time. Hopeless and hopeful.

"Mr. Black?" Her expression was schooled, not an ounce of shock showing through her composed features. "Can I help you?"

He squared his shoulders and tried to relax. Tried and failed spectacularly. "We n-n-need—" *Fuck.* He hated that sound. Despised it. There wasn't an inch of his skin that wasn't crawling from revulsion, but he'd withstand it. He'd do anything. For her. "T-to talk."

She blinked at him, one hand clutching the door, the other pressed against the frame. "Is this about settlement? Because Spencer would be the best person to speak to. I'm only here to ensure all Rydel property is taken from the building and to say goodbye to friends."

Her voice had wavered the slightest bit. She wasn't unaffected by him, and the knowledge encouraged confidence.

"*No,*" he mouthed.

"Everything under control, Savannah?" The male voice carried from her room, practically neutering him.

She kept her gaze trained on his as a large, familiar frame came up behind her.

Spencer.

Fucker.

The guy placed a hand on her shoulder, a protective hand Keenan would've wanted to break on a good day, but when it caused Savannah to stiffen, he itched to fracture every bone in the man's body.

"I'm fine." She stepped to the side, letting the asshole through. "Can you give me a minute?"

"Sure." Spencer jerked his chin in greeting. "Good to see you both again." His tone implied otherwise.

"You, too," Penelope added after seconds of awkward silence.

Keenan sensed the guy's departure but didn't take his focus from Savannah who stood tall before him, waiting for answers.

"Can we come inside?" Penelope broke the silence.

"Why?" Savannah addressed him. "If it's not about the settlement, then there's nothing else to discuss."

"Quit the charade," Penelope muttered, "and just let him explain."

"The charade?" Savannah shot a glare at her cousin. "That's rich."

He pulled his cell, prepared to type whatever he could to gain enough trust to buy some time.

"Save it."

He glanced up to see her eying his phone. There was no malice, no anger. She was devoid of emotion. Entirely flat.

"I don't want any more explanations."

Penelope sighed, long and pained and deep. "Don't you care about what he's been through?"

"What he's been through?" Something formidable sparked to life in Savannah's eyes. "Are you oblivious to what *you've* put *me* through? What you put the staff through? *Christ.* How can you think I'd even want to speak to you after what you've done?"

"I felt the same way when you came back to Seattle. So please forgive me if I lack sympathy. But this isn't about me. It's about Keenan and how he risked his health to be with you. Didn't you notice how tired he was from the drugs? How he—"

Fuck. He grabbed the crook of Penelope's arm and gave her a squeeze of warning.

The woman who had become his closest confidant looked him in the eye. "I knew, Keenan. And I hated every minute of it. You put yourself through hell and you did it all for her."

"You need to leave," Savannah murmured.

Hell, yes, she did. Penelope wasn't doing him any favors. He tightened his grip, pleading. "*Go.*" He released his hold and jerked his head toward the elevator. "*Please.*"

"She needs to understand," Penelope continued. "Maybe then she'll let go of her pride."

"*Go*," he mouthed again. This wasn't about anyone else's pride. Only his.

"All right." She nodded, her eyes filled with regret. "I'm sorry. But please tell her." He watched her retreat down the hall, his courage leaving with her.

Tension surrounded him. It was thick and tangible in the air. Nothing he did would get rid of it. There were no words, no actions. Nothing.

"Drugs?" Savannah murmured.

He sighed and met her gaze. She'd leaned against the door jamb, her arms crossed protectively over her chest.

"Medication," he whispered, ensuring his voice remained strong.

If he could continue to speak like this, he could tell her everything. She could have all his secrets. All his promises. He'd never considered the ability to sing or whisper as a saving grace. He still didn't because it didn't change a thing in the professional world. But he'd do anything today. He'd whisper to Savannah until his dying breath if he had to.

"Those last weeks, you were always exhausted. Was that from the medication?"

He inclined his head. The same side effects had plagued him as a child, when his father had tried to medicate the stutter out of him with Xanax. Lethargy, nausea, and insomnia were all he got out of it. Both times the treatment failed.

"What was it meant to do?"

"Lessen the stutter," his voice was barely audible. "Make it easier for me to face you when I finally explained."

"You were going to tell me?"

He looked into those hazel eyes and gave an honest shrug. "I don't know. I wanted to."

She released an impassive breath of laughter.

"Well…" She shoved from the wall to stand tall. "Thanks for the clarity, but I don't know what you expect from me."

She knew. He could tell by the tremble in her fingers and the nervous swallow of her throat.

He chanced a step closer and leaned into her with his heart in his hands. "I expect nothing. But I would love your forgiveness." He remained in place, so close to the soft temptation of her skin.

Her breath hitched, her chest expanded. "Is that all?"

She inched back, ripping the floor out from beneath him. He'd thought all he needed was to see her, to explain face to face. To whisper those words he'd wanted her to hear over and over again. But her expression was indifferent. Unemotional. She was successfully cutting him off.

She'd moved on.

"Please..." His throat was hoarse, from the influx of work, or maybe it was from fear. "Give me another chance."

"I don't think I can." She shook her head. "I don't think I want to."

"*Just one*," he mouthed. That's all he needed. One more chance. One more opportunity to share all of him and prove he could make her happy.

"One more to go with the two you already destroyed?" She quirked a pained brow. "Fool me once, shame on you. Fool me twice, shame on me. But a third time? Come on, Keenan. I'm not that stupid and neither are you. You knew what you were doing and the results it would have if I found out."

There was no denying the truth. He'd had one too many opportunities already.

"*Okay.*" Pain ricocheted through him with his stiff nod.

He'd never hated his inadequacies more. And compounding his self-loathing was the knowledge of his idiotic behavior—the ego, the need to protect his secrets.

He wanted to hug her. Just once. To kiss her cheek and inhale the scent of her that would never be comparable. Instead, he pivoted on his toes and stalked toward the elevator, determined not to look back.

"Keenan?"

Fuck. He stopped. Turned.

She stepped into the hall and gave him a sad smile. "Just so you know, I adored you, too. I adored everything about you. The stutter wouldn't have changed a thing."

Then she was gone, slinking into her room and shutting the door on the only thing he'd ever cared about.

Email Correspondence

Date: 30th December

Subject: Chances

Dear Keenan,

I'm finding it hard to gain closure. Something in my chest isn't sitting right. So I was hoping this email might help.

I want you to know that I did fight for you. You just didn't see it.

The battle was internal. I combatted the pain of not being good enough, and the heartache of humiliation. I brawled with self-doubt and struggled to overcome things that were out of my control. But now I see that you've been trying to conquer all those things for a lot longer than me.

Please know that I did read your emails, your texts, and kept all your gifts. You words—written or otherwise—have always meant the world to me.

You also mean the world to the Augustines, so please don't shut them out.

Over the past two weeks, I've been given a wealth of information on all things Keenan Black. My aunt calls me incessantly. It seems she picks up the phone whenever she's reminded of something you've done to make her smile.

Apparently, you've made her smile often.

She wants you to be happy. And believe it or not, Penny and

Dominic do, too. I never thought I'd see the day when the cousin who hates me and the one who warned me away from you would both team together to play matchmaker.

No matter how alone you feel, you have some truly great friends at your side. Please don't push them away. I know Dominic is giving you a hard time, but he'll get over it. He can't be too angry if he's leaving messages on my voicemail that pertain to your sexual prowess and how I'll soon learn that I can't live without it.

Anyway, I better get going. I just wanted you to know there's no hard feelings on my side. And I hope there's none on yours.

I still think you're remarkable.

And, hey, maybe it shouldn't be a case of two chances too many. Maybe it's third time lucky. Who knows?

For now, I'm going to take a break from Rydel and see where the world takes me.

Savannah

Thirty-One

"She hasn't left Seattle."

Keenan kept his attention on the road, pretending he didn't know who Penelope was talking about as he drove her ass home. Her broken down car story was a load of shit. Her problem was a case of wanting to drink for New Year's and the expectation that he would be her chauffeur.

Not likely. He was going to dump and run.

Spending the night at Mrs. Augustine's, drinking with Dominic who wanted to gut him, and Penelope who was suddenly more overprotective than usual, was as inviting as a prostate exam from his high school gym teacher.

"Mom said Savannah's not handling losing you." He could see her shrug in his periphery. "I don't blame her. Been there. Done that. Created the theme park in my mind so I never forget it."

Fuck. He ground his molars and pressed his toes harder on the accelerator, a one-track mind set on getting the fuck out of this conversation. The settlement had been hard enough. He'd had to sit across the table from Spencer, his imagination running wild with all the ways the asshole would've comforted Savannah. And he would've comforted her. He could see it in the man's eyes. Could tell the guy was out for blood and pleased he was on the winning team.

"I know you didn't want to tell me how you ended things the other day, but maybe you should get in contact with her again. Just once. Ya know, for closure."

Nope. Not going there. He'd been castrated by the email Savannah sent yesterday. Castrated over and over and over again until he was certain he'd never regain his masculinity. A reply wouldn't gain closure. It would only prolong the misery and the unending loop of castration.

"Would you want to see her again?"

Fuck. He slammed his palms against the steering wheel and shot her a glare.

"Just asking..."

He turned onto Mrs. Augustine's street and contemplated booting Penelope out the door without slowing. He wouldn't even pause. Before him, the tree-lined street housed less than the usual herd of cars associated with an Augustine party. There were only one or two. Dominic's Mustang included. The subdued gathering wouldn't change his mind, though. Anything less than solitary confinement would be a chore.

He pulled into the drive, stopped before the garage, and waited for Penelope to get the fuck out.

"You're not coming in?"

He was still glaring at her. How could she not see that?

"Mom will be furious. I think she prepared something special in the hopes you'd show."

He jerked a thumb toward the house, telling her to get out.

"Fine. Be a dick." She shoved open the passenger door and slid from the car. "But before you go. You might want to check out the porch."

His gaze traveled to the place in question, where Dominic stood before the front door, scowl in place, beer bottle raising to his mouth.

Nope. Definitely not a welcome party he was willing to be greeted by.

"Is that enough inspiration to hang around?"

He glared at Penelope, signed fuck-no and jammed the gearstick into reverse.

She gaped in return, her surprise catching him off guard. "You really don't want to see her?"

Her? He looked again, scouring the porch from one side of the building all the way along to the lone figure standing at the far corner. At first, he thought it was a trick of the dwindling daylight. An apparition. But the more he narrowed his eyes, the clearer the vision became.

And she was a vision.

A sight to behold.

"Savannah," he whispered her name and felt it echo through his ears. What the fuck was she doing here?

He couldn't tear his concentration from her as she came to stand against the railing, her lips parted slightly, her eyes wary. There wasn't an inch of him that knew how to react. He was frozen in confusion. Mesmerized. Completely awestruck by the simplicity of her gloved hands clutching the balustrade and her pink cheeks framed by the raised collar of her jacket.

Why? he signed.

"Like I said, she's having trouble letting go. I don't think it helps when Mom, Dominic, and I are berating her to give you another chance."

He pulled his focus from the porch and met Penelope's gaze.

"You do love her, don't you?" Her heartache was evident. Her resolution, too.

There was no need to ponder. He nodded, slow and confident. "*I do.*"

She smiled, but the happiness didn't reach her glassy eyes. "Then give her everything this time. More than you give my mom, or Dominic, and even me. Be yourself, Keenan. And let her love you back."

She shut the door between them, leaving him to sink into his seat, the engine still rumbling beneath him as she walked toward her brother, then into the house. He still didn't need to contemplate how he wanted this night to end. The outcome his heart pounded for was set in stone. But for the first time in years, he questioned his worth.

It seemed he'd spent a lifetime trying to prove himself to others, to convince them of his value. Now he was the one who couldn't see it. He wasn't entirely sure that 'being himself' was going to be enough. Not for her.

He wondered if she considered his silence petulant, like his father did. Or if she'd give him ultimatums to ensure he spoke aloud, like his mother had. No. He shook his head and cut the engine. He would never have fallen in love with a woman capable of that. And he was in love—wholeheartedly, undeniably, even unintentionally.

He grabbed his cell from the center console and slid from the car. His expression was devoid of the hope he carried in his chest as he came to stand before Dominic, waiting for the inevitable assault he wasn't sure would come in physical or verbal form.

"I'm not warning her anymore." Dominic took a gulp of his beer, his scowl fixed. "I'll warn you, though. Do right by her this time or we're done. You hear m—"

"Dominic," Savannah's soft plea carried from the corner of the porch. "I can look after myself."

"Yeah." His friend gave him a look brimming with silent threats and then reached for the door. "You've done a great job of that so far, Savvy."

It was a modest warning, definitely less than Keenan expected or deserved. He'd take it, though, and remember it nonetheless. There would be no more contemplation of an imminent end. If given the chance, he would aim for a relationship without an expiration date. He was striving for forever, the target forging itself into his mind as Dominic slammed the front door.

His throat tightened at the first step onto the porch and grew painful when he faced her. She turned to him and leaned her back against the railing. There was no greeting. No welcome or murmured hello. She didn't say a thing, merely eyed him, the careless whisper of her lashes sweeping back and forth as her chest rose and fell with heavy breaths.

He felt awkward in the silence he'd grown to derive comfort from. He'd kill to give her his words. The real ones. Not whispered, not typed. But the desert in his mouth assured him he'd slaughter everything that left his lips.

"A-are..." Yep. He wasn't wrong.

She shook her head, denying his failed attempt to connect. Instead, her gaze spoke to him with fluency. She told him a story of heartache and loss, yearning and anger. She laid her pain at his feet and he took it in, letting it destroy him all over again.

"A-are..." *Fuck.* He chanced a step forward, one foot in front of the other, again and again in the hopes she was here to let him salvage something he didn't deserve to have.

"It's okay. You can use your phone if you want."

No. He shook his head. His cell would be a last resort.

Her shoulders tensed the closer he approached, the depth of her inhalations growing once they came face to face, mere feet apart. He'd caged her into the corner, and still she didn't move, didn't slide away. She kept screaming to him with her expression. Beseeching him for his carelessness and begging him for his affection with the shiny glaze in her eyes.

He conveyed all he could with his returned look. He tried to tell her of his unending regret and the enormity of his love. His heart was pounding rapidly behind his sternum with the physical need for her to know. He couldn't live without her witnessing his agony and vulnerability. Everything was hers to take.

She could have it all.

He took another step, the last step, and brought them toe to toe. Adrenaline poisoned his blood at her mere proximity and the accompanied perfume teasing his senses. He leaned in, testing the boundaries that should've been thick and impenetrable and stopped close to her ear.

"Are you here for me?" he whispered.

He retreated at her silence, his stomach rolling from the weight of the assault. Her pained expression didn't give him a clue to her answer. It could be yes or no. Hope or defeat. Heaven or more torturous hell.

"Yes," she murmured. "In my email, I told you I was going to see where the world takes me." She lowered her gaze. "Apparently, it doesn't want to take me anywhere without resolving this. I got as far as the airport before I had to turn back."

Something hard slammed into his chest. Regret, maybe. Or overwhelming optimism. He straightened, needing to see her, all of her, before he could truly believe he had a chance.

She swallowed under his attention, her gorgeousness increasing with the impressive show of vulnerability. "I want to trust your emails, Keenan. Aunt Michelle even tried to convince me of your sincerity, but I need you to look me in the eye and tell me they were truthful."

His palm itched, his hand rising of its own accord to approach the stray strands of hair framing her gorgeous face. He waited for her to slap his touch away, only to be greeted with a slight tremble of her lips as he gently cupped her cheek. There was never anything more profound or punishing than her fragility in that moment.

She was pliable under his touch. Broken under his attention.

"Truth," he mouthed with solemn conviction.

A lone tear ran down her cheek. He couldn't stand it, couldn't protect himself against the miniscule amount of liquid that inspired nausea and almost brought him to his knees. The evidence of her pain hit his thumb, landing a punishing blow with such sweet efficiency.

He was so sorry—for the lies, for the betrayal, for the weakness. He didn't want to hold back anymore. He needed her to see everything, to cast her gaze upon him with unfettered scrutiny and see everything he'd hidden.

"I wish I didn't believe you."

A shuddering breath left her lips and he leaned into it, sucking it into his lungs as he rested his forehead against hers. He stared into eyes that spoke to him on every level, and failed at holding in a tremble when she placed her gloved palm around his neck, holding him close.

Her touch burned him, even through her glove. Everything she did marked him. Scarred him. He inched closer, brushing their noses briefly, still waiting for her rejection as his mouth brushed hers. There was nothing more life changing than that kiss. His world shifted, his focus for the future narrowed entirely on one person. One remarkable woman.

His love was etched into every movement of his lips, into the glide of his tongue and the delicate sweep of his thumb over her cheek. He told her he adored her with every beat of his heart and the way he pulled their bodies close with his free arm, hugging her.

When they broke apart, she blinked back at him, her meaningful expression softening in what he hoped was reflected affection.

"I need you to promise me one thing."

He nodded, willing to give up his soul if she asked.

"I want you to trust me. Maybe not right away...but soon. I need your trust really soon."

"*I will.*" He nodded again, over and over. "*I do.*"

Her brows drew close, her gaze searching for the truth. He was sure she could see it laid bare for her to take. Nobody knew him like she did. Even through the deception, she still held more of him than anyone else ever had.

"Okay." Tentatively, she buried her face in his neck, the action filled with nervous apprehension. "I feel like such an idiot for falling for you, Keenan. But I did. I love you, no matter how hard it is to admit."

He stiffened, every inch of him taut. He'd heard the declaration before, from numerous women. Never from her. Never when the meaning laid a lifetime of happiness at his feet.

She'd broken him with three words.

Three syllables.

He pressed her back into the balustrade and rested his hips against hers. "I promise you the world," he whispered.

She pulled away, frowning. "Your exaggeration doesn't fill me with comfort, Keenan."

"I promise you *my* world," he clarified, hoping his almost silent tone didn't lack persuasion. "I'll give it all. I'll give anything. *That* I promise." It wasn't an exaggeration. It wasn't a lie. He was done with hiding from her. Finished with protecting himself at her expense. His life was hers to take, and with it came his secrets and his vulnerabilities.

"Thank you." A smile nudged her lips, her restrained happiness sinking into his lungs.

He entwined their fingers and held them to his chest, hoping to reiterate his vow, not only to her, but to the Augustines who he knew were spying on them from one point or another in the house.

"They're watching aren't they?" she asked, reading his mind.

He laughed, this time not holding in the sound that came with it.

Her lips parted, her surprise evident in her wide eyes and tightening grip. "You can laugh?"

"Yeah, sweetheart," he whispered with a kiss. "I can laugh."

She shook her head, her awe inspiring a harsh pound behind his sternum. "I'm going to enjoy getting to know you again, aren't I?"

He was banking on it. Praying for it. Settling all his hopes on the third time being the charm. "Yeah." He nodded and lifted her off her feet. "I'm going to make sure you do."

Email Correspondence

Date: 26th November

Subject: This is crazy

Dear Keenan,

Are you as nervous as I am?

I woke up alone this morning and couldn't stop wondering what you were doing. Being apart, even overnight, makes me miss you like crazy.

But it won't be long now. I'm in the limousine, waiting to arrive at the wedding ceremony. You're already somewhere in the chapel—at least I hope you are—and I'm dying from the need to see you in your immaculately tailored suit.

I wanted to take this moment to thank you for everything we've shared over the past year. Thank you for your trust and for letting me into your life. Thank you for sharing things with me that you've never shared with anyone else. And for making my reciprocated love so easy to give.

I can't wait for you to sign those two words in front of the crowd. Then to whisper them across my neck at the reception. And speak them aloud against my lips once we're alone in our honeymoon suite, just like you promised.

I do.

I do.

I do.

Because the third time will always be the charm.

Savannah

The end

Please consider leaving a review on your ebook retailer
website or Goodreads

Look for these titles from Eden Summers

Reckless Beat Series

Blind Attraction (Reckless Beat #1)
Passionate Addiction (Reckless Beat #2)
Reckless Weekend (Reckless Beat #2.5)
Undesired Lust (Reckless Beat #3)
Sultry Groove (Reckless Beat #4)
Reckless Rendezvous (Reckless Beat #4.5)
Undeniable Temptation (Reckless Beat #5)

Vault of Sin Series

A Shot of Sin (Vault of Sin #1)
Union of Sin (Vault of Sin #2)

Standalone Titles

Rush of Insanity
Ravenous
Secret Confessions: Backstage - Josh
Secret Confessions: Down & Dusty - Brooke

*Details on more standalone titles
can be found on Eden's website.*

About the Author

Eden Summers is a true blue Aussie, living in regional New South Wales with her two energetic young boys and a quick witted husband.

In late 2010, Eden's romance obsession could no longer be sated by reading alone, so she decided to give voice to the sexy men and sassy women in her mind.

Eden can't resist alpha dominance, dark features and sarcasm in her fictional heroes and loves a strong heroine who knows when to bite her tongue but also serves retribution with a feminine smile on her face.

If you'd like access to exclusive information and giveaways, join Eden Summers' newsletter. Details can be found on her website - www.edensummers.com

CPSIA information can be obtained
at www.ICGtesting.com
Printed in the USA
FFOW03n1307160117
31420FF

9 781925 512021